Scrooge & Marlee

LEE ANN SONTHEIMER MURPHY

This is a work of fiction. Names, characters, places, and incidents are products of the author's imagination or are used fictitiously and are not to be construed as real. Any resemblance to actual events, locations, organizations, or persons, living or dead, is entirely coincidental.

World Castle Publishing, LLC
Pensacola, Florida
Copyright © Lee Ann Sontheimer Murphy 2022
Hardback ISBN: 9798836444754
Paperback ISBN: 9781958336304
eBook ISBN: 9781958336298
First Edition World Castle Publishing, LLC, July 11, 2022
http://www.worldcastlepublishing.com
Cover: Karen Fuller
Editor: Maxine Bringenberg

Chapter One

He wasn't old, and most of the time, he wasn't cranky, but in one way, he was like the fictional Ebenezer — Theo Scrooge disliked Christmas. He hadn't always. As a child, he'd loved the holiday with all the traditions and trimmings, but as he grew up, that changed.

Theo didn't care much for Charles Dickens, either. In lit classes, he'd been forced to read classics like *Oliver Twist* and *A Tale of Two Cities,* but he balked at reading *A Christmas Carol,* taking an F on a class assignment in high school, which brought his grade down by a full letter.

He wished the author had chosen any other surname for the miserly old character who had a life changing revelation after three ghosts came to set him straight. If Dickens had just called him Ebenezer Smith or Sands or Sims, things would have been different for Theo.

Instead, for as long as he could remember, people joked about Scrooge, especially in December. From elementary school through college, Theo always knew when an instructor reached his name on the class roster. There was a pause, then a frown, and then a hesitant, "Theo SCROOGE?" And especially from junior high onward, one classmate pushed hard, and this continued even into adulthood.

It made matters worse that his dad died in December when Theo was still in high school. That sad event provided more reason not to find joy in the Christmas season.

Growing up in a small Missouri river town where most of the residents had German names made Theo stand out even more. Nestled in the Missouri Rhineland, Hermann paralleled the Missouri River, with the older businesses located along First Street and the remainder on the highway that traveled into town over the river and headed north as a two-lane road leading to I-44.

Several wineries were located within the town limits, and others were in the surrounding countryside. One belonged to Theo's mother's family. A drive in any direction on any of the winding country roads was picturesque, with vineyards boasting acres of grapes and old country farmhouses that looked as if they had been transported from Europe.

Hermann had an Old-World atmosphere as well, from the brick courthouse towering over the river to St. Morand's (the patron saint of wine) on another hill to the downtown district. In the spring and summer, the town bloomed with flower gardens in almost every available space. Multiple bed and breakfasts and two motels provided tourists the chance to stay, and many did. The Amtrak train also roared through town, traveling between St. Louis and Kansas City. Some of the older residents still spoke at least some German.

Theo loved his hometown most of the time. He hadn't intended to stay. He had once thought he'd move off to a city, maybe St. Louis or Chicago or Los Angeles, or even New York. Despite his old English surname, his mother's family had been descended from the early settlers who came from Germany. His mom had been raised at one of the smaller wineries outside town, where she now lived with his grandmother, Oma. His dad, who bequeathed him the Scrooge name, had died during his senior year of high school.

Although it was early April, spring sunshine brightened up the old town and chased away the shadows as Theo made his morning walk down to the river. With coffee in hand, he made his way along the bank and then settled down on his favorite bench to enjoy a few quiet moments before his day got underway.

"Morning, Theo," Abe Tucker, who ran Brunhilde, one of the most popular B&B's, with his wife, called out as he bicycled past. "How goes it?"

"Good so far."

Theo watched the never-still surface of the river as the waters flowed past, en route to join the Mississippi near St. Louis. The Missouri was far from placid. There were always eddies and a strong current that could turn deadly.

Lisa Muller sat down on the opposite end of the bench, her leashed dog in tow.

"Hi, Theo," she said. "What's the special today?"

"Beef rouladen," he said. "And bangers and mash."

His restaurant, styled after a traditional English pub, offered both German and English dishes. He served German beer and wine but also some English ales. And, with more than a little sarcasm and some wicked humor, he called it Bah Humbug! The idea had first been his late grandfather's.

"I'll be there for lunch," Lisa said.

"I'll keep your favorite table open, then."

Theo ambled his way back to First Street, where Bah Humbug! stood at the end of the block. The front faced the main thoroughfare, and the back overlooked the Missouri. A wide covered area to one side offered seasonal outdoor dining. Across the street, Lisa's florist shop and an auto parts store stood, and down the block, there was one of the town's only two grocery stores. Since Bah Humbug! wouldn't open until eleven, Theo dashed up the stairs to his apartment above the place. He spent thirty minutes on the computer, checking emails and posting the day's special on the Facebook page. Then he headed down the back stairs to his restaurant.

Theo had multiple roles—owner, chef, wait staff, and even dishwasher. He did whatever needed doing. His mom, now in her fifties, would arrive soon. Theo got started with some of the basic prep work. Although rouladens often included pickles as one of the ingredients used to stuff the beef, Theo seldom used them. Oma had told him that every German cook put their own twist on the dish, and he'd created his own version that included chopped onions, mushrooms, and a bit of bacon with some seasonings.

As he chopped the veggies, his mom came through the back door, arms filled with two containers of cookies. Theo took the load from her and kissed her on the cheek.

"What kind of cookies?" he asked. She and his grandmother often baked cookies or other sweets at home to serve.

"Gingerbread and vanilla crescents, and keep out of them."

Theo laughed as he popped the lid and snuck a gingerbread cookie. The tender, spicy treat melted in his mouth. "Taste test."

"Do they pass?"

He put his thumb up and nodded. "Specials are rouladens plus bangers and mash. I started on the filling for the rouladens. Do you want to help?"

"You're the boss," she said, and donned an apron. In her late fifties, Liesel Schubert Scrooge remained slender, her hair lightly touched with gray.

Theo pounded round steaks thin and then cut them into portions that would be filled. He peeled potatoes to mash later and signed for a delivery of black bread from a bakery in

Jefferson City. By ten, the rest of the staff had arrived, so Theo headed for the front of the house, where he made sure every table had folded napkins and silverware in place, that each vase held a fresh flower dressed with greenery, and that the daily specials had been written on the chalkboard.

"Ready to unlock the door, Teddy?" Autumn, the youngest of his servers, asked. He wouldn't allow anyone else to call him anything but Theo, but she'd been like a younger sister to him. Her parents and his had been close friends, the kind that spent every Saturday night together dining out or playing cards.

"Yes, but don't call me that unless you want to look for a job on campus."

Autumn was in her second year at Columbia University in Jefferson City. She giggled and unlocked the front door with its etched glass. "We're open!"

Although most tourists wouldn't arrive until Memorial Day, there were always a few in every season. Theo counted on their business and local repeat trade. A few people would make a day trip from either of Missouri's largest cities to visit some wineries and eat at Bah Humbug! The spring sunshine after a week of rain would bring the locals out, Theo thought and prepared to greet them.

The first sour note of the day arrived when local insurance agent and alderman Todd Blevins walked through the door, his too small slacks hitched up beneath his burgeoning belly. Theo caught the overwhelming stench of Blevins's trademark cheap cologne and held his breath. They were familiar, classmates who had grown up together, played on the same youth teams and served on various local committees together. Since the sixth grade, Blevins had been a pain in his life.

"Well, if it isn't Scrooge himself," Blevins blared, his eyes small in his wide face. "And not even Christmas time."

Theo tamped down instant anger and forced a faux smile.

"Table for one?"

"No, the mayor and his staff are joining me," Blevins said. "I'm working on an insurance deal for city employees."

"Will a table for six work?" Theo asked. Blevins, back in the seventh grade, had been the worst one to stir the Scrooge pot, and Theo hadn't forgotten. "If so, follow me."

He led the other man to the far corner and seated him. He listed the specials of the day, but Blevins snorted. "I'll choose from the menu. But hey, Scrooge, bring me a Newcastle Brown Ale."

Although he wasn't a server, Theo did, and by the time he returned with menus, the others had joined Blevins.

"Thanks, Ebenezer," Blevins said. "Don't overwork Bob Cratchit."

He tittered at his own remark, but no one else laughed. Theo shot him a long look but kept his lips together. "Traci will be here to take your order in just a moment," he told them.

Theo took up a position at the door after beckoning to Traci. The seasoned staff member nodded, and he didn't doubt she'd handle Blevins and his group with the right blend of distance and professional courtesy.

After that, the restaurant got busy, and he almost forgot about Todd. After the rush, Theo visited the kitchen. His mom's shift ended now, and he always took a few minutes to eat lunch with her. He fixed his own plate with rouladen and mashed potatoes, a blend of both cuisines.

His mom ate bockwurst on a bun, smeared with mustard and topped with a heavy dose of sauerkraut, then another. If he ate that much kraut, he'd suffer from indigestion all afternoon, but it never seemed to bother her.

"This is good," he said, indicating the rouladen.

"Isn't it always?"

"Of course. The cookies were a hit—I believe they sold

out."

"I'll bake more soon, but for tomorrow, I'm making apple strudel. Will that work with the specials?"

"Yes, tomorrow is pork schnitzel and potato dumplings."

She nodded. "And for the English side?"

"Shepherd's pie, I thought. It's supposed to rain, so I thought comfort food would be a good choice."

Theo ate the two cookies he'd saved. Liesel removed her apron and hair net, then plucked her purse from the shelf by the back door.

"Did Todd give you his usual nonsense? I saw he was here with a group."

He shrugged. "A little, but he always does."

She patted his shoulder. "You shouldn't let it get to you."

"I don't." But he did, and Theo knew it.

"I'll see you tomorrow, *Schatz*."

"*Jawohl, Mutti*."

Theo usually kept the specials the same for dinner, although the evening menu also included some steaks, chicken, and seafood dishes. He usually did most of the cooking, although Liz Vogel, a widow in her late forties, would arrive at two to assist.

Bah Humbug! closed between three and five each afternoon. Around four-thirty, Theo made a ham sandwich on black bread with a side of German potato salad. He ate, savoring the taste. Just before he reopened, Jonas Kaiser strolled in through the kitchen, still in uniform.

"How goes it, Theo?"

"It goes, Sheriff Kaiser, it goes. Are you off duty?"

"Not until eight, so no wine with dinner. Can I get a bratwurst and some of that potato salad?"

"Sure. Got plans after work?"

"Not yet. What are you thinking?"

"Chess and wine upstairs at my place after I finish here," Theo told him.

"Sounds like a plan."

Jonas and Theo had grown up together, classmates from kindergarten through high school, in church together on Sundays. They grew up two blocks apart in town. Summers, Jonas spent almost as much time at his grandparents' winery as Theo did, chasing through the arbors and hunting in the woods when they were older. They'd fished in the little stream that ran across the Schubert's property and later in the Missouri River. They'd camped out, discovered girls, tasted their first beer together, and double-dated at prom. Even though they went in different directions after graduation, Theo to study business and culinary arts at MU, and Jonas to earn a law enforcement degree, they remained friends, brothers of the heart.

With the restaurant about half full, the evening crawled, but finally, around a quarter to ten, Theo hung up the last dish towel, washed his hands, and headed up the interior back stairs. A short hall led to a compact kitchen. With a full restaurant downstairs, he only needed space for a stove, fridge, a microwave, a wine rack, a few cabinets, and a coffee maker. A tiny table rested against the front windows that overlooked Front Street. Across from the kitchen, his living room held a leather couch, a matching recliner, a big-screen television mounted on the wall, and some bookshelves.

His bedroom, the largest room of all, faced the river with fabulous views. The small bathroom had enough space for a walk-in shower, sink and vanity, and a commode. A stackable washer and dryer stood in one corner. The place was large enough for Theo but far from spacious. He had moved in when he opened the place almost ten years earlier.

He figured it would be temporary until he found a house he liked and a woman, but neither had materialized. Theo dated, but few of the women from his hometown appealed. The ones who didn't marry at a young age moved to one of the big cities.

By the time Jonas, changed into cut-off denim shorts and a St. Louis Blues T-shirt, arrived, Theo had the chess board set up in the kitchen and wine ready to pour.

"I thought a dry white?" Theo said. "Or would you rather a sweeter Vignoles?"

"Let's go with sweet," Jonas said.

They played four games, and Theo won three. By then, it was midnight, and Jonas yawned. "Good thing I'm off tomorrow," he said. "I'd never wake up to the alarm, although I'm on call."

"Aren't you always?" Theo had a nice buzz from the wine, pleasant and warm.

"Most of the time, but tomorrow I'm taking Shannon to St. Louis."

"Cardinals playing?"

"Probably, but she wants to go to the aquarium at Union Station, so I said okay," Jonas said. "You're still on for best man, right, with the reception at your place?"

"Yes, to both."

Jonas and Shannon, his long-time girlfriend and high school prom date, were getting married on June 12 at St. Morand's, with an evening reception at Bah Humbug! Theo would stand beside his friend, wear a tuxedo, and drink toasts to the bridal couple's future, but his heart wouldn't be in it. Once married, Shannon would come first, as it should be, but Theo had few other friends.

"Good," Jonas said, rising and stretching. "I'm heading out. Thanks for the chess and the wine, Theo. Got a hot date for next weekend yet?"

Theo laughed, but it rang hollow to his ears. "Not yet, but it's only Monday."

"Dude, you need to get back in the saddle."

His cheeks flushed hot, but it was probably the wine. "I've

dated since Theresa."

"Yeah, about every blue moon or so. How many years has it been since her, anyway?"

"Three or four," he replied, although he knew it had been six. "It's not like I have a lot of free time."

Jonas smirked. "Make some."

After his best friend left, Theo finished the second bottle of wine and sat, staring out over First Street, empty at the late hour. Sometimes he craved a woman, someone he could cherish and kiss, laugh with, and share his deepest thoughts. His mostly full life still had empty places, but at thirty-five, Theo had settled. This was his life, and he expected this was how it would always be.

If not for the loneliness, it would be tolerable, he thought. But then that old Ebenezer had been a bachelor too. *Maybe I'm cursed, after all, just a sour old Scrooge.*

Chapter Two

He woke to the sound of rain and wished he could stay in bed to savor it. One look at the clock told him it was a no-go. Theo rose, stretching, his mouth dry and head aching, the result of too much wine. It didn't help he'd stayed up late, but he'd enjoyed the respite from the daily routine.

Because of the rain, he didn't take his usual walk, but he showered and drank black coffee until he felt human. Theo craved a big breakfast, with sausage and eggs, maybe pancakes. Although the downpour hadn't slacked, he decided to head across the street and down the block to a small, classic café. Maybelle's dated back to the 1920s or 1930s—he never could remember which—and although the owners had changed over the decades, the menu hadn't.

The cap he put on failed to keep him dry, and Theo dripped as he entered. He took the far corner table, tucked at the end of the counter, and used some napkins to dry his face.

"You look like something the cat dragged in, Theo," May, the owner for the past thirty years, said as she poured him a cup of coffee. "I haven't seen you in two weeks."

"I manage to stay busy," he said. "I want a Farmer's Platter, eggs over easy, sausage, pancakes, no biscuits."

"You want the hash browns with gravy too?"

Theo shook his head. "I'll pass, or I'll be too full to walk back to my place."

"I'll have it out in a few."

He sipped the coffee, dark and robust the way he liked it. The café was less than half full, probably due to the rain and the fact tourist season hadn't started. Theo nodded at the familiar faces but paused when he glanced at a table for two across the room. The woman who sat there solo caught his eye, and Theo stared.

Her light brown hair, close to the color of maple syrup with lighter strands, was twisted up with a clip at the back of her head. Her petite nose turned up slightly at the end. She studied the menu, her full lips pursed with concentration, and when she glanced up to give her order, Theo noticed that her eyes were a deep blue. *Pretty*, he thought, *so pretty*.

Theo wondered if she were a tourist. If so, she'd be passing through, and he'd never encounter her again. But it was early in the season, he thought, and she didn't fit the usual look. A number of the visitors who came to Hermann were mature, often retired. A few families came, some with young kids, and so did the occasional honeymoon couple.

The arrival of his breakfast platter interrupted his musings.

"Thanks, May," he said, inhaling the delicious aroma.

"You're welcome," she replied as she refilled his cup. "Need anything else?"

He almost said no, then he asked, "Do you happen to know who she is?"

Although there were several women of various ages in the café, May knew who he meant.

"No, Theo," she said, shaking her head. "But she's been in

before, yesterday, maybe the day before."

"Tourist?"

May shrugged. "Search me, I don't know. Want to know what she orders?"

"Of course not," he said, flustered.

"If I find out anything about her, I'll let you know."

She winked and whirled away.

His eggs were perfect, and the sausage tasty. He ate them first and finished with the pancakes, rich with butter and syrup. As he ate, Theo sneaked a few more glances at her. She ate coffee cake with a fork and bacon with her fingers, her movements graceful. She finished before he did and blotted her lips with a napkin. When she stood to leave, her eyes met his for a brief second.

Theo squelched the urge to toss down his silverware and introduce himself, but that would be too much like a stalker, so he watched her go. When she reached the sidewalk, she turned left and headed west up First Street.

If it's meant to be, I'll run into her again, Theo thought.

She intrigued him more than any woman had in months, maybe more. He had to concentrate to remember the last date he'd had. After some thought, he realized it had been the previous Fourth of July. Too long, much too long.

He made the pans of shepherd's pie before his mother arrived. Liesel came in, closing her umbrella as she entered the back door. Theo realized not only was it still raining, but he'd walked back to work in it.

"Your shirt looks damp," his mother told him. "Have you been out in the rain?"

Theo shrugged. "I walked over from the café after breakfast."

Her gaze focused on him, and she nodded. "I see. You got much done?"

In the uncanny way she'd always had, he figured she probably did see more than he would like.

"Just the shepherd's pie," he said. "It's simple. I thought you could do the potato dumplings, and I can start on the schnitzel. What's the dessert?"

Her gaze narrowed. "Apple strudel, like I told you yesterday. Maybe you should put on a dry shirt first."

"It's not that wet." He touched it to prove the point and found it damp. "All right, I will."

Upstairs, he switched shirts and marveled that he hadn't noticed. As he worked side by side with his mom doing prep work and talking, Theo still wondered who the girl was and if he'd see her again.

With the rain, the lunch crowd was heavy, and the comfort foods proved popular. His mother ate early and left by one, but Theo didn't have a chance to sit down until almost three. His feet hurt, and his back ached as he ate a serving of shepherd's pie, analyzing whether he'd used too much onion or just enough.

"Theo?" Autumn stood beside the table in the back. "If you want to go up, grab a nap or something, I've got this."

"Why would I want a nap?" he asked.

"You're distracted. I thought maybe you're sick or something."

He laughed. "I'm fine. I'm almost never sick."

"Are you sure? You've been quiet."

"We've been swamped, and I was thinking."

Autumn sat down across from him and reached for his hand. "Your mom noticed, too. Is something troubling you?"

"No, no, there's nothing." *Except wanting to know the woman's name and where I can find her.*

"Theo, you're making me worry. You're like my big brother, you know?"

He squeezed her hands and released them. "I promise I'm

fine. But if it will make you calm down, I'll take a walk by the river. It was raining too hard this morning, but it's quit now."

"Take your time, clear the cobwebs," she told him. "I've got this."

Since they closed each day from three until five, he had the opportunity.

Theo grabbed a jacket as he headed outside. Wharf Street lay between the back of his establishment and First. The sun peeked out from the clouds, and the sight lifted his spirits. A walk and some fresh air was exactly what he needed. He strolled along the riverbank, hands in his pockets. Theo cleared his mind of the mystery woman and savored the light wind on his face.

Jonas had annoyed him by bringing up Theresa. His ill-fated relationship with her was ancient history. He didn't pine for her, never really had. She'd humiliated him, however, and caused him to question his worth. Theo was wary of relationships now, and even a casual date made him tense. It wasn't logical, but a date could turn into two, or a dozen, and then he'd be in a relationship. At the same time, he craved a companion.

Until today, he hadn't seen a woman that intrigued him in a long time. Whoever she was, she evoked old daydreams he'd almost forgotten. Since he didn't know her name and might never cross paths with her again, Theo reasoned he would be wise to forget about her.

Struggling with his thoughts, he tromped all the way down to the end by the bridge, idled for a few minutes on a bench overlooking the Missouri, and then started back. By the time he got there, he'd have to scramble to get ready for the evening trade. Even so, he didn't really hurry.

Two junior high kids on bikes whizzed past, riding too fast on the pedestrian path. Theo turned, thinking he might tell them to slow down, and saw her. The same woman he'd admired at the café stood near the river. The late afternoon sun accentuated the lighter strands of her hair. He paused, transfixed by the sight of her, just as the bicyclists neared her. Theo realized their path had veered toward her, and he started to run, shouting, "Stop!"

Whether she heard him or not, Theo didn't know, but the two boys didn't, and he saw her look up with an expression of horror. She leapt forward, out of harm's way, but one of the kids swerved toward her. She lost her footing and tumbled onto the grassy strip on the bank. Theo had almost reached her when she stood up, then lost her footing and slid into the river so fast she barely had time to scream.

At her cry, Theo kicked out of his shoes and dived into the river. His heart pounded as he hit the murky water, colder than he expected, and fought the swift current as he swam toward where she'd fallen. She surfaced, arms flailing, crying out for help as she bobbed, helpless. The current took her under as she struggled against it just as he reached her.

Aware of the danger, he ducked his head beneath the surface and saw her. Theo swam forward, put his arms around her, and kicked to the surface. She struggled against him, and as he broke through the water, he said, "Stop, or you'll drown us both. Just be still, and I'll have you on the land."

Her head moved against his shoulder in what he took to be a nod, then he swam toward shore, weighted with her. It was farther than he expected — the river had carried them almost ten feet out into the swifter current. Before Theo made it, she went limp in his arms, and he pushed hard, fetching up on shore, gasping. The taste of the brackish water was unpleasant in his mouth.

A crowd had gathered, and one man stepped forward, offering him a hand up. He grasped it, still holding tightly to the woman.

"Did she drown?" Mrs. Ketterick, who had been his third-grade teacher, asked, her forehead bisected with a worry line.

Theo glanced down and realized she was still. Fear shot through him, icier than the spring wind that chilled him in his wet clothing. "Hey," he said, nudging her. "Hey, wake up. You're safe now."

If she died despite his efforts, it would mess him up for an awfully long time, but she coughed, spit up some river water, and opened her eyes. She moaned, then turned her head to retch, spewing river water in a small stream. Theo changed position, got behind her, and raised her head, letting her rest against his knees so she wouldn't choke.

She hacked again, then frowned. "I fell in the river, didn't I?"

Theo stroked her face. "You did, but you're safe now."

"You pulled me out." Her voice cracked a little. "Thank you."

She shivered hard against him.

"Someone get her a blanket," he said, and shuddered.

"Paramedics are on the way," old Henry Miller said. "Should be here any minute."

With his head muddled and ears filled with river water, Theo hadn't really heard the sirens until that moment. Within minutes, he had a blanket wrapped around his shoulders, and so did she.

"Theo, we're going to take you and the lady here over to the hospital to be checked out," Andy Jackson, paramedic, told him.

He shook his head. "No, I'm good. I need to go clean up before the dinner rush starts—"

"Your staff can handle it."

A sharp protest died on his lips when Autumn pushed through the crowd.

"Theo!" She knelt beside him and threw her arms around him in a tight hug. "Are you all right?"

"Perfect," he said through chattering teeth. "I'll be there in a few minutes."

"No, you won't. We can handle dinner. Go to the hospital."

"I don't think that's necessary," he said, then stopped. Less than three feet away, the mystery woman was giving Andy her name.

"Marlena Dupree," Theo heard her say. She used a German pronunciation for her name — Mar-lane-a — but the surname was French.

Marlena. He savored the name now that he had it and liked it. It suited her, Theo thought and decided if she were being taken to the hospital, then he might as well go too.

"All right," he told Autumn. "Promise me you'll do everything you can so that dinner runs smoothly."

"Of course," she replied. "It'll be fine."

Theo lacked her complete confidence, although he knew he could be a control freak. His desire to see more of Marlena outweighed his business concerns.

Five long hours later, clean, dry, and warm, Theo prepared to walk out of the hospital. The wait had been extended after other patients arrived at the emergency room with more life-threatening cases — a heart attack, a snakebite, and a car crash victim. His hopes to see how Marlena fared had been dashed when she was taken to one cubicle, and he went to another.

Fatigue dogged his steps. It had been a long day anyway, and his efforts to save Marlena had taken their toll. If being tired wasn't enough, his stomach rolled and cramped. The physician on duty had told him he'd most likely suffer a round of gastroenteritis from the nasty Missouri River water.

"My orders are to take a few days off," he told Theo. "Your body needs the rest, and you shouldn't be around food when you're sick."

"But I run a restaurant," Theo said.

"I know—best schnitzel in town. But you wouldn't want to work with the crud, would you?"

Theo sighed. He wouldn't.

"So go home, get some rest."

Dressed in loaner scrubs, his damp clothes in a bag, Theo wandered out to the admissions area and asked to use the phone. His cell had been in his pocket, and he figured it was kaput. Bummed that he hadn't seen any more of Marlena, he called Jonas for a ride.

"We're on the way back," his friend said. "It'll be twenty minutes, maybe a little more, so hang tight."

Theo found a seat and slouched in the hard plastic chair to wait. He craved his own clothes, a long hot shower, and his bed. Although he hated to admit it, he didn't feel well at all.

Ten minutes into his wait, Marlena appeared, also in scrubs. She searched the room, located him, and sat down.

"You look like I feel," she said with empathy. "I wanted to say thank you again for saving my life."

He shrugged. "You're welcome. I'm Theo, by the way."

"Marlena."

"It's my pleasure, Marlena," he said. "Do you need a ride home?"

"Home is St. Joe," she said, naming the old river town north of Kansas City. "But I'll take your offer if you can drop me at The Vogel Haus. It's where I'm staying."

"Sure," he said. "My best friend will be here soon, but I'm sure he won't mind dropping you off on the way to take me home. So, you're just visiting then?"

Although he'd expected that, it came as a letdown. Up close, she was even more beautiful than he'd realized. He liked the quiet sound of her voice, and he would like to get better acquainted, but he didn't want a long-distance relationship.

"Yes and no," Marlena said. "I came to check out the town

and for a job interview. If I get hired, I'll be moving here. Do you live here?"

"Born and raised here," Theo told her. "I live above my restaurant, Bah Humbug!"

Marlena nodded. "I love the name. I haven't been, but I was hoping to try it out. Why did you call it Bah Humbug!?"

Theo hesitated for a moment, then spilled it. "Because I'm Scrooge, Theo Scrooge."

In his experience, most people laughed or made a joke, but she didn't. "It's a fine old English name," she said. "I won't forget it, that's for sure."

No lame jokes about being stingy or Christmas or Tiny Tim. He liked her more for it.

Jonas arrived a few minutes later with his fiancée Shannon. Although Theo had explained in brief on the phone, Jonas looked him up and down with a frown.

"Can't leave town for the day without you diving into the river," he said, shaking his head. He smirked at Theo, but his eyes were dark with concern. "Are you okay?"

"*Ja*, I'll live," Theo said. "Probably gonna be sick from the water, but it could be a lot worse. Do you mind taking Marlena by the Vogel Haus? She's staying there."

Jonas appeared to be about to laugh but contained it. "Sure, no problem. Let's get both of you out of here."

His stomach twisted in a harsh cramp. "I'm ready," Theo said before he vomited or worse in front of Marlena.

At the bed and breakfast, he walked her to the front door, wishing he felt better and that he had something more to say. "How much longer are you here?"

"Till Tuesday," she answered with a grimace. "I have a feeling I'm not going to enjoy it, though."

"I'm on orders to stay away from my restaurant," Theo told her. "I hope you get the job. What was it again?"

"I'm a teacher," Marlena said. "A boring old teacher."

"Let me know if you move here. I'll buy you dinner or something."

Her lips curved upward. "I'd like that…someday."

Then she put a hand on her belly, and he understood. His own guts were in knots.

"Thanks again," she told him.

Theo cupped her face in his hands. He wanted to kiss her, but they both felt rotten, and it might be too soon. "No big deal. Go get some rest, Marlena."

"Most people call me Marlee," she told him. "You get rested too."

She leaned forward and planted a swift kiss on his cheek, then left him on the porch, wondering.

Chapter Three

As predicted, the dunk in the mighty but filthy Missouri River made him very sick for a couple of days. Theo suffered violent bouts of vomiting and diarrhea. He also ran a fever and had some respiratory issues. All that combined to make him sick enough, he thought he would rather just die, although rationally, he knew he wouldn't. His mom and grandmother took over Bah Humbug! Oma sat on a stool behind the cash register and bossed the entire staff while his mom carried most of the cooking with Liz Vogel's able assistance. She also made soups for him once he could keep more than broth and a few saltines down.

On Tuesday evening, the fourth day after he'd dived in after Marlena, Theo decided he felt almost human again. He wondered if she were still in town or if she'd made the trip home. *I'd hate to make the trip in this condition,* he thought, wishing her well. He'd looked up the distance and calculated it would take her three and a half hours, maybe longer depending on route and traffic, to reach St. Joseph.

Until now, Theo had lacked the energy or inclination to do anything, but with his tablet in hand, he did a few Google searches with her name. Her hometown had three high schools, and he checked the staff list on each one until he found her, a history teacher at Lafayette High School. In her photo, she had her hair pulled up into a high ponytail. A few more searches brought results that she was active in community theater and had graduated from Missouri Western State University. Assuming she'd finished at the average age, it put her just a few years younger than Theo, probably in her early thirties. He liked that — he'd thought she might be younger.

A couple of key clicks, he found her address. He'd expected an apartment, but Marlena lived in an old frame house on a narrow street in the heart of the city. Theo didn't know much about St. Joseph, although he'd visited twice, just that outlaw Jesse James was killed there and that it was where the Pony Express started their short-lived existence.

He wished they had exchanged phone numbers, but they didn't. Maybe she'd get the local job and come to town. The possibility both thrilled and scared him.

Lost in thought, Theo failed to hear his mom come upstairs and jumped when she entered his bedroom with a tray.

"I didn't mean to startle you," Liesel said. "Did I wake you? I have your supper."

"Good, I'm hungry," he replied. "And, no, I wasn't asleep. Actually, I feel a lot better."

Her expression brightened. "That's wonderful! And you're hungry — that's a good sign."

His stomach quivered a little. "It is, although I need to go slow, be particular about what I eat," Theo said. "What is it?"

"Potato soup." She raised the lid on the dish, and he inhaled the aroma with interest.

"Here, I'll take it to the kitchen. I'd rather eat at the table. Can you stay a few minutes?"

Liesel smiled. "As long as you'd like, son."

He ate the soup by slow spoonfuls, savoring the creamy taste. "*Sehr gut*," he told her. "Was this the special too?"

"No, that I made just for you. Do you want more? I can go downstairs and get some."

Tempted, he decided not to risk it. "No, I'll quit with this. What was the special?"

"Cheese spaetzle and Cornish pasties. Black Forest cake for dessert."

Theo nodded. "How's business? I thought I'd come back down in the morning."

She made a dismissive gesture with one hand. "That's too soon. No, no, you're just now recovering. Business is good — Saturday is soon enough. Besides, Hanna is coming, and she'll help."

"Hanna is coming. Why?"

As fair as Theo was dark, his favorite cousin had the classic Teutonic beauty with blonde hair and light blue eyes. He saw her a few times a year — she worked as a flight attendant for Delta and lived in Atlanta. They'd grown up as close as brother and sister, a bond that remained.

"Her favorite cousin almost drowns, and you wonder why she's coming?" his mother asked with a grin.

He laughed. "Then it's a good thing I'm out of bed, or she'd be trying to spoon-feed me. How long is she staying?"

"Only till early Sunday," she said, rising. She leaned down to pat his shoulder. "I'm going home now — I will see you in the morning. If you get hungry, there's lemon sorbet in your tiny freezer."

"And Gatorade," he said, although now he'd had his fill of the sports drink.

"There's ginger ale, too, now," she said.

"Ah, *Mutti*, thank you."

"Get more sleep — you need it."

Theo promised he would, but he didn't. He took a long shower to wash away all the sickbed stench and shaved. Then he sprawled out on the couch and watched most of a movie before he drifted to sleep. He woke cold past midnight, so he stumbled his way to bed and slept.

He took another day to sleep and to eat sparingly with caution. Then Theo descended downstairs, not to work but to escape isolation. His staff, the lunchtime customers, and a few friends greeted him with enthusiasm.

"You're here," Autumn squealed. "Do you want something? Coffee? A beer?"

He laughed. "No to both. If there's any ginger ale, I'll take a small glass."

Her face clouded. "I don't think we have any."

"Yes, we do," Theo's mom called from the kitchen. "Have a seat, Theo."

"I didn't come down just to sit," he told her.

"Jonas went to pick up Hanna at Lambert," she said. "They should be here in an hour or so. Take it easy while you can—she'll talk your ears off."

He retreated to his tiny office, tucked behind the small staff break area. A stack of mail waited on his desk, so Theo worked through it, filing bills and tossing junk mail. A bright blue envelope stood out, and he pulled it free, curious. His name was written across the front c/o of Bah Humbug!, and when he noticed the postmark, he started to grin. He flipped the envelope over and saw her name and address.

The "thinking of you" card was simple, with artwork that depicted a boating scene. Marlena had signed it, but there was also a letter penned with a neat, precise script.

Dear Theo:
I just wanted to drop a note and say thank you again. I would

have written sooner, but I was under the weather. I hope you were not as ill as I have been — I wouldn't wish it on anyone. Never realized river water had so much nasty or that it could make someone sick. I remembered the name of your restaurant — still think it's awesome — and I liked your town very much. I almost felt like I'd been to Europe, and I hope more than ever I might be hired by the local school district. You probably have a terrible impression of me, but you are my hero now! I hope to meet you again if I move there. Till then, you're someone I will never forget. Best, Marlee. P.S. if you ever wanted to call me, here's my cell number.

Theo read it twice, pleased she'd written and more smitten than ever. Warm pleasure washed through him, and he decided to act before he changed his mind — or his cousin arrived. He booted up the laptop he used in the office and brought up a page for floral deliveries. Roses seemed too over the top, far too romantic; daisies were too basic, and lilies reminded him of funerals. Theo wanted something pretty yet simple. A multi-colored tulip arrangement caught his eye, and he liked the Mason jar vase. He ordered it with hopes she did live at the address he'd found online, typing a simple message for the card. "Have a beautiful day! Fingers crossed you get the job, Theo."

He hit send before he lost his nerve. Theo indulged in a few brief moments imagining Marlena's response when the tulips were delivered, then shook himself out of the daydream. He folded her card and stuffed it into his back pocket. Delightful anticipation lingered as he imagined what might happen if she moved to Hermann, and he liked the possibilities.

Oma stuck her head in the door. "You look peaked, Theo," she said, her voice quivery with age.

He rose and hugged her, as careful as if she were made of fine porcelain. "I probably do, but I'm fine now."

"Don't let Hanna keep you up all hours of the night

talking," she told him.

Theo laughed. "I won't. Isn't she staying at your house?"

"*Ja,* but that won't stop her. I know the two of you." His grandmother waggled one finger at him, grinning. "You're grown up now, but you haven't changed that much."

He agreed, but before he could tell her, he heard a rush of voices at the front of the house, Hanna's among them.

"She's here," he told Oma and waited to follow her.

Hanna stood with Jonas and his mom, surrounded by local folks welcoming her back. Her blonde hair had darkened from the near white shade of early childhood to a golden color, he noticed. She glanced up and saw him.

"Theo!" she cried as she maneuvered toward him.

"Hey, short stuff," he said. "I see you haven't grown any."

At barely five feet tall, she didn't even reach his shoulder.

"And you haven't got any smarter," she returned. "Jumping into the river was stupid. Fool!" She punctuated the last with a swift punch to his left shoulder, then she enveloped him in a hug. "Your stunt took years off my life," she said low into his ear. "You could have died, Theo."

"True, but I didn't."

When he'd leapt into the Missouri after Marlena, he hadn't thought, just acted. But since he had realized they both could have easily drowned.

Hanna pulled back to look at him. "Are you all right? I mean, really, all right?"

"I am. I'd be in the kitchen cooking, but no one will let me yet."

"You should take the time you need to recover. Besides, I can help with the food prep."

Theo put on a shocked expression, then laughed. "Maybe. Come on back, we can talk."

She shook her head. "I want to eat. Can't we grab a table

out here?"

"If you want, sure."

He led her to one in the back, close to the kitchen, and pulled out her chair. Hanna slid into it.

"Thanks. What's the special?"

Theo shrugged. "I don't know, but we can find out."

Autumn arrived, pad in hand. "It's *Marsch* or steak pie, a trifle for dessert."

"So, beef stew or steak pie?" Hanna said.

"Order anything you want from the menu," Theo told her.

"What are you going to have?"

He hadn't planned to eat, uncertain if his belly was ready or not, but this was Hanna. She had the family trait of stubbornness. If he didn't eat, she probably wouldn't either.

"*Marsch*," he said. "Small bowl, please."

"I want *frikadellen* with bread and butter and potato salad," Hanna told Autumn. "And a beer, please."

"Sure thing. Theo?"

"Another ginger ale."

Although he hadn't really been hungry yet, the aromas wafting from the kitchen awakened his appetite. Theo figured he'd do well to eat the stew without suffering any problems.

As they waited, the cousins talked. Their bond had always been one so deep that once together, it was as if they had never been apart. While Jonas was his brother from another mother, Hanna had been like the sister he never had, closer than most cousins.

"So, tell me about the woman you saved."

"What's there to tell?"

"How did it happen? Did she jump in or what?"

Theo sketched out the details, and when he described the boys on bikes, she frowned.

"Who are they? They should have some consequences for

their actions."

"I didn't recognize them," he said. "But I don't know many kids, not unless I know their families or go to church."

Her lips pressed together tight. "Hmm. Maybe I should try to track them down."

"Don't," he told her, then repeated their grandmother's often stated fact. "I have to live here."

Autumn delivered their food. Hanna sighed with pleasure. "I've missed food like this. German food isn't popular in Georgia."

"It wouldn't be like this, anyway, without family recipes or my touch," he laughed.

"True but vain," she said.

Theo tasted the *marsch* and savored the flavors of beef, carrot, onions and more. The rich stew included *spaetzle,* and it rested easy within. He doubted he could have managed a larger portion, but it was delicious and nourishing.

Hanna complimented her food and finished it before he'd eaten all the stew. She put the beer bottle to her lips and drank.

"Perfect," she said. "Now, tell me more about Marlena. Did you already know her?"

He had a suspicion that Jonas might have provided too much information. His friend knew him well and had realized Theo had an attraction for her.

"No, she's not from here. She's a tourist."

"That's too bad. You haven't dated for how long now?"

Theo tried to stare Hanna down, but she never blinked. If he didn't answer, she would hound him relentlessly.

"Nosy of you to ask, but about three weeks."

Her surprised look wasn't flattering. "Really?"

"Yes," he said, but it wasn't so. "I date, Hanna."

"But you haven't had a girlfriend since Theresa, have you?"

"Is that all you and Jonas had to talk about on the way here from the airport?"

She signaled Autumn for another beer and nodded. "One of the things, yes. He's concerned you're so alone."

Theo swore in German, which meant he was perturbed.

"I'm not alone," he said, offended because, in some ways, he was. "Or lonely. I don't have time to be lonely."

"Oh, Theo," she said. "It's been so long since Theresa. Do you ever see her or hear from her?"

"No." He spat out the single word. "I don't, and that's how I want it."

Theresa Duncan was his past, not future or present. He had dated her for almost a year after she'd come out from Kansas City to do a travel piece on Bah Humbug! for a regional magazine. The article had brought him increased business, but the relationship had been toxic. After her initial delight in the tiny German-style town, Theresa had wanted Theo to move, first to Kansas City, then to either Seattle or Los Angeles. Hermann was Theo's home. He was grounded here. Family, friends and his business were all there.

After the first six months, their relationship became long-distance, which meant Theo drove to KC every week, at least once and often twice. Although she wrote the story and took the photos in early January, the piece ran during October along with other Oktoberfest and German-themed pieces. At first, he enjoyed the novelty of the urban scene, but his absences soon affected his business, which Theresa failed to grasp.

The more she demanded his presence in Kansas City, the more reluctant he became to go. Opa had still been alive then, although his health had become precarious. The weaker his grandfather grew, the closer Theo stuck to home, realizing Opa had months, not years, left.

By then, he knew Theresa and he were not compatible.

At Thanksgiving, he had invited her to share the holiday with his family, and she agreed, but nothing went as planned. Theresa refused to stay at the winery and insisted she stay with Theo. The small space proved not to be large enough, and worse, she tried to get involved in Bah Humbug! She wanted to play hostess while mocking the town and the customs.

When Oma served the traditional goose at Thanksgiving dinner instead of turkey, Theresa had complained and refused to even try it. She monopolized the conversation, tried to make Theo take her to St. Louis to see a movie on Thanksgiving evening, and once back at his place, bitched about everything from the wine to the dessert. If that hadn't been enough, she got up on Friday and hauled in boxes of holiday decorations from her car.

"What is all that?" Theo had asked, arms crossed.

"I'm going to decorate your restaurant, darling," Theresa replied. "You'll love it!"

"No," he had said. "*Nein.*"

The celebration of Christmas was a long-standing sore spot for Theo. He didn't put up any holiday decor in his restaurant or apartment. The only way he acknowledged the holiday was with a few gifts for his family and dinner at his grandparents' house. He'd had his fill long since of the Scrooge jokes and references, both of which spoiled a celebration he once enjoyed. Most years, he went to Midnight Mass because it pleased both his mother and grandmother.

Theresa knew all that. They'd discussed it many times, but on that Black Friday, she was determined not to respect his feelings.

"Don't be silly, Theo," she had told him, pursing her crimson lipsticked mouth into a pout. "Think how pretty it will look, and I bought all these things."

She held up ornaments and wreaths, Santas and snowmen, stockings and strings of multi-colored lights.

"Put that stuff away," Theo said. "Take it back to your car."

Ignoring him, she grinned. "We have to go get a fresh tree somewhere. I was thinking a big Douglas Fir would be nice, but I'd settle for a Scotch Pine."

His simmering anger boiled over. "No, no, and no," he said, voice raised. "No tree, no wreaths, no Santa, none of it, Theresa."

Her eyes flashed hot with rage, and she tried to sidestep Theo. He put up one arm to stop her, and she danced sideways, losing her grip on the box she carried. Her grip faltered, and it dropped. The sound of breaking glass filled his ears, but he wasn't sorry.

"You made me break the ornaments," she screamed. "I ordered those online. They were hand-blown glass from Germany. Do you have any idea how much they cost?"

"*Na, ja,* I don't care. Now clean up this mess and put the rest of it back in your car. I've got to prep for lunch."

Theresa's face turned red. "Ohhh!" she cried. "You have the right name, that's for sure. Scrooge! Ebenezer Scrooge! You're as mean as he was!"

For Theo, their relationship ended the moment she spoke. He could tolerate a lot and had over the past few months, but for her to hit his Achilles heel and then hammer it was unacceptable.

"Theresa." With effort, he had throttled his voice down to almost mild. "You need to go home now. Don't bother with the mess—I'll take care of it—but pack up these things and go."

Her mouth opened wide. "Go where?"

"Back to Kansas City," he'd replied. "Or go to the devil. I don't care."

Although he spoke English, he used the usual German wording, go to the devil, not go to hell.

Theo remembered much too well how her face had

hardened when she realized he meant what he said and how she'd tossed the decorations into his dumpster, overfilling it. Then she'd stared at him.

"I'll go, Theo, but this is it. We're over. Stay here in your stupid little burg and be mean, *Scrooge!* Don't ask me to come back—I won't."

"Good," he had said.

She had departed within minutes and didn't look back. He'd heard she eventually moved to Seattle, but Theo didn't care. If his life was empty, it was still an improvement over sharing it with Theresa.

Caught up remembering, Theo had tuned out Hanna and his surroundings. Shaking his head, he realized she was still talking.

"So, do you ever think about her, Theo?"

"I don't unless someone brings her up," he said. "Hanna, let it go. Theresa wasn't right for me. It just took me too long to figure that out."

Still tired after his illness, Theo stood up. He'd heard more than enough about the woman he'd rather forget ever existed, and his stomach was a little uneasy.

"Theo, I didn't mean to make you mad," Hanna said, and her expression confirmed it.

He shrugged his shoulders. "I think I could use a nap," he told her. *"Ich bin krank im Magen."*

With that, Theo walked into the kitchen. His mother must have overheard, because she reached out and grasped his arm.

"Theo, don't you feel well?"

"I've been better," he told her. "I just need to sleep a little more."

Theo kissed her cheek and continued upstairs.

Before he shut the door, he heard Hanna's voice raised and his mother's less shrill reply. He had no doubt that she regretted bringing up the past, but Theo needed a little space, favorite cousin or not.

Instead of lying down, he picked up the new cell phone Jonas had dropped off yesterday to replace the one lost in the river. Theo had programmed it, and now, with Marlena's card in hand, he added her number. Then he texted his new number to her. Without waiting to see if she would respond, he removed his shoes, stretched out on the bed, and went to sleep. *Might as well,* he figured, *now that I've shot the day to pieces.*

Chapter Four

Later, in the afternoon, Marlena called, and that was enough to salvage Theo's day. His cell phone rang, rousing him from a sound sleep, and without bothering to read the caller ID, he answered.

"Theo."

"It's Marlee."

He sat up, realized his stomach had calmed and tried to gather his wits. "I got your card. How are you?"

"Good," she said. "Theo, thank you for the flowers. I love them — they're just what I needed to brighten up my day."

"You got the tulips, then?"

"I did. My favorite flower, especially now."

Theo sighed with relief. She could have hated them. "I'm glad."

He wanted to say more, to keep the conversation going, but he lacked words. He liked this woman, from what he knew about her, which wasn't much. Her beauty had attracted him, and when he pulled her out of the river, it made a bond. She must have had similar thoughts because when Theo was about to wrap up the call for lack of anything to say, Marlee asked a question.

"What do you serve at Bah Humbug! I was curious. Is it meant to be like an English pub or what?"

Theo rolled over and sat up, finding a comfortable position against the pillows. "It's more or what," he said with a chuckle. "It's modeled after an English pub, that's true, but we serve both English favorites and traditional German food. I have a special from each cuisine every day and a dessert, plus a menu with items from both. Plus a few American standards like steak and burgers and such."

"It sounds interesting. I wish I'd had time to eat there."

"Next time you're here, it's on the house," Theo said with an effort to sound casual. "Do you think you'll be back, or did the dunking ruin the place?"

"Oh, no, not at all. Yes, I plan to come back. I think I told you — maybe not, it all runs together in my head — that I applied for a teaching job. If I get hired, I'll be moving there."

A wild hope made his head whirl and his heart pound. "You did mention that."

"I really hope I get the position. I think I fell in love with your town. It's like a little piece of Europe in the middle of Missouri. There's a lot of history here in St. Joe, but it's larger, and it lacks that Old World feel, I think."

"I liked the Patee House and the Pony Express Stables. I could imagine the Old West days."

"You've been here! That's awesome."

"Just a couple of times. Once to buy some restaurant equipment when I was getting ready to open, once just to see the sights."

The second time had been with Theresa, but he'd rather not recall that trip.

"If you come back sometime, let me know. I'll show you all the sights. If you like history, there's some other sites, and we have some awesome parks. I teach history, so it's a passion."

On impulse, Theo decided he might make a trip to her hometown. "That's great. I may be there over Memorial Day weekend."

"Really? That would be wonderful."

Until his recent days out of commission, Theo couldn't remember when he'd last taken leisure time off, but he decided he would. They talked for a few more minutes and mutually agreed to hang up.

"Now you have my number. Call me anytime, Marlena," Theo offered.

"Thanks, I will. Please call me Marlee," she replied.

Encouraged, Theo took a shower and headed downstairs just before the dinner rush.

His mom pulled a pan of gingerbread from the oven as he walked into the kitchen. Across the room, Hanna, now clad in an apron, wrapped silverware. Both glanced up as he entered.

"Look who's back," his mother said.

"The triumphant return," he returned. "That smells good."

"If you want some, I can cut you a piece. There's whipped cream, too, if you think you can handle it."

"Maybe after a while," he said. "Hanna, I need to apologize."

His cousin faced him. "No, I do. I got pushy and nosy where it's none of my business. I never really knew what happened with Theresa, but Tante filled me in a little. I'm sorry, Theo."

"Me, too." He opened his arms, and she stepped in for a hug. "Are we good?"

"Of course."

Theo grinned. "Better be—we reopen in fifteen minutes. Where's Liz?"

"It's her day off," his mother said. "But with Hanna here, Oma and I are leaving very soon."

"I can help, if I need to."

Liesel removed her apron. "If you do, go slow. See you tomorrow."

She kissed his cheek, and he hugged her.

Business was steady but light, the average for a Wednesday night when half the town attended midweek church services. Hanna did most of the kitchen work, dishing up the specials until they were gone. She managed most of the menu orders, but Theo helped with two. His evening servers, single mom Constance and Eva, handled the diners with ease.

Just before nine, Jonas strolled in, and when he saw Theo, he grinned. "Can I get a beer and a steak?"

"Sure, on the house even."

The sheriff raised one eyebrow. "Cool, but why? Are you delirious and giving food away?"

"No, just returning the favor. Thanks for picking me up at the hospital."

"Thanks for not drowning. Good to see you on your feet. You should know better than to drink the river water."

Theo laughed. "It wasn't intentional. Strip or ribeye?"

"A thick KC Strip will do."

He gave Constance the okay to lock the front door, and while Hanna cleaned up the kitchen, the servers left, and Theo cooked two steaks. He served Jonas a medium-rare steak with a baked potato and salad on the side. Eva had provided him a beer. His own plate held just a steak, medium. Cooking the steaks made Theo hungry, but he wanted to be wary. He thought he could handle the meat, but he didn't want to overload.

Hanna hovered, so he waved her over. "Want to join us?"

She shook her head. "No, if you don't need anything else, I'll head out to Oma's. It's been a long day. I just need a ride."

Jonas put down his knife and fork. "I can take you."

"Finish eating first."

Theo reached in his pocket for keys and came up empty. "You can take my truck," he said. "The keys are upstairs. I can go get them, or you can."

Hanna beamed. "I can find them. Kitchen counter?"

"That or by the bed, beside the alarm clock."

The truck in question was in a free-standing garage behind the place and was vintage. The 1953 3100 Chevy Pickup had been Opa's, bought used in the late fifties, then driven for decades, and handed over to Theo when he turned sixteen. He had learned how to work on motors with the truck, kept it running enough to drive back and forth to Columbia for college, and restored it once he made enough money. Now in mint condition, the truck was a deep forest green with tan leather seats and an engine any car enthusiast would envy.

"You're letting her take the truck?" Jonas asked.

"One time, just to out to Mom's," Theo replied. "I trust her to manage that."

Hanna rocketed down the steps from his apartment, keys jingling in her hand. "I heard that. But thank you, anyway."

She rushed him, planted a smacking kiss on his cheek, and headed for the door.

"Hanna." His solemn tone halted her. "Don't put a scratch on it, okay?"

Her fingers traced an X across her chest. "Cross my heart and hope to die."

"And bring it back in the morning," he called.

Jonas shook his head with a smile. Theo ate his steak in small, slow bites, savoring each one. While they dined, his friend told him local highlights.

"Did anyone invite you to town council yet?" he asked, after he'd finished eating.

Theo stilled. "No, why would they?"

The last time he'd been summoned to a meeting, Blevins

had attempted to stir trouble about some code violation, something about occupancy. It had gone nowhere. Theo had been precise in his remodeling of the old building, which had once housed an old-fashioned grocery store.

Jonas smirked. "They're going to give you some hero award for saving a life," he said. "A week from Friday."

"I don't want it—I did what anyone would do."

"Really? I didn't hear about anyone else jumping into the damn river. Let them give it to you—you earned it. Make being sicker than a dying dog count for something."

"I'll think about it. Want to play some chess?"

"I'll take a raincheck. Shannon's coming over, and you look like you need the rest."

Hoping he didn't look as haggard as he felt, Theo agreed. As soon as he stacked their dishes in the dishwasher and put the kitchen to rights, he headed upstairs, ready to sleep. Instead, he found himself wide awake, so he went online, checked out St. Joseph's tourism site, and perused the hotel selection. After an hour or so spent making tentative plans for a late May trip, he yawned and retired to sleep until morning.

Theo made coffee before heading downstairs. Early enough, he beat his mother, grandmother, and cousin. Since he hadn't prepared menus, he did so, deciding on pork schnitzel sandwiches with *Bratkartoffeln* or an English bacon butty. Dessert he left up to his mother's choice. He also, in the interest of planning ahead, chose Friday's menus—breaded trout served with a warm apple and cabbage slaw or traditional pub-style fish and chips.

Despite the medical advice he'd been given on Monday night, Theo started cooking. He enjoyed his work, and although his mother could cook equally well, he had culinary arts training that he liked to think gave his food a little pizazz. He turned on the radio to his favorite classic rock channel and blasted it loud. Although there were times when he could listen to German music or Bach, Theo's personal preference reflected rock tastes.

Theo thought about Marlee as he worked, remembering his first sight of her on Monday. Hard to believe he hadn't known her more than a few days, or that in that short span of time, he'd saved her life, or that they were in the early stages of something. He couldn't name it yet, but his heart knew what he wanted. He hadn't known such a pull to any woman since long before Theresa, who had been more convenience than crush.

He sang along with some of his favorite tunes, uninhibited. With the music blasting, he didn't realize his mother had arrived until she turned down the radio.

"So, it's *schnitzel* today?" she asked, without a word about the rock and roll.

"Good morning," he said. "Yes, as sandwiches with *Bratkartoffeln* and bacon butty sandwiches. What's the dessert?"

"*Zwetchenkuchen,*" she said.

"Plum cake!" he replied. "That's one of my favorites."

Liesel laughed. "I know. That's why I made it."

Theo envied her the dedication it took to rise early six mornings out of seven to bake. Sometimes she baked after she returned home for the day, but he knew the effort it required.

"Can I have a piece?" He hadn't had breakfast yet.

"*Jawohl,* you can."

"Good, then I'll start the bacon," he said. "But one question—where's Hanna and my truck?"

"She'll be here soon, I think."

He didn't worry—much. Hanna arrived just before he opened for lunch.

Somewhere between all the hectic bustle of rush, between plating specials and smiling, Hanna persuaded Theo to take a break, which by then he needed.

"So, it's Thursday," she said after he sat down across from her.

The way she said it, Theo figured she had a reason, but he was clueless. "And that means what?"

"I leave early Sunday morning," she said. "I only have the rest of today, tomorrow, and Saturday to spend with you."

Now he understood. "We should do something. But what?"

Hanna grinned, the mischievous smile that had so often got them both in trouble during their shared childhood.

"I have a few ideas."

Her ideas turned out to be spending the day in St. Louis, hiking at the Grand Bluffs Conservation Area, horseback riding, or taking the Amtrak to the Light and Power District in Kansas City. Theo lacked enthusiasm for any of those possibilities, but he tried to pretend interest. One, he hated to spend time away from Bah Humbug! after his mom had taken up the slack for most of the week, and two, he preferred simple pleasures.

"What about a picnic in the park?" he suggested. "Or spend the day out at the family winery."

Although his grandmother and mother lived in the vintage farmhouse, his cousin Thomas Schubert, Hanna's brother, ran the actual winery. Unlike most of the local wineries, he kept it small, but the wine produced was exquisite, and Theo took pride in serving it.

She wrinkled up her nose. "That's so basic. We could go up to Jeff City and tour the old penitentiary."

"I'd rather take a picnic to the shrine."

The Shrine of Our Lady of Sorrows at Starkenberg across the river was one of the most peaceful places Theo had ever been. After his close encounter with the wicked Missouri River, he craved calm. To his surprise, Hanna nodded.

"That could work. We could take a picnic, eat on the grounds."

"When do you want to go?"

She countered him. "When can you go?"

He smiled. She knew him too well, committed to his work.

"If I get the specials ready to serve tomorrow, we could go right after we open and be back by five."

"All right. But I put together the picnic."

Theo agreed. He might have said more, but Blevins strolled in with a group that included the mayor. Again.

"Well, if it isn't our local hero!" the man said with a sneer. "Scrooge, back at work."

Although anger flared like a struck match, Theo schooled his expression to stay benign. "Our specials today are schnitzel sandwiches or bacon sandwiches," he said as he led them to a table. "And of course, we offer our full menu as well. Autumn will be here to get your order shortly."

"Missed a chance to decrease the surplus population by one, didn't you?" Blevins asked. "But I guess even a Scrooge will save a pretty gal."

Theo gritted his teeth. If he didn't walk away now, he'd punch him and go to jail for assault. He held his tongue and turned away as Autumn approached with her order pad and a bright greeting.

It's not worth it. The hassle isn't worth it, he thought as he stalked back to the kitchen. But the one thing he did know was that Marlee was.

In the kitchen, he busied his hands to avoid thinking about Todd Blevins, but his mother, intuitive as ever, put her hand on his arm. "Don't mind him," she said. "He's nothing and nobody."

He forced a laugh. "I know, but—"

"But after— How long has it been? More than twenty years? It shouldn't matter."

Theo nodded, then sighed. His mother remembered, and so did he.

On a cold winter day during his fourth-grade year, Theo had been changing after P.E. in the locker room. He had moved slow, aware that if he happened to be tardy to his next class, he would be excused. He had glanced down at his left wrist where he sported the new watch he'd received for Christmas. The Timex Indiglo watch lit up with the press of a tiny button and was the first adult watch he'd had. Theo took both pleasure and pride in the watch.

Todd Blevins emerged from the showers, dripping and without any modesty. He jiggled when he walked, but Theo couldn't fail to notice that the other boy wasn't as physically developed as he was. To be polite, he glanced away.

"Hey, you got one of those watches!"

He had nodded. "Yes, for Christmas."

"I want it — give it to me!"

"No," Theo had said.

Blevins grabbed his wrist, Theo had pulled away, and they ended up tussling, Theo landing a few good punches the way Opa, a one-time Golden Gloves champion, had taught him. Coach had heard their scuffle and broke up the fight. They both got in trouble at school, but before, Blevins had been just an annoying kid. Afterward, he had become an enemy bent on revenge. There had been a few Scrooge jokes before, but after the fight, Blevins stepped up his game and had never stopped.

"He knows what pushes my buttons," Theo said. "I'll try harder not to let him."

"*Sehr gut,*" Mutti said. "Now, catch up. We've got people to feed."

Theo fell into the familiar rhythm and pushed Blevins out of his head. Instead, he indulged in a few thoughts about Marlee. Maybe later, he'd give her a call.

Chapter Five

On Friday, although gray skies foretold rain, the weather held off until after Theo and Hanna had their picnic at the shrine. Our Lady of Sorrows lay across the river from town in the hills. The church and outdoor stations of the cross remained, and as soon as he climbed out of the truck, Theo found the peace he'd always found here.

Hanna carried the old wicker picnic basket from Oma's house, and so far, she hadn't revealed the contents.

"I'm glad we're doing this," he told his cousin as she handed him a faded quilt. "And I'm glad you came."

She shrugged. "It's been good to be home and to see you. I couldn't live here like you do, but sometimes I need to come back and get grounded, put my feet on the earth for a few days."

Theo thought about Atlanta, how the traffic roared down the interstates and major thoroughfares with speed and shook his head. "I couldn't live there."

"Atlanta?" she asked, pausing at a shady spot. "Does this work for our picnic?"

He nodded. "Sure. Yes, Atlanta. I'm not cut out for urban

life."

Hanna rolled her eyes. "Why couldn't you be? You like to go to St. Louis or KC, don't you?"

Theo did, but he also liked to return home and told her so.

"If you had a place like Bah Humbug! in Atlanta, you'd be rich."

"I make a living, and that's enough. I like it here."

She opened the basket and handed him a piece of cold fried chicken. "Yes, I fried chicken," she told him. "Oma's recipe."

"Thanks, I love fried chicken."

"I remember," Hanna said. "And Hermann suits you. I am sorry that I said your life was empty and lonely. It's not—it's full."

Theo bit into the chicken. "That's delicious. I am lonely sometimes, Hanna. I do want to be married and have a family someday."

He had, for as long as he could remember. There had been a time when he thought the city would be the place for him and his dreams, but he changed his mind. When Ted Scrooge, his dad, died during Theo's senior year, he'd realized he needed his strong family. Scrooge Senior had been a long-haul truck driver. His dad had always come in and out of their life like the seasons. He'd always known, though, that he'd be back until the accident on an icy bridge near Springfield ended Ted's life.

"I don't," Hanna said. "Or not for a long time yet. Maybe you'll find your happily ever after, Theo. For your sake, I hope you do."

He thought of Marlee and smiled. Hanna, who'd known him forever, caught the expression and read it correctly.

"It's her," Hanna exclaimed. "Isn't it? The woman you saved?"

"Marlee," Theo said. "I barely know her."

Although he schooled his voice casual, he didn't fool his

cousin.

"That doesn't mean you aren't interested, though."

"I am," he admitted. "We'll see."

And although Hanna teased and begged for more, Theo wouldn't talk about Marlee. Instead, they shared memories from their childhood and enjoyed the food she'd prepared. By four, the clouds had darkened, and Theo could smell rain.

"We need to get back," he said. "It's going to pour any time now, and it's almost time to open for dinner."

The skies opened and emptied rain until they were both soaked.

Traci had everything under control, so Theo took over the kitchen. The peace he'd known at the shrine evaporated in the steam, and by the time they closed, he was as worn and crumpled as the dish towel he'd just folded.

"I'm heading out," Amber said. "The sheriff's here, waiting for you up front."

Without asking, Theo opened two beers and headed for the dining room. Jonas grinned. "Thought you'd never ask," he said.

"As long as you're off duty, always," Theo said as he sat down. Jonas pushed a folded newspaper toward him. "What's that?"

"This week's paper. There's a brief about the award they're giving you."

Theo read the few lines and shook his head. On impulse, he pulled his cell from his pocket and snapped a photo, then sent it to Marlee with a message, *Only on a slow news day!*

He didn't expect to hear back, but within ten minutes, his phone tinkled like a spoon tapped against glass. When he glanced down and saw she'd replied, a warm delight made him smile as he read her message.

Awesome! Well-earned. Can I come?

Figuring she was joking, he texted back. *Absolutely.*

When he glanced up, Jonas grinned at him. "From your lady?"

Theo shrugged. "*Non wegen!* I barely know her."

"But you want to, don't you?"

Jonas knew him far too well. Theo spread his hands out. "Maybe."

"Then best of luck," he said, raising his bottle in a salute. "*Prost!*"

Theo touched his bottle to his friend's and drank.

He rejected the idea of another chess match, so Jonas suggested a fishing trip on Sunday.

"Maybe. I'm driving Hanna to Lambert early."

"So, we'll go in the afternoon."

"At the river?" Theo wasn't sure he wanted to give the Missouri another shot, not yet.

"Little Bear Creek." Theo hesitated, and Jonas glared. "Come on, this place is closed, so come out, do something fun for a change."

"All right — unless it rains."

"If it does, we'll play chess."

On Saturday, Theo always had specials worthy of a celebration, whether it was a date night or a special birthday or anniversary. Some diners anticipated the Saturday night specials at Bah Humbug! So, after Jonas departed, Theo decided on English pub steak made with chuck, with oven fries, and a chicken breast schnitzel. For next week, he started sauerbraten, a favorite of his, always popular in the restaurant.

Liesel brought apple strudel because it was Hanna's favorite. Although business was brisk, the sun shone for an almost perfect late April day. Theo couldn't shake a little sadness. He would miss his cousin after she returned to Atlanta, although he knew if she stayed, they would sometimes disagree. The last week and a half had been intense — meeting Marlee, rescuing her from the river, and his subsequent illness, along with Hanna's visit combined, almost overwhelmed his emotions. Maybe he should be delighted about the award, but Theo would be relieved when the presentation was done.

On Sunday, he rose at 3 a.m., showered, downed some coffee, and picked Hanna up at the winery. In the cool, quiet darkness of early morning, she waited on the porch with her bags and yawned as he got out to load them into the truck. She cradled a travel mug of coffee in her hands, and for the first few miles, neither said much until they reached the interstate.

Theo, still sleepy, turned on the stereo to a favorite hard rock CD, and Hanna jumped at the first guitar riff.

"I'm awake," she said.

"Good," he replied. "I'm trying to stay that way."

"I should have picked a later flight."

He laughed. "Look at it this way — traffic's light early."

At the next exit, Theo bought them both more coffee at a truck stop, then they rolled into St. Louis as the first light tinged the edges of the sky. Theo stayed on I-70, and they crossed over the Mississippi at St. Charles.

At the airport, Hanna suggested he drop her off near the Delta terminal, but Theo refused. "I'll see you to your gate."

He parked and paid, then they entered the airport. After checking her bags, Theo walked with Hanna as far as he could go.

"I guess this is it," he said. "I'm glad you came. Don't be such a stranger."

"I won't. I'll come for your wedding."

Her light tone made it a joke, but Theo wondered where in the hell that came from. He ignored it and hugged her instead. They said a brief farewell, and she walked away from him without looking back. He watched her go, then returned to his truck for the trip home.

On the way, he stopped in St. Charles long enough to grab a fast-food sausage biscuit and more coffee. Although lighter than on a weekday, traffic increased by the time he took the exit for the two-lane highway that led back to Hermann. Once back, Theo headed upstairs, intending to crash until mid-afternoon. But as tired as he was, he had trouble falling asleep.

He thought about Hanna, tucked into a seat on a jet, probably curled up asleep or gazing out the window. Theo didn't fly much, but when he did, he enjoyed the view of the clouds and, when possible, the land spread out below. Her words lingered — that she would be back for his wedding. Although he'd long hoped to marry, it had been abstract. Women, he thought, were the ones who dreamed of veils and gowns, flowers, and cakes. He could remember when Hanna brought home bridal magazines and when her older sister, Trudi (short for Gertrude), got engaged. The talk had been centered around the upcoming ceremony.

Theo had never daydreamed about a wedding or thought much about it beyond the fact he would be a groom someday. But now Hanna's teasing remark made him think about weddings and about Marlee. They'd barely met, and despite his attraction, it was much too soon to think about marriage. Or so he told himself as he lay awake. The more he tried to sleep, the wider awake he became.

He'd seen St. Morand's decorated for weddings, both when he was an altar server and as a guest. When Jonas and Shannon tied the knot, he would stand beside Jonas as the best man. For the first time, Theo imagined himself dressed in a tuxedo, waiting at the altar for a bride to walk down the aisle. He ached to have a deep relationship, and now he realized he wanted a wife. Someday he wanted kids, too.

Never with Theresa or in any other relationship had Theo

given a thought to marriage. The idea both exhilarated and terrified him. The broad spectrum of emotions kept him stirred and unable to relax. When he finally did succumb to sleep, he had no more than three hours when his phone woke him with his AC/DC "Highway to Hell" ringtone. He rolled over to answer.

"Theo."

He expected Jonas, but it wasn't.

"It's me," Marlee said. "Did I wake you? You sound sleepy."

He sat straight up in bed and ran a hand through his tousled hair. "No, no, I just had an early start. I drove Hanna, my cousin, to the airport in St. Louis this morning. Her plane left at five-thirty."

"Too early for me. About that award you're receiving. Is that Friday?"

Theo almost groaned. "Yeah, Friday at the town council. The meeting starts at seven."

"I thought I'd come if you don't mind."

Her voice carried a tentative note. *She was serious,* he thought.

"I'd love it," he said, totally honest. "That would be great."

Her sigh of relief was audible. "Good, because I bought an Amtrak ticket. I thought I'd come on the train on Friday, stay the weekend maybe."

"That sounds like a plan." Theo's head whirled with possibilities.

"I just wanted to be there—it's my life you saved, after all."

"True."

"Would you meet me at the station?"

"Of course, Marlee."

So, you'll pick me up at the train station around noon on Friday?"

"Yes."

"Okay, I'll find a place to stay, and maybe we'll talk before."

"I hope we do."

And he did. He wanted to keep talking to her, even though a quick glance at the clock confirmed Jonas would be there any time. "What are you doing today?"

"I planted some flowers this morning," she told him. "That and reading on the front porch. What about you?"

"Jonas and I are going fishing."

"Your friend, the sheriff."

"*Ja*, you remembered!'

They talked for a few more minutes. Theo dressed quickly in old jeans, ones with one knee worn through, and an ancient plaid button-down shirt. He dug in the closet for worn boots and gathered his fishing gear. This time when his phone rang, it was Jonas.

They fished along the banks of Bear Creek, one of several streams that flowed into the Gasconade River, which in turn joined the Missouri River. Although they caught no more than a few small bluegills and no keepers, the expedition was pleasant. They talked a little, but mostly the two men savored the day beside the creek.

It was almost dark when they called it quits. Famished since he hadn't eaten since the sausage biscuit, Theo suggested supper at Maybelle's, and Jonas agreed. After a thick cheeseburger with hand-cut fries, Theo headed home, and Jonas to see his bride-to-be.

Theo opened a bottle of Riesling and sat in the open-air dining area. He drank two glasses as he pondered the week ahead, mentally planning menus and with Marlee on his mind. The sweet white wine proved to be an ideal relaxation aid as he wound down and prepared for the coming days.

He sat in the cool darkness, relishing the spring wind against his skin, and let his mind drift, blank. Memories drifted into his mind, and Theo remembered.

***

The night before he opened Bah Humbug!, he'd sat here with a bottle of wine. It hadn't yet become an outdoor dining space, just a side yard, but Theo had dragged a lawn chair out to survey his new domain. He'd been twenty-five, and reflecting back, it seemed now that he'd been impossibly young. He'd graduated first from high school with honors, despite his father's death, then from MU with a business degree and another in culinary arts. Then he'd worked at a bistro in Jefferson City, where state representatives, senators, and even the governor had been known to dine. Theo had honed his cooking skills, lived in a tiny apartment tucked over the garage over one of the fine old homes above downtown on High Street, and skimped to save for his own place.

Jefferson City was a small town, especially for a state capitol, but it had amenities like a mall, numerous chain retail stores, and history. When the building that now housed Bah Humbug! went on the market in his hometown, Theo kept an eye on it. After it had been listed for more than a year, the owner dropped the price, and he made an offer. Once the deal was done, he'd borrowed more money to renovate it into what he imagined. Opening his own place had been a risk, but he'd gambled, and so far, he'd been successful enough to stay open and make some profit.

Ten years later, Theo reflected he'd settled into life in his hometown well, maybe too well. His routine had become all but carved in granite. Although he could envision living his life here and growing old, he realized he wanted more, not in another place or in a different business, but with a family.

Someday, although he hoped that time was distant, his

mother and grandmother would join his father and Opa in the cemetery at Starkenberg. Hanna's life was elsewhere, and he wasn't as close to any of the other cousins. Jonas would always be his brother, but he would soon have a wife, then probably a family of his own.

Ten years later, Theo realized he had a successful business to show for his efforts, but he needed to make new steps. The profit margin was thinner than he'd like. Most of the time he came out in the black, but a few missteps could change that. He planned to hold a tenth birthday bash for Bah Humbug!, maybe in October. Planning would need to start now, he realized, and the ideal time would be October. That month, each weekend became a German party like no other.

"I'll do it," he said aloud. Maybe Marlee would help. At the very least, she could come and be part of the celebration.

Despite the plans he'd spawned, Theo slept well and long when he retired. In the morning, he woke ready to begin a fresh week. Knowing Marlee — how that name suited her, he mused — would be here at the end of the week improved the outlook.

Without any Monday morning blues, Theo started his week with smoked pork chops with potato pancakes and sauerkraut and cottage pie with braised vegetables.

And he counted down the days until Friday.

Chapter Six

The first three days of the week crawled past. Theo opened the restaurant, he cooked, cleaned up, waited a few tables, and more. He mentioned his idea of a ten-year event for Bah Humbug! to his mother, who applauded the idea. Each night the long hours made him ready for bed by eleven, and he slept most nights without waking. Marlee and he texted a few times a day, and he'd talked to her twice.

Thursday morning, Theo was deep in the preparation of *Leberknödel*, a liver and dumplings dish he didn't make often. Too many customers shied away from anything that involved liver, but he had a few who asked for it. It wasn't on the menu as a regular item, so once every six months or so, he'd served it as a special. To him, raised on the stuff, it tasted rich and delicious with little hints of liver. The other special was a simple but classic Salisbury Steak served with mashed Klondike gold potatoes. The dessert, provided as always by his mother, was an English trifle, pound cake served with whipped cream, fresh strawberries, and vanilla custard.

"Theo, the sheriff is on the phone."

He glanced up. "Thanks, Autumn. Give me a second or two."

"He says it's important," she said, and handed him the cordless phone.

He wiped his hands and put it to his ear. "What's up, Jonas?"

A small knot formed in his stomach, wary of bad news. Theo couldn't imagine what it might be, but Sheriff Kaiser wasn't in the habit of calling during the workday.

"Can you spare a half hour or so and come up here?" Jonas said. Although he kept a professional tone, there was a hint of amusement too.

"Now?" Theo wanted to throw up his hands. "We start serving in an hour."

"It's important, or I wouldn't ask. Can you?"

Theo blew air through his pressed lips with frustration. "All right, I'll be there in five."

He undid his apron, told his staff he'd be right back and gave a few directions. Although he could have walked, he drove the truck and parked at the courthouse. Inside the majestic stone structure, complete with a lightning rod on top of the tallest of three domes, he hurried down the corridor to the sheriff's office.

His friend sat at his desk, fidgeting with a pair of handcuffs. Across the room, on a wooden bench that had to be almost as old as the courthouse, two young teens sat, faces grim. A man leaned against one wall, wearing a sour expression.

"Come on in, Theo," Jonas said. "I have two young men who want to meet you. Boys, this is Theo Scrooge. Your irresponsible actions caused him to dive into the river to rescue Marlena Dupree, who was here to visit our town. His quick thinking saved her life, but both were extremely ill afterward. Theo, this is Logan and Lucas Becker, ages fourteen and fifteen. They are the bicycle riders whose careless and imprudent ride caused Ms. Dupree to fall into the Missouri River."

Although Jonas maintained a serious expression, Theo knew him well enough to know the sheriff was both amused and annoyed. Theo stared at his friend, wondering just what the hell Jonas expected him to do.

"They can be charged with reckless endangerment," Jonas said. "Along with public endangerment, speeding, careless and imprudent driving.... That's just for starters. Now, if you wanted to pursue a civil case for damages, then that's another option, but it's up to you. And Ms. Dupree, of course, if you want to press charges."

Did he? Theo had no idea. It seemed like more of an accident than deliberate action. He was unaware of what kind of punishment the charges Jonas listed would bring, but he was hesitant.

"How did you apprehend them?" he asked.

The man leaning against the wall came forward. "That would be me. I'm Frank Becker, these kids' dad. I brought them down after they told me what they'd done."

Theo needed a few moments to process all the information. "It's been more than a week."

Jonas stood up. "True. So, Theo, what do you think? Press charges?"

The two teens were pale, and the slightly smaller of the two couldn't keep his hands from shaking.

"What's the alternative?"

"Well, if you don't press charges and Ms. Dupree doesn't, then I would suggest community service. Their dad here says they both want to apologize, and he thinks they need some consequences from their recklessness, or they won't learn."

In seventh grade, Theo had had to turn in an insect collection, and right now, he felt as pinned in place as the poor bugs he'd put on the Styrofoam background. He couldn't see sending the brothers to some juvenile detention facility or even probation.

"I don't want to press charges," he said.

The sheriff nodded. "I'll need to talk with Ms. Dupree."

"Marlee will be here tomorrow," Theo said.

His friend's eyes widened and then sparkled. "That's convenient. Can you bring her by to talk to me then?"

"Yes," Theo said. "Are we finished for now? I've got the lunch rush about to start."

He glanced over at the Becker boys, noticing they had relaxed a little.

"Mr. Becker, is that fine with you?" Jonas directed the question to the parent. "If she feels the same as Theo, then maybe the boys could attend town council and make their apologies there, right before the lifesaving award."

Becker nodded. "That works. Boys?"

"Yeah," one whispered.

After a round of handshakes, the Beckers departed, and Theo turned to Jonas.

"Just what was that?"

Jonas shrugged. "I thought it was obvious, Theo."

"You blindsided me with it."

"It's my job. Besides, since when is her name Marlee, and why is she coming?"

Theo's mouth widened in a grin he couldn't contain. "It's what she goes by," he said. "And she's coming to watch me get the stupid award. Want me to save you a bowl of liver and dumplings?"

At the suggestion, Jonas made a face. "No, thanks. I'm brown bagging it today."

Theo laughed and left.

Although he figured he could enter unnoticed from the rear of the building, his mother was waiting, her forehead creased.

"Was ist los?" she asked, reverting to her first tongue.

"Nothing's wrong," he said, and told her about the boys.

Her expression eased, and she smiled. "Oh, it's good you won't send them to court. What kind of public service do you think they will do?"

"No idea, but Mama?"

Most of the time, Theo called her Mom or Mutti. When he said Mama, it was something important, and she knew it. Her eyes narrowed.

"Was?"

For almost a week, he'd tried to casually mention Marlee's visit, but the time never quite seemed ideal, or he'd been too busy. With a mere twenty-four hours until she'd step off The Missouri River Runner, Theo knew he'd better speak up now or cause an emotional storm. Still, he tried to ease into it.

"You know the town is giving me some award tomorrow night, right?"

"Of course. Oma and I are coming back to town to watch you get it."

Theo should have known, but that might be a good thing. "Someone else is coming to watch, too."

Her bright eyes glared at him and narrowed. "Hanna's coming?" she asked, playing dumb. He could tell from her tone she knew it wasn't his cousin.

"Marlee's coming."

He expected an immediate reaction, but Mutti stared at him. After a few seconds, she frowned. "Who?"

"Marlena Dupree—Marlee, the woman I fished out of the river," Theo said. He hadn't told her about the nickname.

Theo anticipated that she'd fuss and fume, that she might list the reasons why a woman he didn't really know should come for a visit. Liesel surprised him, however, and smiled.

"Oh, the teacher, the pretty one," she said, nodding.

He didn't remember ever mentioning that Marlee taught. "That's her."

"Is she driving down from St. Joseph?"

Theo knew he definitely hadn't mentioned where she lived.

"She's taking the train from KC," he said, torn between being glad and exasperated. "Who's been talking?"

"Didn't you tell me? I thought you did."

Hanna, then, or maybe even Jonas, he thought, unless there was more gossip than he'd been aware of. "Maybe so," he said, although he knew for certain he hadn't. "I need to get to the kitchen before anything goes wrong."

"We managed fine when you were sick," his mother said. "But no problem. We can talk more later about this, Marlena. What did you call her? Marlee?"

"Yes, Marlee."

"I like the name," Liesel said. "It suits her."

Theo rolled his eyes. "You haven't met her yet."

She offered him a small, mysterious smile. "But I will."

Before he could summon a response, a pot clattered to the floor with a crash and his afternoon assistant Liz Vogel shouted, "Theo!"

"I need to see what happened," he said, and exited.

He found a mess but no damage and assisted with a quick clean-up. He worked distracted, his mind more on Marlee than meal preparation. Theo nicked his finger twice and forced his mind to stay on task.

When he took a break around three-thirty, Theo retreated to his office with a plate of Salisbury steak, ready to rest his weary feet for a few minutes and to breathe. He also wanted to plan a special menu for Friday because it would be the first time Marlee would dine at Bah Humbug! He wanted her to like it — to be honest, he wanted her to be wowed.

As he debated what to prepare, his mom stuck her head through the door. "Oma and I are going. I will be here a little early so you can take off when the train arrives."

There were several things he wanted to say, but all he said was, "Thank you."

"What are the specials?"

Theo sighed. "That's what I'm trying to decide."

"What does she like?"

"That's the question."

Liesel laughed. "Instead of worrying about it, why don't you ask her?"

He swallowed a bite and shook his head. "Why didn't I think about that?"

"You make things too complicated, Theo," she said. "I'm baking snickerdoodles. *Tschüss.*"

"See you tomorrow, Mutti."

Theo finished his meal, closed the office door, and picked up his phone. If he hesitated, he wouldn't call.

She answered after two rings. "Theo!" she said. "I can't wait until tomorrow."

"I'm looking forward to it," he said. "I called because I wondered what you like to eat. I'm about to plan the daily specials, and I thought I could cook something you like."

"Oh, wow, thank you. I'm not all that picky."

"Give me an idea or two."

Marlee laughed, a merry and delightful sound he'd already come to like very much. "Anything chicken or seafood," she said. "I'm not very familiar with German food, but I've liked what I've tried."

Theo scribbled a few notes, listening. "Is there any food you absolutely hate or are allergic to?"

"No, not really," she said. "I'm not too fond of liver in any form, though, or turnips. Did I tell you I booked a room?'

"No, where?"

"The Frau Haus," she said, naming a local bed and breakfast operated out of a charming older home. "I have one of the attic rooms. On the website, it looked small but clean and quaint."

Theo knew the owners well. "It's a great place. You'll like it."

They chatted for a few more minutes, then hung up, both anticipating Friday.

With her preferences in mind, Theo decided he would make *Hühnerfrikassee, a* traditional German chicken fricassee that bore no resemblance to the American version. He'd seen it served with fried chicken smothered in a cream gravy and cringed. Done right—or German-style—the dish included deboned chicken and a variety of vegetables, including carrots, mushrooms, and onions or leeks simmered into a rich, not quite stew. Theo's version was thickened with a cream-based roux, and he often added asparagus tips to dress it up.

For the English-style entree, he would make a fish pie—nothing fancy, just shepherd's or cottage pie with fish, usually cod, in place of lamb or beef. Either dish would make an impressive, delicious noon meal. And in the evening, the focus would be on the town council meeting. He thought perhaps he could take her out to dine afterward and made a mental note to check if other local restaurants had extended hours in the last weeks before full tourist season arrived.

Both entrees could be paired with seasoned rice and creamed peas for perfect comfort food. With the meal planned, that left the remainder of his day free to think about ways to make Marlee's visit memorable.

On Friday, Theo woke early and couldn't manage to go back to sleep. He rose and took his coffee with him for a stroll along the riverfront as the sun rose. His nerves were on edge.

Despite his eagerness for Marlee's visit, Theo couldn't help but worry about how it would go. Although he hadn't known her long, he hoped to build a relationship with her, so a lot depended on how well the visit went. He also wondered if she'd heard whether or not she would teach in Hermann.

He saw Lisa Muller and her dog Fritz. Flowers! He wanted a bouquet for Marlee.

"Good morning, Lisa!"

"Hey, Theo. Excited about tonight?"

"*Na, ja,*" he replied. "Not really. You open the shop at nine, right?"

"Six days a week."

"I'll be over to pick out a bouquet, and I'm open to suggestions."

"I can help with that, sure."

After another cup of coffee, a light breakfast of wheat toast, and a shower, Theo dashed across the street to Blooms. Out of his element, Theo walked around looking at fresh flowers and became undecided. He'd thought to buy tulips since the ones he sent were a hit, but the sight of numerous blossoms in various colors and varieties confused him.

"So, Theo, do you have an idea of what you want?" Lisa asked.

He shrugged his shoulders. "I thought maybe tulips, but now I'm not sure. I have no experience with flowers."

She laughed. "But I'm an expert, so let's get started. Who are the flowers for? If it's your mom, I know she loves bright yellow, so I'd say mums and maybe lilies with some carnations."

"They're not for *Mutti,*" he said, shifting from one foot to another. "The woman I pulled out of the river is coming to visit. They're for her, for Marlee."

He thought he saw amusement in her faint smile but chose to ignore it.

"You said tulips. Is that your choice or hers?"

"I sent her some tulips once, and she liked them, but I don't want to be boring."

Lisa walked over to the cool case where she kept fresh-cut flowers. "Tulips aren't boring," she said. "They're a perfect spring flower. I can arrange them with other flowers too. I could do white tulips with pink peonies, that's pretty, or white tulips with lavender lilacs. Or I can mingle tulips and any flower—roses, carnations, lilies. What's her favorite color?"

Theo shook his head. "No idea. I think either the peonies or the lilacs with tulips would work."

After more discussion, Lisa decided to blend white tulips with both peonies and lilacs, dressed up with some greenery and baby's breath. She created a large bouquet, wrapped the stems together, and placed it in a green paper cone.

"*Volia!*" she said, handing it to him. "What do you think?"

"It's gorgeous, and I think she'll like it."

Lisa grinned. "I know she will."

Theo carried the bouquet with him to Bah Humbug! and placed them in one of the coolers. Then he got busy with preparation. His mom arrived with dozens of cookies, so he showed her the flowers.

"*Sehr Schön,*" Liesel cried. "Theo, they are perfect and so pretty."

"I hope she likes them," he muttered. "I felt silly buying flowers."

"Son, she will, I'm sure."

Since he would meet the train, Theo had arranged for Liz to come in early to assist with prep and plating the food. Autumn would be working, and so would both Constance and Eva. Since the weather was fair, Theo took time to set a table on the outside patio, which would not be open to the public. Maybe he should have bought a posy for a centerpiece, but a quick glance at his watch told him there wasn't time.

Theo rushed upstairs and changed into a fresh black shirt and jeans. He combed his hair, added some cologne, and hurried downstairs. He avoided any fanfare by slipping out the rear door. Even though the station was barely two blocks away, he drove the truck, flowers on the seat.

At the compact station, he sat in the truck until he saw the Amtrak approaching. Most often, the trains rocketed through town en route to St. Louis, but today, the train halted, and a few passengers disembarked. Theo saw Marlee immediately and grinned when she waved at him.

"You look beautiful," he said when he reached her. Her light brown hair was swirled high on the back of her hair with a clip, and if she wore make-up, it was light and natural. Her khaki slacks were paired with a floral print blouse in pastel pinks, blues, and yellows. A purse hung from one shoulder, and she had a single carry-on bag in the other. "You put the posies to shame."

Before he could hand them to her, Theo leaned down and kissed her. He'd meant it to be light, no more than a greeting, but once his mouth met hers, a fire kindled, and he kissed her deeper, longer. When they broke apart, she smiled at him and, heart beating faster, Theo realized he was falling in love. To be honest, he thought he'd already fallen.

"For me?" she said, nodding at the bouquet.

"Yes." Theo handed her the flowers and watched her bury her nose and inhale the sweet fragrance. His head still whirled from the kiss.

"Thank you, they're lovely."

He reached for her carry-on bag and offered her his arm. "I thought you could check in, and then we'd have lunch at Bah Humbug!"

"I'd like that," Marlee said. "Oh, is that your truck?"

Her tone held awe — so she liked it.

"Yeah, it's mine," Theo said, trying to sound humble even though it was his pride and joy. "It used to be my Opa's, my grandfather's farm truck.

"Is it a '53?"

He nodded, put her bag in the bed, and opened the passenger door so she could climb into the seat. Marlee scooted over to sit beside him, so close he could smell her perfume—lavender, he thought. On the short drive to the Frau Haus, Theo pointed out a few of the sites of town, although he was aware it wasn't her first trip. He said so, and she put her hand on his thigh.

"You make a great tour guide," she said. "I didn't really see much of the town before."

At the inn, a small brick house painted white, a path led through a garden blooming with spring flowers. A pair of dogwood trees were in full blossom, along with some lilacs, both white and purple, at the edge of the walled garden. Theo knew the place by sight, but he'd never stepped inside, although he was familiar with the current owners, Fritz and Francine Lautner. Francine had conceived the idea to turn the old home into an inn, which explained the name—Frau Haus.

Although Theo could have waited outside, he insisted on carrying her bag up the stairs and the narrow short flight that led to Marlee's attic room.

"It's small," she said, glancing around the space. "But it's cozy. I like it."

"Are you hungry?"

"I'm starving. I had coffee and toast for breakfast."

"Then let's go eat."

Together, they stepped into his truck, and he drove her back to Bah Humbug!

Chapter Seven

At Bah Humbug! Theo saw his place through her eyes, or at least with a fresh perspective. The black and white square tiled floor, the vintage square tables with traditional Bentwood chairs, the short bar and the dark woodwork worked, he thought and were appealing. It wasn't as dark as an English pub or a German tavern because Theo liked the light, and there were many windows. The green plants he kept and tended in the corners and other spots were his touch. On the shelves that lined some of the walls, he had not only English trinkets but German beer steins which had come from Opa's collection. The pressed tin ceiling provided a vintage look, and the old pictures of Hermann were a view into the past. He brought her through the front entrance so she could get the full effect but now wondered if that had been wise.

The Friday lunch crowd packed the place, leaving only a few empty tables. With Marlee's arm linked through his, it seemed as if everyone paused, freeze framed with fork or drink in hand. To him, the place fell silent. Theo wanted to see her expression, but he was afraid to look in case she was underwhelmed.

"Oh, Theo," she said, her voice light and soft. "It's marvelous! It is like an English pub, but with a touch of Germany too. And the food smells so good."

Now he heard the usual murmur of voices, the clink of silverware against china, and the other sounds that were so familiar. If anyone stared, he didn't notice because now he looked at her face and nothing more.

"Do you like it?"

"I adore it. I didn't know quite what to expect, but this is beyond anything I had tried to imagine. You captured the authentic look."

"Do you go to many English pubs?"

"There are a few in KC," she said. "Although they're nothing like this. This is more like a pub in England."

Theo wondered if she'd been. As much as he'd always wanted to travel, he hadn't made it to Europe. Before he could think of a way to ask that didn't sound lame, she confirmed it.

"When I went to England a few years ago, my friend and I visited a few pubs. Yours is amazing!"

He wanted to kiss her, but not here with a full house watching.

"So, let's go eat. You can tell me what you think about the food," he told her as he navigated the room. "I thought we could eat outside on the patio. The weather's good, and it's more—"

"Private," she said. "I like that."

In the outside dining area, the table he had set waited. Theo pulled out a chair for Marlee, and as she scooted to the table, his mother appeared with a tray that held a bottle of his favorite Riesling and two chilled wine glasses.

"Welcome," Liesel said. "I thought you might like a glass of wine to start."

"That's perfect. Thank you, *Mutti*. This is Marlena Dupree, who prefers Marlee. Marlee, this is my mom, Liesel Scrooge."

His mom bowed her head in a polite nod. *"Freut mich,"* she said. "I am very pleased to meet you."

"I'm honored," Marlee said. "You have an amazing son. He saved my life, you know."

"I do."

His mother uncorked the wine and poured it into the glasses, then backed away. "Your meal will be out very soon."

Theo, torn between admiration and exasperation with his mom, raised his glass, and Marlee did the same. He touched the glass to hers. *"Prosit!"*

"Cheers," Marlee responded.

They drank, the white wine a sweet whisper on his tongue.

"This is delightful," she said as she sipped. "Sweet, a little citrusy, and a bit crisp. Is it local?"

Theo nodded. "Yes. It's one of my favorite wines."

"I want to tour a winery if we can. I wanted to before and didn't have a chance."

"Probably because you ended up in the river."

Marlee laughed, not quite a giggle. "Exactly why. That was spring break when I was here before. It started out so well, too."

"Until you almost drowned."

She finished her glass and held it out for more. Theo poured.

"True, but if I hadn't, you wouldn't have saved me, and I wouldn't have met you, so I'm glad it happened."

It might have been a sharp, cool April breeze, but a frisson shuddered through him. Being with Marlee had a fairy tale quality, but nothing had ever been as real to him.

"Then I'm glad too."

Autumn, not his mother, appeared with their food. He hadn't even had time to tell Marlee the specials so she could choose.

"Hello," she said. "Our specials of the day are chicken fricassee and English fish pie. Your mom plated both. I hope that's all right."

"It's fine," Theo said. He wished he'd thought of that. "Thank you."

With the plates on the table, he reached for a fork, but Marlee shook her head and held out her hands.

"Let's say grace," she said, and did after she made the Sign of the Cross. "Bless us, Oh Lord, and these thy gifts which we are about to receive from thy bounty, through Christ, Our Lord. Amen."

Theo said the words with her, a prayer he'd known for as long as he could remember. He grasped her hands a moment longer than necessary. "You're Catholic."

Marlee nodded. "And apparently, so are you."

He grinned. "Yes. Would you like me to say it in German?"

She smiled back. "Later, maybe. Right now, I want to eat. Tell me about what we're having."

Theo did, describing the dishes and what went into each. She complimented the cuisine, and he could tell she meant it. Just as they finished the meal, his mother and grandmother appeared, Liesel with coffee, Oma with cookies.

He introduced Marlee to his grandmother. Although Marlee protested how full she was, she ate a cookie and drank a little coffee. Relaxed, Theo decided to share all the details with Marlee.

"So, you know about the award," he began.

"Yes."

"Well, there's a been a new development."

Her expression shifted. "Such as?"

Theo told her about the phone call he'd received from the sheriff and about the Becker boys. "So, they'll be there, and they want to apologize."

Any expectation she would have the same reaction he had faded quickly.

"They were reckless!" she exclaimed. "Either of us could have drowned."

"True," Theo replied, choosing his words with care. "But we didn't. And there's more than just an apology — we have to decide whether or not to press charges."

Marlee's lips were tight. "What charges and what repercussions?"

"Reckless endangerment, mainly." He tried to remember the full list and failed.

"Are you pressing charges?"

With an overwhelming sense she wouldn't approve of his decision, Theo said, "No, I'm not."

She glared at him. "I think I will. I don't think I've ever been that frightened. I really thought I would die in the river. And I believe I would have without you."

An image of the brothers, white-faced and terrified, popped into his head. "I know, and I understand, but they didn't intend to knock you over."

"But they did. And they need to understand their recklessness had consequences."

"I think they get that, now. And even without charges, they'll perform community service. You'll see them both tonight at the town council."

"I don't think that will make any difference to me."

She's stubborn, he thought, *and tenacious*. Theo realized that the woman across the table was much more than a pretty face. He hoped, however, that she possessed some compassion and would be fair.

"Maybe not, but will you at least consider not deciding until after their apology?"

She had an open face, and he observed the various

emotions that shifted her expression. After a long minute or two, she nodded. "All right, that's fair. But no promises, Theo."

"Agreed."

"So, what now?"

He grinned. "I need to do some work. Want to come watch?"

Her frown cleared, and Marlee nodded. In the kitchen, he provided her with a mandatory hair net and an apron. Then Theo parked her in a corner out of the way and got busy. He did some additional cooking for the dinner rush, and when it came time to plan the Saturday specials, Theo handed her a menu and asked her to choose.

"Does it matter what I pick?"

"Not really. Just one German, one English."

"What if I don't know what things are?"

Theo laughed. "The menu has a description of every dish," he told her.

Marlee studied it for a moment. "I don't suppose I can pick something like meatloaf? That's one of my specialties."

Intrigued, he asked, "Do you cook?"

She nodded. "Sometimes. But only traditional, very American things. Is there even a German version of meatloaf?"

Theo didn't realize that his mother was in the kitchen until she spoke. "There is," she said. "It's called *Falscher hase.*"

"It translates as 'false hare,'" Theo added. "It's not an old traditional dish. It became popular after World War II when there were meat shortages. It's made with hamburger, not hare, but it's different than American. For one thing, it has hard boiled eggs inside, and is usually covered with bacon. Meatloaf—not German style—is one of my favorites."

Her face lit up. "Could I make it for Bah Humbug!?"

This was a first. No woman he'd ever dated had ever shown interest in cooking, and Theo liked it. "Can we make it together?"

"Sure, we can."

"Then we will," he said. "I just have to figure out how." Marlee appeared confused, so he added, "I don't have much ground beef here, but I can get it, even if I need to go to the store. Can you write down the recipe from memory?"

"Just give me pen and paper."

Deciding to make Marlee's meatloaf changed Theo's plans, but he was willing. Other than the meat, he had everything else on hand necessary, so they made a trip to one of the local markets and almost bought them out of ground meat. Theo wanted ground round and got it but had to also settle for some ground sirloin and ground chuck. Back at the kitchen, he stowed his purchase and turned to Marlee.

"We close from three to five every day," he said. "It's after three—town council isn't until seven. Afterward, I want to take you out for a late dinner, if that works, if you can wait until then."

"I can."

"What would you like to do now? I can take you on a tour, drive out to the family farm to show you around, or we can do a quick winery or two. Or, if you want some time to rest or whatever."

"What about making meatloaf?"

"We'll do that in the morning, early. I've already asked the kitchen staff to come in earlier than usual, so I can take most of the day off," Theo said.

Oma appeared, tying on one of her head scarves, a sure indication she and his mom were about to leave. "What's the English special?" she asked. "I didn't hear what you picked for it."

Marlee hadn't, but Theo, aware of what he had on hand, said, "Bangers and mash."

"I'll make a butter pound cake," Liesel said as she came

toward the door with her purse over one arm. She paused to kiss Theo's cheek. "We'll see you tonight, both of you."

Aware of both Marlee and the meeting, Theo pondered what to serve as sides. He decided that mashed potatoes would do for both, something he did occasionally, with red cabbage for the German orders and peas for the English. As long as no one ordered anything too complicated from the full menu, he would be able to prep and leave his capable staff to serve—after he'd tasted Marlee's meatloaf.

With the afternoon at hand, they walked the short distance to the closest winery, which also happened to be one of the oldest. The red brick structure dated back to before the Civil War, and Marlee appeared to be enthralled with the history as they did the tour. The proprietor, an old school German American gentleman that had known Theo since birth winked at him, well aware that Theo could have probably led the tour competently.

After seeing the step-by-step process of making wine and the oversize casks where it aged, they partook in a tasting. Normally Theo never drank during the day or while working, and he'd already had two glasses of Riesling with their noon meal. Still, he doubted the small amount to taste would do any harm, so he said nothing and sipped. After they left the winery, though, he resolved he wouldn't drink anything more until after town council. He wanted his head and senses clear. Besides, he wouldn't want Marlee to think he might be a heavy drinker.

They strolled, hand in hand, back past Bah Humbug! and through town. The sunshine touched their shoulders with warmth, and Theo admired the way the rays brought out bright highlights in Marlee's hair. They walked beside the river, although he made certain to keep a fair distance from the edge, unwilling to have a repeat. Theo told her about the original silver bridge that had been replaced by a standard highway bridge.

"It was unsafe," he said with a sigh. "I understand that,

but it was much prettier than this one."

Marlee squeezed his hand tight. "I get that. St. Joe used to have one, the Pony Express Bridge, but it's long gone too. I like the old bridges. They were almost magical."

Theo stopped and stared at the river. "True. The Missouri River has its own mystery and magic when you're not fighting drowning in it. But it's treacherous, too. I've always liked to come down here to watch the river traffic. These days it's mostly tugs and barges, but I could always imagine the steamboats."

"Or Lewis and Clark paddling upstream," she said. "I teach history because I love it."

"There's plenty of history here."

"I've been reading about some it."

They exchanged a long look, and he faced her. Theo lowered his mouth and kissed her again, slow and sweet but with heat. Marlee kissed him back, her arms around him. He inhaled the sweet fragrance of her perfume, something vanilla and pleasant, with a hint of citrus, he thought, almost as delicious and intoxicating as the wine. Theo ached to go deeper, but he stopped. They were in public view in his town, but he wanted more.

His apartment was close, but time was short. Theo held her for another moment, then released her. "It's almost five-thirty if you want some time to go change or freshen up," he said. "I can pick you up around six-thirty."

Marlee offered him a smile. "That works for me."

In that hour, Theo took a shower, short and cold, then donned a pair of khaki slacks with a button-down shirt and a casual jacket. He popped into the kitchen downstairs long enough to be sure that everything ran smooth and that no problems had developed.

At the Frau Haus, Marlee waited in the garden. She wore a blue dress with bold pink flowers and a matching pink jacket. The garment favored her figure, although the skirt belled out wider to the knee. Theo noticed she'd changed into heeled sandals, and when he greeted her with a brief kiss, he realized she stood inches higher.

"You look fantastic," he told her.

She grinned. "Thank you. Theo, I'm so excited."

"About town council or the award?"

"No," she shook her head. "I checked my phone for messages, and I had a call. The school district hired me!"

It took a few seconds for that information to sink into his brain, and then he whooped. Theo picked her up and swung her around in a circle. Marlee laughed and protested.

"I'm moving here," she cried when he set her down. "I can't wait. I'm going to love it."

And I love you. Theo almost said the words aloud but didn't. She might think he was crazy or something. Most women would think it was too early for such a declaration, but Theo knew. His admiration and interest had grown into something deep and full. After the kisses, he wanted to make love to her with a slow hand, but he would wait. He also wanted to share his life with her.

"I'm glad," he said. "We're going to be late if we don't go now, though."

The council chamber doubled as a municipal court once a week. A single aisle divided two areas of folding chairs, set in four rows on either side. At the front of the room, a long desk held places for each of the council members and the mayor.

Theo steered her to a pair of seats in the next to last row on the right. Across from them, Frank Becker sat, flanked by his boys. Both wore dress shirts complete with ties and worried frowns. Theo nudged Marlee. "There's the two boys, Lucas and Logan, with their dad."

As he spoke, Jonas, in full uniform with a Glock holstered on his hip, strolled up. "I thought you were bringing Ms. Dupree to see me," he said.

"I forgot about that," Theo said. "Marlee, do you remember Sheriff Kaiser?"

She extended her hand to shake. "Of course, I do."

"Now that you're here, can we take a minute? The kids want to apologize in person, and I need to know whether or not you want to press charges."

Theo stilled, remembering their earlier conversation. He still hoped she wouldn't decide yet.

"They look so young," Marlee said. Her expression had softened with compassion. "They're younger than I expected."

Jonas drummed impatient fingers on the back of an empty chair. "There's just about fifteen minutes before the meeting starts if you two want to come back into one of the offices with me."

Theo stood and offered Marlee his hand. Jonas nodded at the Beckers, who followed. In a small, mundane office space, Theo introduced them to Marlee.

"Thank you for this opportunity, Sheriff," Frank said. "My sons have something they want to say." He nudged the boys, who stepped forward to face Theo and Marlee.

"We just want to apologize," Logan said. He was taller by a few inches. "We didn't mean to run you down."

His brother Lucas spoke up too. "It was an accident."

"We're both sorry," Logan added.

At a look from his father, Lucas spoke again. "It was very irresponsible of us. We had no business riding our bikes on the walking path, and we shouldn't have gone so fast. You could have died, and so could Mr. Scrooge."

He recited the words as if he'd been made to memorize them. Remembering Marlee's reluctance to not press charges, Theo tensed. The kids' plaintive apologies moved him.

"Can you forgive us?" Logan said.

Marlee stepped forward, and Theo saw tears in her eyes.

"Of course, we can," she said. "It was an accident, and I imagine you learned a lesson from it."

"Apology accepted," Theo told them.

The boys and their dad lost their tense posture. "What about some kind of community service, Sheriff?" Frank asked.

Jonas shot a glance at Theo and lifted an eyebrow in inquiry. Although he hadn't really considered it until that moment, Theo spoke up.

"You can work for me at Bah Humbug!, in the kitchen, for a few weeks," he said. "It'll be clean-up, scrubbing pots and pans, taking out the trash for an hour or two a day. Will that work?"

Both kids wore small grins and nodded.

"Come by after school on Monday then," he told them.

The city clerk stuck her head into the office. "They're ready to call the meeting to order, so you need to come out here."

When they did, Theo saw Todd Blevins seated on the alderman's platform, his usual smirk on his face. Any hope that he might not notice Theo ended when Blevins came to his feet.

"There's Scrooge now," he cried. Even across the room, Theo could smell stale beer on his breath. "From zero to hero."

Although Theo tensed, he refrained from an answer.

His mother and grandmother came through the door, so he greeted them with a hug. "Come sit with us," he said. "The meeting should begin soon."

Marlee lifted one of the agendas from a vacant chair. "The award is not too far down the agenda."

"Good," Theo said. "We can leave after it, if you'd like."

"Is that why we sat in the back?" she asked.

"One of the reasons."

"Don't mind him," Liesel said, leaning over and lowering her voice. "Ignore him."

"Trying," Theo said.

The mayor called the meeting to order, and the chief of

police led all present in reciting the Pledge of Allegiance. The award was the third item on the agenda. Although he'd dreaded it, the ceremony was brief, and afterward, Theo remembered little except that he was handed a plaque and the local newspaper took photos. Marlee and his family clapped. So did a few others.

As he walked back to his seat, Blevins shouted out, "Way to go, Ebenezer."

Resisting an urge to punch his nose, Theo handed Marlee the plaque and certificate. "Do you want to go eat? We can, or we can stay."

She glanced at him, then over at Blevins. "Let's go before you get into a fist fight. Besides, I'm hungry."

Hand in hand, they filed out, followed by his mother and grandmother. Once they were alone in his truck, Theo kissed her. "I'm glad that ordeal is over."

"It wasn't so bad. It was nice of them to give you this award," Marlee said. "But who's the half-drunk idiot?"

Although he'd rather not think about him or talk about him, Theo explained. "Todd Blevins, local insurance agent. We went to school together, and he decided years ago to make fun of my last name, tying it with Dickens."

"I thought you were going to punch him."

He flexed his fingers against the steering wheel. "I'd like to, very much. He needles me, and he knows it gets to me."

"You shouldn't let it."

His laugh was dry and forced. "That's what *Mutti* says too. Easier said than done."

Marlee put her hand over his. "It really bothers you, doesn't it?"

"Yeah, it does."

"Why?"

Theo sighed. "It's hard to explain, and I know it probably sounds like I'm a pathetic loser. It's just that it's gone on for so many years, back to the sixth grade. He's mild with it now, but back in school, he tormented the devil out of me. It started with the Scrooge thing and escalated."

Because it was Marlee, he sketched the watch saga for her. Then he told her how one year, the high school drama club put on *A Christmas Carol* and how Blevins ramped up the insults and commentary.

"It soured me on Christmas," he admitted. "The December of my senior year, my dad — he was a truck driver — jackknifed on an icy bridge near Memphis and was killed. It was a hard time for all of us. My mother and I moved out to my grandparents' farm. I finished my last year of high school and had Blevins on my back about the Scrooge connection. I'm trying to let it go."

"You need to," Marlee said, in a noticeably quiet tone. "Let's go have some dinner."

Theo released a long breath. "Let's go. I know just the place."

And they went, with Theo hoping any talk of Blevins was finished.

Chapter Eight

The town's solitary steakhouse sat at the far end of First Street, just down the hill from the county courthouse, with views of the Missouri River. Theo's place was trendy, but the Munich Steakhouse offered upscale dining at a price. Although he could have cooked them an excellent steak at the pub or upstairs in his compact kitchen, Theo sometimes craved a change of pace.

Any lingering distaste from Blevins evaporated once they were seated and their focus turned toward celebration. For Theo, the fact that the award had been given and was now over brought relief. For Marlee, that she would be teaching in town this fall brought happiness.

Their table overlooked the river. As dusk began to fall, the water reflected the glory of a summer sunset and turned the Missouri shades of orange.

"What a beautiful view," Marlee said.

Theo nodded. "It is. I'm glad you can see the beauty even though we could've drowned in it."

She laughed, and he was glad to hear it.

"The important thing is that we didn't. It's funny — St. Joe is on the Missouri too, but there's no place like this to dine and view the river. There's the casino, I guess, but most people never look outside when they're there."

"Do you go there much?" Theo made his tone casual, but he wondered. Casinos lacked any appeal, just a place to lose money.

"No, I don't," she replied. "It's not my thing. There's a trail along the river, Riverwalk. It's nice, but I don't like to go there alone. It's pretty isolated, and I worry about staying safe."

The image of Marlee taking a solitary stroll or run disturbed him. "Good. There's no point in taking chances."

Marlee sipped wine and smiled. "True, but I'm taking a chance coming here, too."

Theo could almost hear the unspoken *and with you.* "Very different, though. You're not in danger moving here."

Not physical anyway, he thought, because fever shimmered between them, almost tangible the way the summer heat rippled and rose from the pavement.

Their steaks arrived, cooked to perfection, and they ate, talking about the town and their preferences in books, music, movies, and television. Neither watched much TV, which was a relief for Theo.

After the meal, although it was almost dark, they walked along the river for a few minutes, Theo's arm around her. Marlee leaned against him. They paused at a bench and sat. Around them, the spring night came alive with the noise of the river, whippoorwills, and crickets.

"So, tomorrow, what time do I need to come to make the meatloaf?" Marlee asked.

"By nine or so," Theo replied. "Once that's done, and we have everything ready, we can go. My staff promised to take over so I can take the rest of the day off. Then we'll figure out what we're doing, where we're going. I hope I'm wrong, but it looks like it could rain."

Her bottom lip jutted out just a little in a pout. "Why do you think that?"

Theo pointed at the cloud bank to the west. The dark gray mass hadn't been there when the sun set, but it loomed there now. "Those are rain clouds, probably storm clouds. I haven't checked the forecast, but I'd say it's going to rain tonight, possibly tomorrow."

"And what if it does?"

He shrugged. "It won't matter."

By the time he dropped Marlee off at Frau Haus, the rain seemed likely. Theo had kissed her but resisted the temptation of visiting her room.

The sound of rain pelting down hard was the last thing Theo remembered before he fell asleep sometime after midnight, and when he woke on Saturday, rain still fell. Although it was past seven, the weather kept it dark, and so he lingered for a while, savoring the sound of the rain. Since childhood, when he'd had to rise for school or church on Sunday, Theo had always longed to have the luxury to linger cozy in bed and savor that sound.

If it hadn't been for Marlee's visit, he might have indulged for an hour. But instead, Theo rose. Once out of bed, eagerness for the day ahead overcame his reluctance. He showered and dressed, then made coffee and carried it in a mug with him downstairs.

Maybe I should make something for breakfast, he thought but didn't. Marlee might eat at the bed and breakfast. He knew they put out a spread each morning with sweet rolls, juice, and coffee. If she wanted to eat, he would whip up something. He could make do on coffee.

Theo's eating habits probably left something to be desired. He ate when he was hungry and seldom else. When he craved a big breakfast, he went to Maybelle's. When he cooked, it was as much art as work. Like most chefs, he tasted as he worked because it was necessary. He sometimes ate lunch, more often not, and he seldom ate an evening meal until after the place closed. There were times when he ate with gusto, and moments when he didn't.

Some career cooks and chefs became heavy, too fond of the food they prepared. Theo managed to stay lean. His erratic appetites and his daily walks along the river helped him stay trim. So did his heritage, he figured. Some Germans were large, others tall and angular. His family ran to the thinner, fortunately for him.

Theo thought if the rain didn't slack down, he would go pick up Marlee. But it wasn't quite eight, so he kicked up some music and peeled potatoes for the mash. John Fogarty's vocals sang out with classic Credence Clearwater Revival as he worked. Theo sang along with "Have You Ever Seen the Rain?" perfect for the rainy day. He was chiming in with "Long as I Can See the Light" when he heard someone bang through the rear door. Expecting his mother, Theo turned down the music as Marlee staggered into the kitchen, soaked clothes dripping onto the floor, her hair wet and streaming.

"Hi," she said, with a tiny flicker of a smile. "I'm a little wet."

"You're drenched," Theo replied. "I could've picked you up."

She held up a broken umbrella, turned inside out. "I had this, but the wind tore it up," she told him. "It was fine until then."

It was past repair, he noted. Theo also saw that Marlee trembled.

"You're cold," he said. "Let's go upstairs and you can change into something dry."

Marlee shook her head. "I don't have any other clothes.

You'll have to drive me back to Frau Haus."

"You can wear one of my T-shirts or something while your clothes dry," he told her. "Plus, you can see my place." She hesitated, and he took advantage of it. "I think I have a robe somewhere," he said. "Your clothes will be dry in half an hour. Otherwise, we'll get behind on making meatloaf, and I really want to try your recipe."

Theo offered her his hand, and she took it. He led her upstairs and ushered her into his bedroom.

"Let me grab some towels," he said. He also found the robe, something his mother had bought him one Christmas that he'd never worn. He gave her several thick towels and the robe. "Go ahead and change. Put your wet stuff in the hall, and I'll dry it. Do you want some coffee? I can make some."

"Yes, thanks," she told him. "So, you live above Bah Humbug!"

"It's convenient."

"It's compact," she said. "I like what I've seen so far."

"I'll give you the grand tour in a minute."

In the kitchen, he stared out the window overlooking the street at the rain that still cascaded from a dark sky. Water gushed down the street in small streams that made him think about the river. It'd been a rainy spring, and the river had been running bank full. It wouldn't take much to flood, and if it did, his pub was too close for comfort.

Theo made two cups of coffee and started down the hall. Before he reached the bedroom, Marlee emerged wearing his robe. Although she had belted it, it hung loose with sleeves that billowed. On him, it was knee-length—on Marlee, the robe came to her ankles. The robe dwarfed her, and she wore her hair twisted into a turban fashioned from one of the towels. Wearing his robe, she looked very feminine, young, and vulnerable.

Theo held out the coffee, and she took one of the cups.

"I'll throw your things in the dryer," he said. "If you want, go to the living room—you can't miss it."

"Thank you."

With one hand holding the mug, the other lifting the robe so she wouldn't trip, Marlee walked down the abbreviated hall. Theo gathered up her discarded garments—a pair of jeans, a Notre Dame T-shirt, thick socks, and her smalls, a pair of bikini pants and a bra. He drew a deep breath as he scooped them up, along with a hooded jacket. Beneath his robe, she wore nothing. Sudden, powerful desire rushed through his body, and Theo shivered.

Once her clothes were drying, he headed for the living room with his lukewarm coffee in hand. He drank it in one gulp and put down the cup. Marlee stood at the window but turned to smile.

Theo acted without thought. He crossed the space between them and took her into his arms. She rested her hands on his shoulders and tilted her face upward. Theo kissed her, his mouth hot and hungry with need. When their lips fused, she moved until there was no space between them. He craved more, but Marlee put her hands on his chest.

"We can't," she told him. "I'm not the kind of woman who would."

Theo sighed, but he knew she'd made the right choice. "I'm not the kind of man who does this either," he told her. "But that doesn't mean I don't want to."

She pulled the robe tighter with a small smile. "We're human, Theo."

Before either could continue the awkward discussion, Liesel's voice echoed from downstairs. "Theo, *wo bist du?* Are you up here?" his mother called. *"Was ist los?"*

Marlee tensed. "Is that your mother?"

"It is," Theo said, and untangled.

"Ich bin hier, Mutti. Alles gut," he yelled, then remembered Marlee probably spoke no German. "It's all good. I'll be down in a few minutes."

"Bist du krank?"

"Nein, no, I'm not sick," he replied.

Marlee sat up and covered her face with both hands. For a moment, Theo thought she was crying, but a giggle escaped.

"It's not funny," he said in a stage whisper.

"It is, in a way."

They burst out laughing, then Theo kissed Marlee again. "I'm going down. Join us after you get dressed, and we'll make that meatloaf."

He took the stairs two at a time, dashing down to the kitchen, but slowed to a stroll when he entered the kitchen. Liesel glanced up and smiled.

"So, there you are," she said. "Where's Marlee?"

Her question shafted him with surprise. "Marlee?"

His mother stared at a purse on the counter, then shifted her gaze to a puddle on the floor. "Isn't she here? I thought that must be her purse."

Busted, he thought. "It's hers. She walked over and got soaked in the rain. I put her clothes in the dryer. She'll be down soon, I think."

Liesel shrugged. "Good, good. I was afraid you'd overslept or that you were sick."

Theo glanced down and flushed. He had an idea his mother suspected what they almost had done. "Thanks for reminding me. What's the dessert?"

"Pound cake, like I told you I would make."

"I like pound cake," Marlee said as she entered the kitchen in sock feet. He'd forgotten her shoes would still be damp. Although she wore no make-up and her hair was pulled back into a loose braid, she was beautiful. "Good morning, Mrs. Scrooge."

"Call me Liesel," his mother said. "I hear you got a soaking."

Her cheeks pinked a little, but she nodded. "I got caught in the rain, and the wind ruined my umbrella, but Theo came to the rescue."

"*Jawohl*," she replied. "I can see that he did."

"Let's make meatloaf," Theo interrupted. "Grab a hairnet and apron, Marlee. If I'm going to take time off, we need to get started."

His mother sliced the pound cake and plated each slice. Then she headed out to the table she reserved to sit with Oma until Theo might need her willing hands. In the meantime, she would do crossword puzzles or play Sudoku.

Together, Theo and Marlee gathered the ingredients they would need to prepare her recipe. As she walked him through the steps to make meatloaf her way, Theo was very aware of her proximity. With her hands encased in disposable food gloves, she blended the ground beef with some lean ground pork, breadcrumbs, eggs, tomato sauce, beef broth, minced onions, seasonings that included some garlic powder and black pepper, a bit of tomato sauce, and some Worcestershire sauce. He watched, committing her process to memory so he could repeat it, but ached to kiss the vulnerable back of her neck beneath the braid. Once he saw how she put together a meatloaf, Theo joined in, and they worked in tandem.

Any fears he'd entertained that Marlee might feel awkward vanished because they talked in easy conversation, nothing strained or stilted. She met his warm glances and touched him casually. Theo turned the music back on but at a lower level, and Marlee sang along to some of his favorite old tunes.

Autumn came through the kitchen just before her shift began, gazed at Marlee, and grinned, offering Theo thumbs up out of Marlee's view. With the meatloaves baking, the mashed potatoes ready to serve with brown gravy or red sauce, and bangers on the grill, Theo headed to the front of the house to unlock the door.

"You're happy," Autumn said as he stopped to straighten some napkins.

"Aren't I always?"

She shook her head. "Not like this, Theo. I've never seen you like this. You're light-hearted and merry and...well, just happy."

Theo shrugged with a smile. "Seems that way."

He did his best to downplay his emotions, but Autumn had nailed it. He wore happiness, a deep kind he hadn't known for a long time, like a warm jacket.

"Stay that way!" she said, and he laughed, shaking his head. "Seriously, it suits you."

Did it? He wondered whether or not he'd been too serious. If Autumn saw a good mood as a major change, he must have been much dourer than he'd realized.

*I **am** happy, though,* he thought. *If I've been unhappy, I never really noticed, but I was lonely. Marlee is what I've needed.*

Before he could think further, Marlee came from the kitchen. "The meatloaf is ready if you want to try it."

"I can't wait."

"Are we eating lunch here?"

"That's my plan unless you just don't want to," he said.

"That's perfect. But afterward, what are we going to do?"

She posed a good question. Theo had planned to take her out into the country, visit a few wineries, including his family's, visit the church at Starkenberg, and take a scenic drive along the river, but the rain hadn't stopped.

Marlee drew closer and put one hand on his arm, casual yet intimate and a little possessive. He liked it. "It's just that it's raining, and I checked the forecast, and it's supposed to rain till tomorrow morning. And not just showers—there are thunderstorms on the way."

"It's just weather," Theo said, fighting an urge to kiss her, resisting because they were in view of the restaurant and the early customers were arriving.

"I don't much like storms." The way she said it made him realize storms made her anxious.

"We can do something indoors," he said, brainstorming. "We could go catch a movie or check out the museum. If you wanted to go up to Jeff City, we could tour the state capitol, go through the state museum."

"Could we just stay in?" she asked. "I mean, we could watch movies, eat popcorn, or you could cook just for me. Do you cook anything besides German and classic English pub?"

Theo caught her free hand and kissed it, light and soft. "Of course, I do, *Schatzi*. I studied culinary arts. I can cook about anything you'd like—cordon bleu, jambalaya, lasagna, pierogis, Asian, Mexican, pizza, a curry—"

Marlee interrupted his list of dishes. "What about good old American cheeseburgers?"

"Of course, with the best homemade fries you've ever tasted, or with a salad, pasta or green."

"Cheeseburgers with fries," she said. "And movies with popcorn. Can you make popcorn the old-fashioned way in a skillet on the stove too?"

Theo laughed. "Not without burning it, but I have a hot air popper, butter, and salt."

"That'll work," she said. "And watch movies. Do you have any?"

"I have Netflix and some DVDs."

Liesel bustled around them, carrying a tray. "*Raus, raus*," she told them, her tone light. "You're in the way. Go eat and get out of here, Theo."

They ate in his office. The meatloaf, prepared with Marlee's recipe from memory, was delicious.

"This is very good," he told her. "The seasonings are perfect."

"Thanks," she replied. "But you're probably just saying that to be nice."

"I'm never that nice."

Marlee laughed. "I think you are. So, what now, after we finish lunch?"

He ate a bite of pound cake and savored it. "I'll need to go to the market, then we'll hide upstairs. You can stay here if you want."

She shook her head. "I want to go. There's somewhere I need to go."

Theo raised an eyebrow. "Where?"

Her cheeks flushed. "I want to check out of the bed and breakfast so I can stay here tonight. I don't want to have a wonderful time then have to go out in the rain back to a lonely room."

He loved the idea and hated it. Of course, he wanted Marlee with him, but the moment she left the Frau Haus, half the town would know she would be staying with him. "If that's what you want, sure."

"Don't you?"

"People will figure it out, but I don't mind if you don't."

"I don't." She met his gaze with hers, unblinking.

So, together under his big black umbrella he usually didn't use, they dashed out into the rain and into his truck. Theo drove her to the Frau Haus and, figuring he was in for a penny, in for a pound, came in with her to carry her bags. Fritz Lautner lounged in the lobby and smiled at Theo, then winked.

While Francine did the paperwork and chatted with Marlee, Fritz asked him, in German, "So, she goes to stay with you?"

"Yes, but it's not what you probably think," Theo replied.

Fritz grinned. "I would hope not, Theo."

On the way to the market, Marlee snuggled close and said, "So what did he say, the owner?"

Theo grinned. "He seemed a little shocked, but like he understood."

"I wish I spoke German," she said. "Will it be a problem in the schools that I don't?"

"Not at all. Mostly older folks speak German, and what they speak here is a watered down, American, Missouri version. Most of the residents are several generations removed from Deutschland. I'm fluent either way, though."

"I took Spanish, but I honestly don't remember very much of it," she said. "Do you speak any other languages?"

He shrugged. "A little French from culinary arts, that's it."

The rain picked up by the time they reached the supermarket, so Theo dashed in alone and gathered the items he needed for the meal he planned, some butter and some popcorn. He got into the truck, soaked.

"Anything else before we go home?" he asked, then realized he'd said home, and it was his, not hers.

If she minded, it didn't show. "Not unless you want to rent movies."

"Not unless you do," he said. She shook her head. "Then let's go."

Thunder growled in the distance, and the first flickers of lightning illuminated the dark clouds. The rain became a heavy downpour by the time he parked the truck. Theo handed her the umbrella.

"Go on upstairs," he told her. "I'll be right behind you, with your bags."

Marlee held out her hands. "I can carry the groceries."

He looped the bags around her wrists. "Okay."

"You'll get wet."

"I'll dry," he said. "Go ahead."

With swift motions, Marlee opened the door, released the umbrella, and gathered the bags in her arms. She dashed to the rear entrance and went inside. Theo drew a deep breath, then stepped into the heavy rain. By the time he pulled her bags from the truck bed, his clothes were drenched, and his wet hair dripped down his face. It didn't daunt him, though, as he sprinted inside and almost ran into his mother.

"Watch your step, Theo," she cried as they danced around each other to avoid a collision. "What are you doing?"

"We're going to watch movies because of the weather."

Liesel nodded and put her hand on her son's chest. "Just be careful, son."

Theo narrowed his eyes. "In what way?"

She rubbed the place where his heart was. "Mind your heart," she said. "Don't get hurt, not like before."

"I won't. Marlee is nothing like Theresa."

His mother nodded. "I see that, and I like her. Oma and I are heading home. Will you be at church in the morning?"

He'd almost forgotten church, but he planned to go. "Yes, we'll both be there."

"I'll see you then, Theo."

"Be careful driving in the rain."

She snorted. "I've been driving much longer than you've existed. Go on upstairs—you're soaked."

Theo grinned and bounded up the stairs despite an armload of luggage. At least she hadn't asked about Marlee's bags, but he figured the sight of them was self-explanatory. He put them inside his bedroom and found Marlee in the living room. The groceries he'd bought had been put away, he noted, and she gazed out the window.

He came behind her and put his arms around her. She startled, then shrieked. "You're wet!"

"I know," he said. "I'll go change in a minute. Go pick out a movie. There's a shelf in the corner, and if you don't see anything, there's Netflix." Theo brushed aside her hair and kissed the nape of her neck. "And don't worry about the storm."

"I'm trying," she said.

In his bedroom, he shucked the wet clothes and put on a pair of gray sweatpants with a favorite KC Chiefs T-shirt, then put his things in the washer. When Theo returned to the living room, Marlee had settled onto the couch with her feet tucked beneath her. Her shoes were on the floor.

He paused, staring at Marlee, a rush of desire rising. He wanted to ravish her, and he ached to cherish her. With a groan, Theo crossed the room and held out his hand. She glanced up with a puzzled look. "Theo, what's wrong?" she asked.

He pulled her to her feet. "Nothing, it's what's just right," he said, and kissed her the way he'd wanted to all morning. Marlee's lips yielded to his, and she wrapped her arms around him, pulling him tight and close. Theo realized he loved her— really loved her, in the way he'd like to keep her forever and spend the rest of his life with her.

That took a little time to process, but once he thought about it, Theo had no doubts. He loved her and wanted to marry her. But some inner inkling told him it was too soon to tell her, so he kept quiet.

Chapter Nine

They watched movies and fell asleep on the couch, cuddled close but separated by both pillows and blankets. By the time they woke, the storms had moved away, and a rainbow could be seen above the river, reflected in the waters. "Come see," Theo told her and led her to his bedroom so she could view the Missouri. Although he'd seen many rainbows during his lifetime, several of them above the river, Theo couldn't recall any with such bright colors.

"A rainbow!" Marlee said with delight. "Oh, it's beautiful."

"It's a sign of hope," Theo said.

She turned so that their eyes met. "And new beginnings."

He knew she feared the river now, and Theo didn't want her to be afraid. The Missouri commanded respect, but it was part of life in Hermann.

A rush of joy filled him, and he grinned. "*Jawohl*, new beginnings. Are you hungry?"

"Very."

"Then I'll cook."

Whenever he didn't work, which was rare, Theo possessed

a keen awareness of time. He knew, almost to the minute, exactly what was happening at Bah Humbug!, or what should be. Even when he'd been sick a few weeks ago, he knew the schedule and the routine and followed it mentally. But now, he paid no attention to the clock and gave no thought to his business beneath them.

By the time Theo had organized everything to begin cooking, Marlee appeared wearing pink floral pajamas with her hair pulled up with a clip.

"You look comfortable," he said.

"Well, we're not going out tonight again, are we?" she asked. "So, I put on my jammies. Can I watch?"

"Of course, I hoped you would. Grab a seat. Do you want some wine?"

When Marlee nodded, he pulled out a pair of frosted wine flutes etched with hummingbirds and opened a red wine he'd chosen. A product of the family winery, it was a medium red, a little dry with a lingering sweet taste, and he savored the bouquet as he poured it.

"To new beginnings," he said, and touched his glass to hers.

"To possibilities," Marlee replied in a soft, husky tone.

Theo took the ground round he'd bought earlier and blended it with a small amount of very lean sausage. He pressed it into two generous patties and placed them in a heated sauté pan with just a glaze of virgin olive oil. Then he added seasoning in small amounts. While the burgers cooked at a low, steady heat, he washed and sliced a handful of small golden potatoes into wedges and fried them in a separate pan until each was crisp. In another small skillet, he melted butter and sauteed baby portobello mushrooms. At first, anxiety that he would fail to impress made him self-conscious, but soon he found his groove and cooked with the grace of a ballet dancer.

Marlee watched, an attentive audience of one, her expression rapt.

He toasted a pair of Kaiser buns, then reached for condiments. "What would you like on your burger?" he asked her.

"I'll leave that up to you," she replied with a smile. "I'll take it however you want to serve it."

Theo nodded as he topped the burgers with a slice of Swiss cheese. Then he spread a little mayo over the bun, then added a small amount of brown mustard. He placed the patties onto the buns, then topped each with a slice of sweet red onion, lettuce, a tomato slice, and the mushrooms. He plated the burgers, then added the wedge fries.

"Let's eat," he said, and placed the plates on his small table. He picked up the wine bottle and topped off their glasses.

Although downstairs he seldom took time for a blessing, it seemed right now, so he reached for her hands, bowed his head, and said, "Bless us, O Lord! and these Thy gifts, which we are about to receive from Thy bounty, through Christ our Lord. Amen."

Marlee spoke it with him, then picked up her burger and took the first bite. Theo watched her face, waiting for her reaction, and he wasn't disappointed.

"That's fantastic," she said, briefly closing her eyes with appreciation. "It's delicious."

He grinned. "I'm glad you like it."

"It's perfection. I probably won't ever enjoy a basic burger as much ever again."

"Once you get moved, I'll make you a burger any time you want," he promised. "Even downstairs."

"I'll hold you to that," she said. "And when I'm settled, I will cook for you, too."

"Your meatloaf was outstanding. I imagine I'll hear some

rave reviews about it on Monday."

"Do you really think so?"

He paused to take a bite, then nodded. "I do. I'll call and tell you whatever is said."

Marlee nodded. "And you'll tell me how the boys do, too."

The boys. Theo choked on a crisp fry. He'd forgotten the Becker brothers would come to Bah Humbug! after school to work for him to make amends. "I will," he said. "I have no idea what I'll do with them, though."

"Give them simple tasks they can do," she said, as if it were easy.

Theo didn't know how to explain kids weren't his forte. He hadn't been around young people very often. "I wish you were going to be here, too."

She polished off the last of her burger with a deep sigh of appreciation. "I wish I didn't have to go home tomorrow, but if wishes were horses, beggars would ride."

Theo would have rather forgotten that she had to leave. "What time is your train?"

"Three," Marlee said with a sigh. "I won't get home until late evening, probably, but I don't care. I wish school was already out."

He glanced at the calendar from a local hardware store that hung on the wall. "Tomorrow is May 1. When does your school end?"

"The Friday before Memorial Day," Marlee said. "It's the last Friday in May. If I have a place, I can move that weekend."

Four weeks. He counted and topped off their wine glasses one more time. He sipped the sweet red wine and contemplated. A month seemed like an awfully long time, but when he considered that Marlee would need to pack and move, it became short.

"I'm still planning to come up to St. Joe over Memorial Day weekend," Theo said. "I can help, maybe even bring some of your stuff back with me in the truck, if you want."

Her eyes brightened. "That would be awesome, Theo."

"Then it's a plan. Let me clean up, and we can go watch a movie."

Marlee stacked their plates and put their silverware on top. "I'll do the dishes," she told him, and when he tried to protest, she shushed him. "It's fair. You cooked; I'll do this. You can go pick out a couple of movies."

"If that's what you want." Theo kissed the nape of her neck, slow and sweet.

"It is," she said. "I'll be there in a flash."

She turned and raised up on her toes to plant a kiss on his lips. His arms went around her, and he kissed her until she broke free, laughing.

Theo perused the movies he'd collected, rejecting the action movies as too violent, the sci-fi films as questionable, and bemoaned the fact he didn't own any rom cons. He had some vintage black and white movies, which might be possibilities, and he had some Westerns, including his favorites, *Silverado* and *Lonesome Dove.*

Considering that Marlee taught history and hailed from a town with some frontier heritage, he decided to take a chance with *Lonesome Dove.* If she balked, there was always *The Ghost and Mrs. Muir* or Netflix. Theo loaded the first DVD into the player and fast-forwarded to the opening scene, then paused it.

She joined him, rubbing lotion into her hands, and the sweet lavender scent filled the room. Marlee kicked off her shoes and curled up beside him. "What are we watching?"

"Something I hope you like." Theo hit play and reached over to turn off the lamp. He liked Marlee, even thought he loved her, but now came the acid test—what preferences they shared and which ones they didn't. If their very new relationship worked, they would compromise, and he knew it, but this moment was the first chance to discover her tastes.

The single street of Lonesome Dove filled the screen, then the camera cut to the Hat Creek Cattle Company sign just before Gus McCrae stumbled outside to chase away two pigs fighting over a dead rattler. Marlee leaned closer and drew a deep breath.

"Ohh!" she said.

"Does that mean my choice is good or that it's bad?"

She turned her head and gazed at him. "It's perfect. This is one of my favorite books."

A small coil of tension in his chest eased. "Have you seen the movie?"

"Once," she said. "It was a mini-series, wasn't it?"

"Yes."

"And you like it?"

"It's one of my favorites," he said. "I like the idea of the Old West. Sure, I'm deep in German culture and history with a little English tossed in for good measure, Missouri Rhineland born and bred, but there's something about the West that I've always been drawn toward."

Marlee touched his face. "Me, too. Let's watch."

So, with his arm around her and with Marlee leaning against him, they watched until they struggled to stay awake. They had made it through four of the six hours, but Theo groaned.

"What's wrong?" she murmured, her voice thick and drowsy.

"Nothing except I can't stay awake much longer," he said. "If we're going to go to church, we need some sleep."

She yawned. "I'm sleepy too, and I do want to go. We can finish it later, next time I'm here, or once I move here."

As tired as he was, Theo grinned. "And then we'll watch *Comanche Moon, Streets of Laredo* and *Dead Man's Walk*, in order."

"Perfect!'

He extended his hand. "Let's go to bed — to sleep."

In his bed, spacious for one, Theo made room for Marlee. Except for a few occasions, he'd never shared mattress space with anyone. As an only child, he'd had his own room and a set of bunk beds, so when he had friends spend the night, each had had their own space. His standard size double bed, usually roomy, became snug when shared, but Theo had no complaints as he held Marlee, her back curled against his belly, until they both slept. The half open window delivered the cooler air left after the storm passed, and with it the fragrance of spring.

For church, Marlee wore a floral print dress, mauve with bright yellow and blue posies. Theo liked the high neck style with cap sleeves. The skirt swirled down to her knees and belled out. Even in her high heels, she wasn't as tall as he, and Theo liked that. He wore a light grey tweed blazer over his quintessential black slacks and a white dress shirt with a tie.

"Sharp dressed man," Marlee said. It took every ounce of his willpower to resist kissing her, but Theo managed.

"You look beautiful."

At St. Morand's, Theo helped her out of the truck.

"Thank you," she told him. "You're very much a gentleman."

"I can be," he told her.

Marlee came to a halt and almost tripped him. She gazed upward toward the white steeple of the Gothic style church and released a slow breath. "Theo, this church is fantastic. Is it as amazing inside?"

Theo's spiritual life had centered around the red brick church for as long as he could recall. The awestruck expression she wore brought the revelation that maybe he'd taken it for granted.

"It's beautiful, yes," he said. "Let's go inside. If we don't go now, we'll be late."

Marlee grasped his hand as she dashed up the steps into

the sanctuary. Inside, she gawked at the stained-glass windows, all imported from Germany around the turn of the century, and the ornate carved altar. Theo steered her over to the font where they each dipped their fingers in Holy Water, then made the sign of the cross. From a middle pew on the left, his mom and grandmother beckoned. Behind them, the priest, lector, and two altar servers prepared for the procession.

"Look later," Theo whispered. "Let's go sit with my family. Mass is about to begin."

She nodded, and after genuflecting at the pew, she slid down to sit beside Liesel and Oma. Theo flanked her other side. For Theo, the words of the familiar Mass served as a balm for his soul. Marlee's presence enhanced that. Afterward, they lingered in the church long enough for Marlee to appreciate the beauty.

Theo nudged her. "*Mutti* and *Oma* are waiting."

"Oh, I didn't realize," she said. "I'm almost finished looking."

"The church will be here," he said.

Marlee turned to him. "You're right. And I have a train to catch this afternoon. Let's go." She linked her arm through his, and they walked to where his family waited.

Liesel smiled at Marlee. "I wanted to ask if you two would like to come to dinner at the farmhouse."

Before Marlee could agree, Theo spoke up. "Her train leaves at three," he said. "I don't want to rush her first trip out there. We're going to Maybelle's for brunch. Would you and Oma like to join us?"

He knew that his mother seldom made a full-scale Sunday dinner, not for two. If she knew Theo or one of the family was coming, then she did.

His grandmother answered. "We would love that, Theo. I haven't had breakfast out in so long."

"We'll meet you there," Liesel said.

At Maybelle's, they ate, but it wasn't food Theo craved. His breakfast platter tasted fine, and it sated his hunger, but watching Marlee, he dreaded her imminent separation. He only half-listened to the three-way conversation she held with his matriarchs, pleased to see they interacted.

"You're quiet," Marlee said softly into his ear near the end of the meal. His mother and grandmother had just departed.

"Just thinking," he said.

"About the fact I'm leaving in a few hours?"

Theo nodded.

"I don't want to go," she said. "But it's time for some adulting."

He laughed and reached for her hand. "True, but we don't have to like it. The sun's shining. Let's go for a drive until it's almost time for your train,"

She'd packed before church, and after a quick sweep to make sure she'd left nothing behind, Theo carried Marlee's luggage to his truck. Then they set off on a Sunday drive, through town and into the countryside. It was a lick-and-promise kind of tour, he thought, but he drove her to see the church at Starkenberg and past the family farm. At first, he played tour guide and narrated, but after a while, he let the music play, and they listened or sang or talked. He ached to take her home and spend more time with her, but Theo realized they lacked the time, and he didn't want her to miss her train.

Too soon, it was two-thirty, so he wound back into town and parked at the Amtrak station. Once her bags sat near the boarding area, they sat down on a bench to wait.

"In less than a month, you'll come to see me to help me move, and then I'll be here," she said. Their hands were linked.

"You could come for Maifest in two weeks," Theo said. The idea had just hit, and he liked it. "That would break it up, and it wouldn't be so long."

"I don't know — maybe," she said. "I have so much to pack, and I'd have to ride the train again...."

"I could come get you," Theo offered. It would make his pub schedule difficult, but he would do it.

Marlee leaned against him. "You're tempting me, Theo Scrooge."

"That's the idea."

"Maybe," she said.

"Call me when you get home," he said.

"I will," Marlee promised. "I'll call every day,"

"And I'll call you, too." Theo stood. "The train's coming."

She rose and faced him. "Kiss me."

He pulled her into his arms and held her, his mouth slow and sweet. His lips cherished her, then shifted into an urgent heated need. The train rocketed into the station, then came to a stop. Despite the noise, Theo didn't stop, not until Marlee broke away.

"I'll miss my train," she laughed.

Theo helped her with the bags, and just before she stepped into the car, he saw tears in her eyes.

"Marlee, I love you," he said. Maybe it wasn't the perfect moment, but the words came from his heart.

Her face changed, and for a moment, he feared he'd made a mistake. But then she smiled, a bright expression that made her beautiful. Marlee put one hand to her heart and said, "Oh, Theo, I love you too, so much."

He thought she might step down from the train, and knew she couldn't.

"Call me, *Liebling,*" he said.

"I will."

Her tears spilled down her cheeks, but her smile didn't dim.

Theo stepped back and watched as the train pulled out,

picking up speed as it traveled along the Missouri River. He'd always meant to take a train trip one day but never had.

He stared at the tracks after the silver cars were gone. Then Theo drove the short distance home, left his truck, and walked alongside the river for a long time, heart brimming full and lonely.

At Bah Humbug! he planned the next day's menus, waiting for a call, wondering and dreaming.

Distracted, he cut his finger when he sliced some black bread for a late sandwich, and worried himself into a stomachache when Marlee hadn't called. Theo had his phone in his hand, planning to dial if he didn't hear in another ten minutes. But it rang, and he forgot everything else but the sound of her voice.

Chapter Ten

Too much coffee and not enough sleep combined to make Theo cross and on edge. He'd decided on *Zwiebel-Schinkenkuchen*, ham and onion tarts for the special, along with a simple shepherd's pie made with ham instead of lamb for the English side. Preparation should have been simple, but he fumbled too often, his mind on Marlee, not the meal.

After he dropped the third dish that shattered, he swore loudly in two languages, managed to cut his thumb picking up shards and debated on whether or not it was too early to start drinking. Since it was not quite ten. Theo conceded that it was.

They had talked far into the night, later than he should have, but Theo hadn't wanted to end the connection. Irritable because he had difficulty envisioning her surroundings, he tried to focus on something else and failed. Marlee could imagine Theo's day since she'd been in the kitchen, the pub, and his place, but with nothing but a handful of online photos, he couldn't visualize her day. Oh, he could summon up images of a standard classroom with a teacher's desk, student desks, a chalkboard, and windows, but he knew it probably was nothing like the reality. Even the night before, he had no notion of her home, and although it didn't matter, he couldn't stop thinking about it.

When his mother arrived, Theo made an effort to appear calm and cheerful.

"I brought gingerbread," she said. "Do you have cream? If not, we need some for the topping."

He inhaled the still warm spicy confection with pleasure. "I do. That smells *wunderbar, Mutti.*"

"I thought you'd like it," Liesel said with a smile. "Take a break and have a piece."

"I might. Where's Oma?"

"She's at the winery with Thomas. She's helping him with ideas for Maifest. Are you planning special menus? You usually do."

Theo hadn't, not yet. He hadn't even thought about it. "Maybe, but there's a chance I may not be here part of the time."

Liesel lifted an eyebrow in question. "No? Why wouldn't you be?"

"I might go pick up Marlee so she can come," he said. "It's not for sure, not yet."

As she spoke, she cut him a generous slice of gingerbread and rooted in the fridge for the cream. She handed it to him with a spoon, shaking her head. "Ten years and you hardly miss a day, only when you're too sick to get out of bed or it's something very important, and now you go when you want."

Guilty, he tried a defense. "But, Mama...."

"*Sei ruhib,* Theo. It's good. It's about time."

Flabbergasted, he stared at her. "You mean it, don't you?"

"*Jawohl!* You've worked so hard and had nothing but work, church, and family for too long. I'm happy to see you this way. I like your Marlee, and even more, I like how you are when you're with her."

"How's that?"

"Happy," she told him. "Now finish your gingerbread. You have customers coming for lunch."

Between the gingerbread and his mom's advice, Theo's mood improved. At twelve-thirty, in the midst of the hectic noon rush, his phone buzzed in his pocket. At any other time, he would have ignored it, but he pulled it out and grinned.

"Hi."

"Hey, Theo. It's lunch break, and I have like four minutes, but I couldn't wait," Marlee said. "I miss you!"

"Babe, I miss you too," he told her. "I've been thinking about you. How's your day going?"

"It goes," she said. "It's fine, just same old, same old. I just wanted to hear your voice so I could be sure it's real."

"It's as real as it gets."

In the background, he heard a bell, and she sighed. "I have to go, but call me tonight, please. I want to hear how the boys do and all about your day."

"I will, I promise." He'd almost forgotten about Lucas and Logan Becker.

Her voice dropped low, just above a whisper. "I love you."

"I love you, too, sugar. Talk to you later."

Theo stood, savoring the words for a long moment. Autumn burst into the kitchen.

"Theo, where's the orders? Everyone's complaining. Why are you running behind?" He grinned, and she gaped at him. "Are you okay?"

"I'm great," he said, and started plating food with speed.

"You're usually the slave driver, and now you're lollygagging."

"Ja, ja, I took a minute," he said. "It's no big deal. Here, order up, and I'll have the next one ready by the time you're back."

Theo pushed his mind back into the groove, and the

remainder of lunch went smoothly. By the time they closed, he had started cabbage rolls and chicken croquettes for the evening meal. He ate a fast, late lunch with Liesel, then tried to determine what the boys could do.

They arrived soon after school ended, both a little pale and wearing scared expressions.

"Hi, guys," Theo said. "Ready to work?" Both nodded. "Then come on, I thought you could wrap some silverware."

He demonstrated how to place a knife, fork, and spoon onto a napkin and roll it tight. After a few klutzy efforts, they got the hang of it. Rather than stand over them, Theo backed off.

Autumn beckoned him over. "So, are they working here?"

"It's probation," he said, and sketched out the bare bones of the story.

Sheriff Kaiser and his wife came for dinner, watching the Becker boys with a keen eye that seemed to make them tense. Theo noticed and pulled them to the kitchen.

"Are you guys hungry? There's cabbage rolls or chicken croquettes, plus my mom made gingerbread."

The younger of the two, Logan, frowned. "Do you have any pizza?"

His brother jabbed him in the ribs with one elbow. "Shut up," he hissed.

Theo wanted to laugh but didn't. "What kind of pizza do you like?"

"Pepperoni," Logan said.

"Or sausage?" Lucas added.

"I'll order pizza this one time," Theo told them, trying to appear stern. "You've worked hard and stood up to people gossiping."

"And the sheriff watching us," Logan said. Apparently, bashful was fading fast.

"He was," Theo stated. "But he's a good man. Not nearly

as mean as he looks."

After it was delivered, he ate a slice of pizza with the kids, then told them they could go for the day.

"Come back tomorrow," he told them. "I'll have something different for you to do."

They left with a chorus of thank yous, Theo shaking his head as they went.

During the remainder of the dinner rush, he planned his menus for Tuesday, choosing Schwäbische Maultaschen, potato dumplings filled with ground meat, spinach, and seasonings, and steak pie — minus the kidneys. He decided to serve both dishes at noon and evening.

Jonas stopped at the end of his shift for a meal, and Theo brought him back to his office to eat.

"How'd they work out?" he asked about the Beckers.

"Good, better than I expected," Theo told him. "It's been a day, though."

Jonas raised an eyebrow. "How so? Lonely?"

"Yeah, missing Marlee more than I thought possible."

"My friend, it happens that way," Jonas said with a grin.

Theo shot him a look. "Apparently. She'll move here at the end of May, but until then, I don't know."

"You'll survive," Jonas said with certainty. "I have. Want to play some chess later?"

"And drink wine, *jawohl*," Theo replied. "After I talk to Marlee. Around ten?"

"Works for me."

As soon as the staff left, with the place sparkling clean and ready for Tuesday, Theo locked the doors and dashed upstairs to the privacy of his apartment. He flopped down on the couch and called Marlee.

"Hi," she answered. "So, Bah Humbug! is closed for the day?"

"Locked and loaded for tomorrow," Theo said. "How did school go?"

"It went. The kids are eager for summer break to start, and we're not doing much, just review, then tests, then we'll probably watch movies. Normally it's a break from routine, but right now, it just seems boring. I found myself wanting to tell them all about Hermann and your pub and everything. I didn't, though. Did the Becker boys show up?"

"They did. They were nervous, but they did good, except Logan wanted pizza."

"Let me guess—you bought them some."

Theo laughed. "Guilty, but just today."

"You're too good-hearted," Marlee said. "But I love you anyway."

Her words delighted him. "I'm glad. I miss you like crazy."

"Same," she said. "Tell me where you're at right now."

"On the couch," he said. "It's not fair, though."

"What isn't?"

"I can't imagine you. You've been here, but I'd love to see your house."

"So, I'll send you a picture. I'm out on the front porch because it's so nice. There's an old-fashioned glider I sanded and repainted red, and a trellis. It has clematis growing up it. I'll take a selfie as soon as we hang up, I promise."

"I'd like that."

He told her what specials he planned for the next day, and she shared that her classes were heading out on a field trip to see the Pony Express stables, the Jesse James house, and the Patee House, a museum.

"I wish I could go," Theo said, and meant it.

"When you come, I'll take you to see all of it."

If Jonas hadn't arrived at exactly ten o'clock, Theo thought he could have talked to Marlee all night, but he explained, and she sighed.

"Go play chess, Theo. I have an early start tomorrow. I'll call, or you can call me. Probably not at lunch because of the field trip, but if I get a chance, I will."

"I'll have my phone with me. I love you, Marlee."

"Love you, too. Good night."

Jonas arrived and set up the chess board. Theo provided the wine — sweet red — and a few snacks. The soon to be bridegroom offered some sage advice for the lovelorn. Although Theo joked it was just to distract him from the game, he listened and took the advice to heart, along with the wine.

"You've just realized this is the woman," Jonas said. "And it's life changing, and in your circumstance, you have to be apart for a short time. Just deal with it, Theo, and instead of focusing on the distance, celebrate the fact you've found each other. You're eating yourself up."

"I'm not."

Jonas laughed. "You are. Anyone can see it — me, your mom, and Autumn, for starters. But stop. You'll make Marlee upset, you'll try too hard, and you might ruin what you have started. I would guess she misses you too, so don't guilt trip her. Now, pay attention to the game, or you'll lose."

Pondering what his friend said, Theo tried but still didn't win.

He lost three chess games but drank four glasses of wine. It affected Theo just enough to be glad he only had to walk a short distance to bed and had no need to drive. He wasn't drunk — far from it, just relaxed to the point of boneless peace. The wine eased his loneliness enough to sleep.

Theo awoke in a brighter mood. While he drank and played chess, Marlee had sent him some photos of her house, including the porch, the kitchen, and her bedroom. Her text promised pictures from school and from the field trip.

Miss you, Theo, she texted with a string of x's and o's.

Once he was in the kitchen downstairs, Theo replied with a selfie as he prepared to cook. For fun, he even donned a black chef's hat that matched his usual ensemble, something he almost never wore. Then, he jacked up this music and sang along with the tunes.

The rouladen turned out nicely, and the steak pie as well. Liesel arrived with a German apple cake, the kind made with yeast and apple tarts.

"That's the perfect dessert for today, Mutti," Theo said as he kissed her cheek. "Thank you."

"You're welcome. So, you're in a good mood, *ja*?"

"*Ja*," he said.

"That's the way to be. Remember, love is patient."

Theo hugged her. "I'm trying, Mutti."

Oma entered. "So, where's the girl, my Theo? The way your *mutter* talked, I thought you probably went to kidnap her and bring her back with force."

He'd been ridiculous and realized it. And he recognized his grandmother's sarcasm when he heard it.

"That comes later, Oma."

His grandmother waved a hand in dismissal. "She'll be here soon enough. You're young. There's time. It's really no time at all until she moves here."

"You're right," he said, and hugged her. "Patience is the virtue I haven't managed to perfect."

Theo sent Marlee pictures of the day's specials, plated, and a selfie of him. In return, she sent back pictures of the Patee House and high school kids sprawled out in a small park with a locomotive in the background. *Call me tonight*, she texted.

Bah Humbug! was busy, and the afternoon passed quickly as Theo prepared the evening specials, grilled *Weisswurst* with spaetzle and shepherd's pie. The noon rush and multiple tasks left little time to daydream about Marlee, and it was almost closing time before Theo realized Blevins was in the house.

By the number of beer bottles on the table, he'd been there a while or drank with speed, Theo noted. As he passed through the dining room, delivering a late order of *Weisswurst*, Blevins called out, and Theo tensed.

"What kind of sausage is this supposed to be?" he asked with a sneer. "It doesn't look German to me—more like some fancy Frenchified food. Are you adding French food, then, Scrooge? Are you going to serve crepes or maybe some snails?"

Blevins's breath carried the smell of beer, and from his belligerent tone, Theo figured the man to be well on his way to being drunk. Doubtful he'd pass a sobriety check, Theo thought as he paused to provide a forced, polite reply.

"*Weisswurst* is Bavarian," he said. "It's a traditional wurst, and no, I hadn't planned to add any other cuisines."

"Is that right? I thought maybe you had to impress your little Frenchwoman."

Theo knew very well he meant Marlee, but he played dumb as he tried to tamp down a red wave of rage. "I'm not sure I know who that is."

"That Miss Dupree," Blevins blared. "What's her name again? Oh, wait, I remember now. How could I forget? It's Marlee, isn't it? Perfect—Scrooge and Marlee."

He burst into laughter, a raucous and rude outburst.

Theo stood, stunned. Until now, he'd never made the leap but remembered that the fictional Ebenezer's late partner was named Marley. His surprise tempered his anger for the moment, and Blevins, aware he'd made a hit with his remark, grabbed his ticket and headed to pay, leaving Theo to bus the table and fume.

The Becker kids helped take his mind off Ebenezer Scrooge and Todd Blevins. They talked more and worked with enough effort that Theo let them do some minimal prep work.

Marlee called early, weary from the field trip but buoyant. Theo said nothing to her about Scrooge and Marlee. While he didn't like the similarity or any reference to her from Blevins, nothing could change how he felt. Still, he failed to fool her because Marlee paused in a story about how some of her students ran into the Jesse James home on the ground of the Patee House through the back door, and said, "Theo? You haven't said much. Are you okay?"

"Just tired," he told her. "And missing you. I might just take Oma's suggestion—to kidnap you by force and bring you back here."

She laughed, and the merry sound eased most of his angst. "I almost wish you would, Theo, but I have to finish the year and pack. But I'm marking off the days on the calendar until you come for the holiday weekend."

"What about Maifest?" he asked. "Have you thought about coming?"

"I want to," she replied. "But Theo, it would be so rushed. I have so much packing to do to get ready to move. So, I don't think so."

Disappointed, Theo understood. "That's fine. There's next year and all the other festivals. But we're still good for Memorial Day weekend?"

"Of course! Are you coming on Saturday?"

"Friday," he said. "The sooner I come up, I figure the sooner I can get your stuff loaded. Have you found a place to live yet?"

It turned out Marlee had not. "I didn't even think about that," she said with a gasp. "Oh, Theo! I'm going to need somewhere to live, or we can't bring my stuff."

Theo did some swift thinking. "What if I find you a place? I can take care of that from here—unless you change your mind about Maifest."

"Maybe I should."

"Either way, you'll have a place. I promise."

Thinking about where she might call home once she arrived kept Theo from thinking about the Scrooge and Marlee thing, at least for the rest of the night.

There was always tomorrow.

Chapter Eleven

Theo scouted out several potential apartments and one small house. They had talked about the possibility of Marlee moving in with him once she moved to town, but decided the small space would be too tight for two. Marlee also thought the board of education might frown on her taking up residence with a single man, and Theo, although he wanted to disagree, thought it was probable. And since both were committed to celibacy while single, Theo kept searching for a place.

She didn't come for Maifest, pleading end of school activities and too much to do to prepare for the move. Theo, distracted by her absence, decided to go big for Maifest. He offered all German specialties for that weekend. Sunny skies and warm temperatures brought out the crowds. Bah Humbug! served a record number of meals both inside and in the outdoor dining area. Keeping the food coming kept him busy, although he talked to Marlee each evening.

He emailed her photos of the rental options, and without seeing them in person, she opted for an apartment within an old house just blocks from his restaurant. The one bedroom, one bath apartment consisted of half the downstairs space. The floor plan was simple—a large living room, a smaller bedroom, a kitchen and bath, with an enclosed sun porch on the back. Acting as her agent, Theo rented it for her and arranged to have it cleaned. Henry Muller, whose wife, Lisa, ran the florist shop, owned the place.

"It will be move in ready when you get here," he told her.

"It's perfect. Thank you, Theo."

Theo didn't tell her, but he'd negotiated a six-month lease rather than a year, in hopes that in that time they might make other arrangements, like marriage. He'd also planted some pansies in the tiny garden space behind it, a spot large enough for two outdoor chairs and a tiny grill.

He sent photos of Maifest and told her how much fun it was. The boys continued to show up to help, and he used them every day during Maifest. Both had become competent helpers, able to bus tables or wash pans, among many other tasks.

Once the festival was over, he waited without much patience. For the first time ever, Theo considered closing Bah Humbug! for the long Memorial Day weekend. His staff, including Autumn, loved the idea, but his mom wasn't as thrilled.

"You'll lose business, son," she told him. "It's the real start of the tourist season. You should be open. Let your Marlee bring her own things down, or hire a mover."

"I want to do this for her, Mutti. I thought you liked the fact I'm not working so hard."

"*Jawohl*, I do, but I don't want you hurt. I hear the talk."

"Talk?"

She put on a mocking tone. "Scrooge and Marlee, Scrooge and Marlee. I don't want you letting it upset you. It means *nichts*."

"I'm not."

Theo was, though, and he realized it.

"I worry you'll drive her away, smothering her and being

unreasonable. She needs her space. If you're meant to be together, it will happen."

"It will all be good," he said.

Liesel glared at him. "So, you've told her this thing about Scrooge and Marlee, then?"

Theo, stubborn to the core, ignored the question and went upstairs to finish packing a bag. He returned to kiss his mother and Oma before they went home. He had also decided to remain open, after his mother offered to oversee operations on Friday and Saturday. Bah Humbug! would be open on Monday, but he would be back long before then.

"I'm leaving first thing in the morning," he told them. "I'll call occasionally, and we'll be back Sunday if not before. I love you both."

Theo departed in darkness, and it was at least a hundred miles before he saw the first hint of sunrise in his rear-view mirror. Traffic was non-existent until he hit I-70, and even then, it remained sparse. By the time he hit the outskirts of Kansas City, however, and headed north, it was daylight, and the morning rush hour was well underway. Theo pushed the old truck up past eighty miles an hour to keep from being run over by the tide and finally took an exit to buy coffee and take a break. As promised, he called his mom and chatted about the cookies she had in the oven for Bah Humbug!

Once he reached St. Joseph, Theo had an idea of where to go to reach Marlee's neighborhood. Since she wouldn't get out of school until early afternoon, he drove around, refreshing his memory of some of the local sites. He managed to find the Patee House, an old hotel turned garment factory turned museum, located a few blocks from the Pony Express Stables, with little difficulty, but his efforts to drive to Wyeth Hill were fruitless.

In the end, Theo navigated to Marlee's address and parked out front. He realized he had no idea what she drove, but then figured his distinctive truck would announce his presence. If he hadn't been concerned the neighbors might peg him as a stalker, he would have taken a seat on the glider he noticed on the porch. Along the way, he'd stopped at a florist and bought a dozen tulips, remembering those were her favorite flower.

He'd known her just short of two months, and they'd been apart for several weeks, which made him both eager and anxious to see Marlee. Reflecting on their relationship, Theo realized most people would think he hadn't known her long enough to want to be married or, to be sure, but he had no doubts.

She arrived, wearing khaki slacks and a dark green polo shirt with the name of the high school where she taught emblazoned on the upper left side. Although he wanted to rush to her, Theo paced his actions and met her on the sidewalk.

"Hi," he said. "I brought you these."

Marlee took the bouquet of multi-colored tulips from Theo and smiled. "Thank you. They're lovely. How about a kiss?"

Theo obliged and put his mouth on hers, kissing her slow and sweet.

"I'm so glad you're here," she said. "I have a lot packed already, but I don't know if it's all going to fit in your truck."

"I hope you're kidding," he laughed.

She shook her head. "Not really. Come see."

Inside the vintage two-story house, Theo goggled at the stacked boxes and the furniture waiting to load. Within the living room, there was a sofa, an armchair, and two tables, plus lamps, framed photos, and a television. Moving through the house, he saw there was a wooden desk and chair, a kitchen table with four chairs, and a tall bookshelf. Upstairs, Marlee had a bed, dresser, cedar chest, and chest of drawers. There were two other bedrooms, one with a twin bed and the other piled full of boxes, each labeled with the contents. He saw boxes holding kitchen stuff, books, and miscellaneous stacked in various spots.

"Does it all have to go?" he asked, wondering not only how it would fit in the truck, but how much would need to be stored.

Marlee nodded. "It does. I know it looks like a lot, but I pared it down. I donated a lot of stuff I didn't need to Goodwill."

Theo spied several large boxes toward the back of the spare bedroom, each one marked "Christmas," and he cringed. The holiday remained a sore spot. "What's all that Christmas stuff?"

"It's my tree, nativity set, wreaths and garlands, and all my ornaments," she said. "And one box has my Christmas movies, music, and books. I love Christmas!"

And I hate it, he thought. "And it all has to go?"

Her eyes grew wide. "Of course, it does."

Theo sighed and blew air through his nose. "All right."

Her lips turned downward. "Is something wrong?"

He shook his head. "Just the Christmas thing. I'm not a fan."

"I remember. You told me that your dad died in December. But I didn't know you had a problem with Christmas decorations and stuff."

"Well, I do," he said. "It's the whole Scrooge thing. I've been made fun of since grade school, and it was so bad, it overshadowed Christmas."

"But you named your place Bah Humbug!"

"Out of sarcasm," Theo said.

"And you get upset when people like that guy—what was his name?"

"Todd Blevins. Pick at me about it? Yeah, I still do."

Marlee shook her head. "That's silly and childish, Theo. You need to let it go."

"Maybe it sounds lame, but…."

She met his gaze without looking away. "It does. Don't

you like *A Christmas Carol* at all? It's one of my favorites, the book and then the various movies made over the years."

"I never read it, and I haven't seen any of the movies," he said. "I never wanted to."

"Do you know even know what it's about?"

Marlee used her teacher voice to ask the question, which annoyed Theo.

"Yeah, it's about a mean old guy who hates Christmas, and he's mean to everyone. He's a lonely old miser with nothing in his life. No need to wonder why I don't like it."

"Oh, Theo, that's just the beginning of the story. And you're not like Ebenezer Scrooge."

"I've heard that I am since the fourth grade, and it's all the worse now."

Marlee stared at him. "How is it worse?"

"Because now Blevins has started with Scrooge and Marlee."

Just saying it brought anger, but Marlee laughed, which rubbed his long-standing wound raw.

"Yeah, it's just hilarious," he said. "So now the town is making fun of us too."

"I hadn't even noticed," she said. "But Marley is spelled different, and Scrooge's late business partner doesn't have anything to do with you and me. It's just a story, Theo."

Theo wished he'd never said anything about her Christmas decorations. "Marlee, let's quit talking about it, okay? I don't want to get into a fight with you. I've looked forward to today for weeks, and I can't wait for you to get settled in Hermann."

Her expression changed. "I don't want to fight either. I'm glad you're here, and I'm ready to get moved. Do you want to start loading or what?"

Theo stepped back into the hallway, relieved she'd agreed to drop the subject.

"I won't be able to haul it all, but you can figure out what needs to go with us and what can go on a moving truck. And I guess we need to find a mover who can drive the rest of it down."

"That sounds like a plan. How about lunch first?"

"I like that idea," he said. "What do you have?"

"The kitchen is packed," she said. "And there's not much food because I haven't been to the store, knowing I'm moving. Let's go out, eat somewhere, and then come back so I can prioritize."

"Let's do it."

Theo, as a chef, was picky about what he ate and seldom lowered his taste standards to fast food. But when Marlee suggested a local favorite, a place that offered loose meat sandwiches, he was intrigued enough to agree. They picked up a sack of the burgers with some fries and soft drinks, then headed to Wyeth Hill for a picnic. They ate beneath a picnic shelter that overlooked a wide vista of the Missouri River, with Kansas visible on the opposite bank.

Spring grass surrounded the pavilion, and irises bloomed in flower beds around the edges, their scent sweeter than candy. A light wind ruffled Theo's hair and touched his face. He liked the burgers, although the meat tended to fall off the bun. In the moment, Theo let go of his issues with Ebenezer Scrooge and enjoyed the time with Marlee.

After they'd eaten, they kissed.

"Let's go back to work, or nothing will get done," she told him. "If we get loaded and find someone to move the rest, we could head out tomorrow."

Theo had planned to go back on Sunday and told her so.

"The sooner we get there, the quicker I can get settled in," she said. "I know school doesn't start back up until August, but I want to get adjusted to living in Hermann and have plenty of time to spend with you."

At her house, Marlee bustled around and prioritized what she'd need first. Theo made several calls to moving companies, but all were booked. The earliest one could take the job was mid-June, and Marlee said no.

"We could rent one of those do-it-yourself moving trucks," she suggested.

"Who's going to drive it?"

She sat in one of the kitchen chairs. "I thought you could, Theo, and I'd drive your truck."

"Can you drive a standard?"

"No."

"Then it won't work. Both a moving truck and my truck are stick shifts. Besides, the idea of you trying to pilot either vehicle through KC traffic scares me."

"Don't you think I can handle it? I have to get my car there somehow."

Theo laughed. "*Liebling*, it terrifies me, but you're right—you'll need your car."

Marlee frowned. "Then I can't move till mid-June?"

"Of course, you can. We can make multiple trips," Theo said. Inwardly he cringed because he shouldn't take that much time away from the restaurant. That reminded him, he needed to call his mother and check in. "Or we'll figure out something. Think about it while I call Mutti and make sure Bah Humbug! is still standing."

From the front porch, for a better signal, Theo called her at home first, certain it was late enough that she would be there, but no one answered. Theo dialed the number for Bah Humbug! and waited. After five rings, he was about to hang up when his mother picked up the phone.

"Bah Humbug," she said. "How may I help you?"

Her stressed tone alerted him. "*Mutti, was ist los?*" Theo asked. "What happened?"

"Oh, it's you," Liesel said. "It's more what didn't happen, Theo. Autumn burned her hand this morning trying to help in the kitchen. Bad enough, she had to go to the hospital. Liz called in, she's sick, and so Eva tried to help with the cooking. When we went to make the *frikadelles*, the meat was spoiled, so we changed the menu. One of the evening servers quit, and it's been so busy we had trouble keeping up with orders, so people were impatient and complained."

Theo shut his eyes and stifled a curse. "I'm sorry it's been like that. Is Autumn okay?"

"*Na ja*, she will be, but she can't work with the bandage on her hand," Liesel said.

"Are the Becker boys coming after school? They can help."

"I told them not to come—we closed at three," his mother said. "Oma is tired, and I'm worn out. There's not enough staff to make dinner, and unless you say different, it will be closed tomorrow."

His profits for the week had diminished, if not vanished. "I understand, and that's fine. I will be home sometime tomorrow with Marlee."

Or without, he thought, if they couldn't find a way to move all her things.

"*Sehr gut*," she replied. "Be careful on the way, son."

"I will. Thanks for holding down the fort."

"*Bitte*."

Unless she'd found a mover, there would have to be a major change in plans, he thought, and he'd have to figure out something, or his business would suffer.

Marlee was on her cell, laughing. "All right, that's perfect. Thank you. Love you!"

Theo stood in the doorway and waited. She leapt up from the chair with a grin.

"We've got someone to drive a rented truck!"

Relief made him sink into the nearest chair. "That's great."

She studied his expression. "Was everything okay?"

"Not really," he said, and filled her in. "But it'll be okay. Who's your driver?"

"My brother, Louis. He'll be here early in the morning after he picks up the truck."

He realized he knew nothing about her family. This was the first he'd heard about a sibling.

"That's awesome," he said. "I didn't know you had a brother."

Marlee smiled. "I have two, both a lot older than me."

"You never told me about your family."

She shrugged. "You never asked."

Theo had been selfish, he realized. He'd introduced her to his family, even his best friend, but he'd failed to find out about her family. For a single second, he wondered if he might be as selfish as Scrooge, then dismissed the thought.

"I should have. I'm sorry I didn't. Will I meet your parents?"

"No, they're both gone," she said. "My dad for five years, Mom for three. But you'll meet Louis tomorrow. He's the oldest, and I'm sure you'll meet Peter sometime. That's about it except for their wives and kids—and a few aunts, uncles, and cousins. Let's get busy. When Louis says early, he means at the crack of dawn."

That was logical, and so they worked late into the night, packing and moving furniture downstairs for loading. It wasn't the night he'd hoped for, but necessary. The only thing they didn't prepare to move was Marlee's bed, so she could sleep in it one more time.

Theo slept on the couch downstairs, surrounded by full boxes and other furniture. Although exhausted, he didn't rest well, anxious about meeting Marlee's brother and eager to begin a new chapter of life, one with Marlee center stage.

Chapter Twelve

Morning came too soon. After a restless night, Theo had gone to sleep around three and woke at six, body stiff from the uncomfortable couch. With everything from the kitchen packed, there wasn't any coffee, so he used Marlee's directions to travel to a busy avenue. Theo brought back a pair of large coffees and some breakfast sandwiches. The coffee was tolerable, the sandwiches edible, but he savored her companionship.

They ate on an old glider on the front porch, behind a trellis where a clematis vine climbed, already beginning to bloom.

"I'll miss the glider," Marlee said. "But it didn't look like there's a porch to put it on at the new apartment."

There wasn't, but Theo had a suggestion.

"Take it. Who knows, maybe eventually you'll find a place for it. You probably won't live there forever."

In his mind, he thought they'd be married at some point down the road and buy a house, perhaps one of the older brick beauties found around town. Another daydream he'd had was to build a house at the vineyard. If possible, he'd love to live in that quiet, fertile place.

"True," she said. She leaned over and kissed him. "You think of things I don't."

Theo finished the lukewarm coffee and planted a much longer kiss on her lips. "I try."

"Will you help me get settled, once we're there?"

"Of course. My place is closed today because of all the issues yesterday, and we're never open on Sunday, so I'll have plenty of time. I thought if you want, after we get there and unload, I could make something to eat for all of us, your brother too, at the restaurant."

Marlee's expression brightened. "That would be wonderful, if you're not too tired."

"I'm never too tired to cook," he said. "Is that your brother now?"

A moving truck pulled to the curb, almost too close to Theo's truck, and a tall man with short-cropped hair stepped out. Marlee jumped out of the glider and rushed to meet him. He grabbed her in a bear hug.

"Hey, Sis," he said. "I'm here. You ready to load?"

"Yes," she said.

Theo had come to the edge of the porch, and she turned toward him. "Louis, this is Theo. Theo, this is my oldest brother."

The man who offered a hand to shake didn't resemble Marlee at all. His grip was strong and powerful. Unlike Theo, who was both tall and lean, Louis had a stocky frame, solid with muscles. Theo wondered what he did for a living to keep so buff. Judging from appearances, he had to be at least a decade older than Theo.

"It's good to meet you. You're the one who saved her from the river, aren't you?" Louis said.

"I am," Theo replied. "I'm pleased to meet you."

"Come in," Marlee said. She went into the house, and they followed.

"What goes?" her brother asked.

"Everything. We have to take down my bed, but the rest is ready to go," Marlee said.

"Okay, but let's make a plan, and decide what to load first. Oh, and Pete's coming too."

"That's awesome," Marlee said. "The more hands, the faster we'll get loaded and go."

By the time Louis knocked down the bed frame and dragged it downstairs, Pete arrived. Although fit, he resembled a college professor more than Louis, who Theo guessed had to be the older of the two. Theo shoved the mattress and foundation down the stairs, relieved he hadn't been the one to take apart the bed frame. Although capable in the kitchen, an accomplished swimmer, able to handle a boat, a decent fisherman, and possessing a good eye for shooting, tools were his downfall. He could make simple repairs, if he took his time and allowed for errors he could correct, but Theo was no Mister Fix-it. If he picked up a hammer or screwdriver or wrench, it seemed as if he had ten thumbs and no fingers.

He could carry and tote with the best, though, and so the three men, with Marlee's help, loaded both the rented box truck and the bed of Theo's truck by nine. No one spent much time in conversation as they worked, other than necessary directions or questions. When the trucks were loaded, Marlee asked Theo to do a walk through with her to check for anything they might have missed. When they didn't find anything, she did a quick cleaning, sweeping the kitchen and bathroom and running the vac over the rest of the house.

"I want my deposit back," she said when Pete questioned her.

"We need to get on the road," he replied. "Louis and I have to come back home this evening. And give me your keys— I'll drive your car."

Thank God, Theo thought.

"I need to drop off the keys to the landlord, and then we can go."

Louis cleared his throat. "We can get started, and you can catch up. If we get to Hermann first, we'll wait at hotshot's restaurant."

"It's not open," Theo said. Being called hotshot rankled him because he thought it was meant as an insult, not a description. "But that's fine. We won't be far behind you. We can find you there."

The Dupree brothers departed, Louis behind the wheel of the rented vehicle. Once they were out of sight distance, Theo pulled Marlee close and kissed her, long and sweet. "I've wanted to do that all morning, *liebling.*"

"I needed that. Theo, now that it's time to go, I'm getting nervous."

"Why?"

"I'm excited but anxious. It's going to be different, moving to a new town, a different job. I don't really know anyone but you. And your mom and Jonas and the Becker boys."

"You'll get to know more people," Theo said. "You don't know them yet, but you've met people at the inns where you've stayed and at Maybelle's, and you'll get to know people at church, too."

"And school, I know. It's just a big step, maybe bigger than I thought now that I'm committed."

Theo understood all too well. "Except for going to MU, then living in Jeff City for a while, I've always lived there, so if I moved, it would be a huge deal. But you wanted to move, didn't you?"

"I did, and I do," Marlee said. "I love the idea of a smaller town, and there's so much more crime here than there used to be. Let's go, Theo."

"If you're sure you have everything, sure."

After he made sure the load was stable, Theo climbed behind the wheel of the truck with Marlee beside him, and they headed out. As far as he could see, despite her last-minute jitters, she didn't look back.

"How long does it take to get there?" she asked as they headed south on I-29 toward Kansas City. "I only went on the train before."

"Four and a half hours, probably," he said. "There'll be more traffic now than when I drove up yesterday. It's almost ten now, so we should be there, unless we make many stops by three this afternoon."

Theo wanted to travel through KC between morning drive time and the noon hour rush. They made it—barely—but he breathed easier once they were on I-70 heading east. Traffic was still heavier than he liked but manageable. Marlee, who he guessed had slept as poorly as he had, fell asleep. She slept until just before they reached Rocheport and crossed the Missouri River.

"Where are we?" she asked, stretching.

"Almost to Rocheport and Columbia," he told her. "Still an hour and a half or two hours away from home. Are you up for a pit stop?"

"I'm hungry. What time is it?"

"Quarter till one."

He didn't mind making a stop, not at all. But Theo, whose stomach still rumbled from the pickup breakfast, didn't want any fast food. So he reminded her he planned to prepare a meal at Bah Humbug!

"I know," she said. "I just want a little something to eat so I can hold out, maybe a value menu sandwich or something."

"I'd rather not grab any fast food. My guts are still complaining about breakfast."

She snaked one hand over to touch his belly. "You have a stomachache?"

"More like a little indigestion," Theo said. "I don't normally eat fast food, and when I do, it doesn't agree with me. Do you like soup?"

"Yes, most of the time."

"I know a great diner in Columbia. They always have a soup of the day, and it's delicious, no matter what kind it is. Do you want to try it?"

"Sure, that sounds good. Do you serve many soups?"

"Sometimes. A potato soup, once in a great while oxtail soup, occasionally German wedding soup," he replied.

At the diner, the retro look didn't stop with the exterior. Alternating black and white floor tiles set the stage for the red vinyl booths and matching chairs. There was a long counter with stools, also red, and behind it, the order window. Appetizing aromas floated through the air as they followed a hostess to a window booth.

"What's the soup today?" Theo asked.

"Creamy portabella mushroom and our lunch special is lemon garlic tilapia with rice pilaf or a baked potato and salad. Today's pies are—"

"Buttermilk, chocolate, or Dutch Apple," Theo said, completing the sentence. Then he grinned. "I used to work here a long time ago. Is Sarge still cooking?"

The server returned the smile. "He's back there now."

"Tell him Theo says hello. I'll have the soup, and can we get a basket of black rolls too, with butter, not margarine, and sweet iced tea?"

"Sure can. And what would you like?"

Marlee ordered the soup with a soft drink. The server brought their drinks within minutes.

"Did you really work here?" she asked, sipping her cola.

Theo smiled. "I did, during college for about three years. I learned a lot from Sarge. It's a cool place. They do serve some quality dishes, along with the expected burgers, fries, and chicken fried steak. The soup will be excellent, and it won't be enough to ruin your appetite for whatever I make later."

As they waited for their order, the double doors to the kitchen burst open and a tall man wearing cook's whites came through. He rushed toward their table, and Theo stood in anticipation.

"Theo Scrooge, it's good to see you, kid," the man said, hugging Theo and pounding him on the back with his fists.

"Sarge, it's my pleasure. I couldn't come through Columbia without stopping."

"And all you ordered is soup! What's wrong with you, kid?"

"I'm cooking for my lady here tonight," Theo answered. "Sarge, this is Marlee Dupree—Marlee, this is Sarge, chief cook and bottle washer of this fine establishment."

"I'm glad to meet you, young lady. but I'm also the owner, and that one used to work here."

Marlee shook the hand he extended. "That's what he said."

"How's your business going, and why aren't you there on Saturday?" Sarge turned back to Theo.

"I'm on a road trip, but it's going well, thanks."

"Wonderful! Well, your money's no good here. It's on the house."

Although Theo protested, Sarge refused to take payment, so they enjoyed the soup and lingered over it longer than they'd planned. Louis called before they left the diner, already in Hermann, waiting.

"We'll be there in about an hour," Marlee said as Theo listened, shaking his head. "No, we didn't start late. We stopped for a quick bite to eat. Yes, I know you have to get back, but...all right, wait a minute. Theo, I don't suppose my brother could pick up the keys to start unloading?"

He held up his keyring. "No, I have them to give to you."

Marlee sighed. "Okay. Louis is mad. They're there, and he wants to unload, but they can't get in without keys."

"Not a problem," Theo said. "I'll call Henry Muller, the owner, and see if he can let them in."

She relayed that information to her brother. As soon as Theo confirmed Muller was on his way over, she ended the call.

"Thank you," she said. "That should make Louis chill out."

Theo thought it sounded like he had some control and anger issues. "Is he always like that?"

"He is, often. He still treats me like I'm a baby with no sense. Pete's not as intense, but he has his moments."

"Where does Louis work?"

"He's the head football coach at one of the other high schools. Pete teaches math at the college."

That explained a lot, Theo thought. No wonder Louis was in shape and thought he could tell his sister what to do. Pete had that academic look, even in jeans and a T-shirt. Theo could imagine him in a tweed jacket with leather patches on the elbows.

"Your brother needs to keep in mind he's not at a game, and you're not one of his players," Theo said. He'd wanted to like Marlee's brothers, but so far, Louis failed to impress him favorably, and right now, he didn't care for the man. He hadn't decided yet about Peter.

"True enough," Marlee said. "He wasn't happy we stopped to get a bite to eat, but he said they'd eaten at Maybelle's."

Her voice sounded fretful, and he wanted her to be happy, not anxious.

"We'll be there in an hour, give or take," he said. "Let me tell Sarge thanks again, then we'll head out."

In a short time, they left the interstate for the two-lane winding road that would take them to his hometown. Marlee marveled at the hills and the way the road curved with the land.

"It's one of the original state highways, so they built around the hills and curves, not like now when they just blast a straight course," Theo told her. "It's good land and beautiful scenery. The original settlers thought it was a lot like Germany, and that's why they settled here. That and the fact the land was right to grow grapes."

"It's so pretty. I had no idea. We never explored this far out."

Theo reached for her hand and took it. "We will, though."

She had two more calls before they reached town, so Theo knew her brothers were waiting at Marlee's apartment. The two men stood beside the rented truck, and when they pulled up, Louis approached.

"It's almost three-thirty," he announced. "It's all unloaded and inside, but we didn't try to place any of it—just stacked the boxes and made room for the furniture. Pete set up the bed so you'd have a place to sleep tonight. We need to head back. It's a four plus hour trip, Marlee."

"I know, and I'm sorry—" she began, but Louis cut her off.

"You shouldn't have stopped for a leisurely lunch, not when you knew we had to get back."

Theo's anger fired, but he forced his tone to be level. "Then you'd probably better get going," he said. He didn't mention he'd planned to cook for them all. "Since it's Saturday, there's probably heavy traffic."

Peter approached his sister. "I'm sorry to leave in such a rush. This looks like an interesting town, and I was hoping to see more of it."

"You'll have to come down to visit me," Marlee replied. "Then you can eat at Theo's restaurant, and we can show you the sights."

"I'd like that. Give me a hug, and we'll get out of here. I'll call you soon."

Louis drummed his fingers against the truck's door as they hugged, then came to Marlee. "I'd forgotten the wonder boy chef was going to cook for us," he said, in a tone that indicated he hadn't. "Maybe some other time. But I'm not into tofu and fancy cuisine anyway. Call me anytime. Now I know how to get here and where you live. It's easy to come."

"Have a safe trip home." Marlee let him hug her, then added, "Theo's food is amazing, and it's not what you think. You'll have to try it some other time."

Theo, upset at being called a wonder boy chef, stayed silent. He joined Marlee, waving as they pulled away, but that was all he had to give in the moment. He put his arm around her shoulders, wondering if she'd be affected by her brother's rude disdain.

"What now?" She answered with a smile, so he kissed her, sweet and slow. "Welcome home," he whispered. Now, he thought, the good times he'd anticipated would begin.

Chapter Thirteen

Her new place was in shambles, just as her brother had described, but the reality was even worse. They had to walk single file to get through the living room and could only stand at the kitchen door gazing inward. In the bedroom, her bed was set up in the center of the floor, surrounded by boxes and pieces of furniture. Hands on her hips, Marlee surveyed the apartment and groaned.

"It's going to take forever to get this place in shape."

"I'll help you," Theo said. "We'll start tomorrow after church and get it done."

"Why not do it now?"

"I'm tired—you're tired. It's been a long day."

"I won't be able to sleep with all this stuff. It'll drive me crazy."

"Come stay with me for tonight." When Marlee said nothing, Theo added, "You stayed before, and if you want, I'll even sleep on the couch, so there's no temptation."

"I'm tempted," she said with a smile that lit up her face. "But I also don't want to have sex, Theo. It's not the way I am."

"I know that, *liebling,* and I'm glad. I'll make an early dinner, we can relax, get some sleep, go to church tomorrow, and then we'll get this in order. What do you think?"

"I love you, that's what," she said. "Okay. Will you make hamburgers?"

"*Ja,* anything you want. We'll stop at the market on the way."

Marlee gathered up a change of clothing, some personal items, and a few other things before they headed out. Theo didn't waste time at the store but fielded several questions about why Bah Humbug! was closed. At the restaurant, it was too quiet as Theo unlocked the door and headed upstairs. Once there, he paused long enough to let his mom know they were back.

"*Sehr gut,*" Liesel said, then coughed hard.

"*Mutti, bist du krank?*" Theo asked, concerned.

"*Na, ja, vielleicht,*" she said. "I think I have caught the same crud that Liz has. Oma also has it. But we will be fine, I think."

"You don't sound fine," Theo said. "You sound sick."

"We'll stay home from church tomorrow and rest, Theo."

"You need some good, homemade chicken soup."

She hacked again, and he winced at the heavy cough. "I think we have some canned soup. I'm too tired to make any."

"I'll make it," he said. "Will you both eat it if I bring some out to you?"

Liesel protested. "It's too much work. You've had a long day, and I know you are tired, son."

"It's no trouble," Theo said. "I'll make it now and have it out there by six-thirty, *ja?*"

"*Ja, ja,* all right, and thank you."

"Do you need anything else? Tissues, medicine, groceries?"

She listed a few items, and he promised he'd deliver all of it.

Once he ended the call, Theo turned to Marlee. "There's a

slight change of plan. I'm making chicken noodle soup, German style."

"Is your mom sick?"

Theo remembered she'd only heard his end of the conversation. "Apparently, both she and my grandmother have caught the crud from Liz. She's coughing a lot already."

"Then let's make soup," Marlee said. "Do you need to go back to the store?"

"I should have everything I need downstairs except fresh chicken," he said. "I'll hurry over there and be right back."

She shouldered her purse. "I can go, then you can get started with the rest."

He hugged her. "Thank you. That helps a lot."

With Marlee's help after her quick trip to buy a chicken, he soon had the bird stewing in one pot along with carrots, onions, just enough garlic to add some flavor, two bay leaves, celery, and a few simple seasonings—thyme, sage, salt, pepper, and a dash of nutmeg. While that simmered, he made very thin egg noodles and let them dry. Marlee chopped some of the vegetables and did the dishes without complaint. After an hour, he removed the chicken and deboned it with deft fingers, then diced the meat to return to the pot. Once he'd brought it to a boil, Theo added the noodles, a few at a time.

"If you still want burgers, I can do them later or tomorrow," he told Marlee.

"Tomorrow is fine. The soup smells delicious. If there's plenty, I'd love some."

Theo smiled and embraced her. "There will be. You look cute wearing one of my aprons, and you're a huge help. I could use you in the kitchen sometimes."

"I'd like that, maybe this summer. So, what now?"

"Let it simmer and cook down, then we'll take it out to the farmhouse."

He put some mellow music on the stereo, and they relaxed on the couch as the soup simmered. Theo tasted it when he judged it done and let Marlee sample it.

"That's good," she said.

Theo smiled. "It will turn you off canned soup for life."

He divided it, pouring more than half into a slow cooker with a lid that snapped in place for travel, then placed it in an insulated carrier. The remainder he put on low to stay warm.

"We won't be gone long," he told her. "I need to stop at the store to pick up a few things. Would you like to ride with me? You've never been out to the winery."

"I would, thanks. Your cousin runs it, right?"

"Thomas does, yes."

He sketched out a brief family history — that the winery had been in Mom's family for four generations, that his great-great-grandfather had planted the original grapes after arriving from Saxony.

"It's Mom's side of the family," he said. "She and Oma live in the farmhouse, even though it's too big for the two of them."

Marlee held the soup while he dashed into the store.

On the way, she admired the scenery and the acres of vines. When they pulled into the yard, there was the winery building, complete with an on-site shop. The two-story house was tucked back behind most of the grapes, reached by a winding dirt driveway.

To Theo, the graceful stone house was as familiar as childhood. Although his earliest years were spent in town in a house overlooking the city park, his grandparents had lived here. After his dad's death, he and his mother had moved here. More than anywhere else, this house was home. It had such symmetry, with four windows on either side of the wide front door, two up, two down, and one more above the door. Chimneys stood at both ends of the house, like sentinels.

"It's beautiful," Marlee cried when the house came into view. "It's like something in France."

"Or Germany," he said with a laugh. "Definitely has a European look."

Liesel opened the door for them. "Come in, come in. I won't hug you, though. I don't want you to catch this."

"Do you want me to take the soup to the kitchen?" Theo said. "It should be still hot."

She waved a hand toward the back of the house. "You know the way."

Theo tried to envision how his old home would look to Marlee, with the dark woodwork and the wooden stairs that ascended upward. The walls were simple plaster, still white as they had always been.

"Where's Oma?"

"She's waiting in the kitchen. She said she's hungry and it's feed a cold, starve a fever," Liesel said. "It's very good to see you again, Marlee."

"Thank you. I'm sorry you're not feeling well."

"*Ach Gott*, it's nothing," Liesel replied. "And it was good of my son to make this soup. Did he keep some for you?"

"Yes, he did."

Theo unpacked the cooker, plugged it in, and reached for bowls. He filled two deep bowls with the rich soup, dug out spoons, and served the older women.

"Marlee helped make it," he told them. "She's a good helper in the kitchen."

"*Danke Schoen*," Oma said from the table. Theo thought she looked very pale except for two pink spots on her cheeks. "Theo, you are my best grandson."

"Don't let Thomas or any of the others hear you say that, Oma."

After they asked a blessing in German, Liesel spoke to

Marlee. "Soon, when we are not under the weather, I will have you come to dinner, and you can see the rest of the house where I was raised, where Theo and I lived after I was widowed."

"I'll look forward to that, very much."

Theo unpacked the items from the store and refused his mother's offer to reimburse him.

"Go home, eat your soup, get some rest," she told him.

He kissed both his mother and grandmother on the forehead. "Feel better, both of you."

The remainder of the weekend passed in a blur. Afterward, Theo would remember they ate the soup he'd made, that after church on Sunday, he and Marlee worked hard to get her apartment in order, and that once they succeeded, he made the hamburgers she had requested.

There was no place to store her boxes of Christmas items, so Theo ended up putting them in the storeroom at Bah Humbug!, along with some luggage and a few more items. Although he wanted to complain, he kept silent rather than cause another disagreement with Marlee. Somewhere within in a place he'd rather not visit often, Theo knew his views about both Scrooge and Christmas were overblown, but he had yet to come to terms with either.

It was evening by the time they had everything in place at Marlee's, and later still when they ate. By then, both were tired.

"Theo, that was delicious," she told him. "I'm wiped out, though. I think I'll go home after I help you clean up."

"I'll take you if you want, and don't worry, I'll put the kitchen in order."

Marlee shook her head. "I can walk. It's a nice evening and not quite dark. I'll call or come over tomorrow, sometime."

"I'll be here," he said. "I'll fix you breakfast or lunch when you do."

She came over, and they kissed, sweet but short.

"What will you do now?" she asked. "I think I'll go to bed and read."

"I've got to figure out menus for tomorrow and get organized," he said. "Then I'll get some sleep."

Marlee stepped into his arms for a moment, then left.

After spending the better part of three days in her presence, her departure made him lonely. He also couldn't help worrying a little about his mother, and especially his grandmother. Theo forced himself to head downstairs, where he decided he'd make bacon and onion pies. Some recipes had a yeast-based bread like crust, but he would do a pastry crust. Since he'd already be making pie crust, he decided the other special would be a steak and mushroom pie.

As for dessert, he'd figure something out in the morning.

Then he groaned, remembering for the first time it was Memorial Day. It was a day he always was open because the tourist season was now underway. If he'd remembered sooner, though, he might have remained closed one more day.

Theo hit the ground running Monday morning, prepping and then preparing the day's specials. Desserts had never been his forte, but he managed to use up some bread that would soon go stale, bread that went unused during the weekend, to create bread pudding with a vanilla sauce.

Autumn came in, hand wrapped in a gauze bandage with a dressing. Although he was short on servers, he shook his head. "Go home, take care of your hand."

"Theo, you don't have enough staff," she said. "I can do something. Maybe not wait tables, but let me help."

He hesitated, tempted, but still refused. "I don't want that burn getting infected. I'll manage."

"But I heard your mom and grandma are sick."

"They are," he said. "But I made bread pudding for the dessert. Constance and Eva will be here," he said. "And after school, the Becker kids. In two more days, school's out, and they can do more."

Autumn raised one eyebrow. "Not today—it's Memorial Day. And anyway, they're kids. They can't wait tables."

Theo had forgotten the holiday. "They can do dishes or wrap silverware or take out the trash when they do come. Kid, go home—I'll manage."

She hugged him. "I will, but call me if you need me, Theo, okay?"

He promised but knew he wouldn't. Autumn was too close to being family, his unofficial kid sister, that he would rather she heal than take a chance.

Thirty minutes before opening time, Marlee came through the unlocked back door. She paused in the kitchen entrance, then put her hands on her hips. "You look frazzled," she said.

Theo glanced down. Stains from a variety of mishaps covered his clothing. He'd burned three fingers on his right hand and had cut his thumb. A slow grin spread across his lips. "I'd say so," he said. "If my hair wasn't short, it would probably be standing on end."

Marlee approached, took his right hand, and kissed the blisters where he'd burned it, taking pies from the oven. "That looks like it hurt."

"It did." He wiped his hands on a clean towel and leaned forward to kiss her. He wanted to take her into his hands, but if he did, he'd dirty her blouse. To gain more sympathy, he held out his thumb. "This did too."

She gave him back the kiss, then said, "Where are the aprons?"

"Marlee—"

"You said sometimes you could use my help in the kitchen. Looks like you need me now."

Theo glanced around. His kitchen was a mess. Dirty

utensils, dishes, and pans littered half the space, and too soon, the noon customers would arrive. He pointed at a series of drawers. "Third drawer on the left."

Once she'd donned the apron, she began gathering up all the used items and piled them near the triple sinks. Theo had an industrial dishwasher, but normally he used it for the silverware, glasses, bowls, and plates.

Constance, one of the evening servers, arrived to work both shifts. At his direction, she unlocked the doors and made sure the front end was ready.

Theo drew a deep breath and exhaled. "Marlee, I love you. Thank you."

"*Bitte,*" she said. "I'm picking up some German as I go. You helped me yesterday. Now it's my turn. We're a team, right?"

"*Jawohl,*" he replied. "We are."

From her sweet lips to God's ear, he thought. They had worked as a team, and someday he planned, they would be more.

Chapter Fourteen

Neither Theo nor Marlee stopped to breathe until after three. Customers came in large numbers and devoured the day's specials as if they hadn't eaten in days. Once they closed, Theo locked the door and sat down for the first time since early that morning.

"I'm starving. Can we eat now?" Marlee asked.

"If there's anything left, yes," he said. "I think I need to do something else for the dinner crowd. It is a holiday, right? Maybe some of these people have to head for home."

"There's a few pieces of both the ham and steak pies left, enough for three."

Constance shed her apron. "For two. I'm going to check on my kids, but I'll be back in time for dinner, Theo."

"Thanks. I appreciate the extra hours."

Marlee and Theo ate some pie, splitting up what remained, so each had a bit of both. In the lull, Theo wished he could unwind enough to take a power nap, but instead, he dug some wurst out of the freezer for an evening special—brats on a bun with a side order of *speckbohnen*, German style green beans cooked with ham.

While he began prep and cooking for the dinner menu, Theo also put together menus for the rest of the week with Marlee's input. Constance and Eva arrived ten minutes before time to unlock the doors, and once Theo opened, it was hectic until closing.

The Beckers didn't show up, but it was a holiday, so Theo figured they would tomorrow. Once he and Marlee were alone, he poured them each a glass of a sweet Vignoles from the family winery.

"*Zum wohl!*" he said, tapping his glass against hers.

"What are we celebrating?"

He grinned. "Making it through the day, although we're not finished yet."

Marlee groaned. "What's left to do?"

"Put the kitchen to rights, for one, and I'd better make a dessert now to make tomorrow less crazy," he said. "I doubt Mutti is up to baking yet."

She sighed with pleasure after taking a sip of wine. "How are they feeling?" she asked, "Any better?"

Theo shrugged. "I thought of them all day, but I never had time to call. I'm glad you were here, but it was strange without them here this morning. I should call, but they may have gone to bed."

"It's only a little after eight!"

"They go to bed early, especially Oma."

"I could make a dessert if you have the ingredients I need, but it's probably not German."

At this point, he'd settle for a tray of bakery cookies if necessary. "What is it?"

"An oatmeal cake with broiled coconut frosting. I'm sure you have the basics, but do you have shredded coconut and pecans?"

"If not, I can go get some. Do you want to bake tonight? I

probably will need at least four cakes, and six would be better."

"If you have enough pans, I can. I can have them baked and topped by ten, probably."

"You're wonderful," he said. "That will go well with *Maultaschen,* and shepherd's pie, the two specials for tomorrow."

"I know what shepherd's pie is, but what's the other?"

"Big dumplings stuffed with minced beef and seasonings," he said. "Since we're shorthanded and it's tourist season, I'm going back to the same two specials for both meals each day. It's easier for me that way. Let me run down to the market before they close."

Theo finished his glass of wine and removed his apron, then retrieved his billfold from the office.

"Theo, Jonas is here."

"Let him in," he called. "He probably wants to eat."

But when Theo emerged and saw the sober expression on his friend's face, he knew the sheriff hadn't stopped by for a meal. "What is it?" he said, coming to a halt.

"Theo, your mom called me and asked me to come by to tell you this," Jonas said. "Your grandmother, she took a turn for the worse, so she's at the hospital."

"*Ach Gott!* I need to go and see what's going on," Theo said.

"I can take you," Jonas said. "Do you need to lock up first?"

Marlee came forward and took Theo's hand. "I can do that if you leave the keys," she said. "I can go with you, if you want, or stay and bake the cakes. You'll need them tomorrow."

He nodded. "You're right. I'll be back, or I'll call you to let you know what's what. Thank you, Marlee. I love you."

She hugged him. "I love you too. Don't worry about any of this — I've got it."

Jonas opened the door. "C'mon, Theo, let's go."

In the sheriff's department cruiser, Theo turned to his

friend. "What happened, exactly?"

"All I know is Liesel called me and said she'd called an ambulance for your grandmother because she'd gotten worse and maybe had pneumonia. I had a deputy go pick up your mom so she wouldn't be driving—she sounded frantic. That was around six, six-thirty. I would have told you sooner, but your mom insisted that I wait."

"I'm sure she did," Theo replied, and began praying the Our Father in German, the way he'd learned it at his mother's knee.

At the small community hospital, the same one that treated Theo and Marlee after their dip in the river, Theo rushed to the desk, gazing around for his mother.

"Theo, your grandmother is in room seventeen," Trudi Braun told him. "Your mom's with her—you can go on back. Good evening, Sheriff Kaiser."

"Theo, I'll go. Keep me updated, and if you need a ride or anything, call me."

"Will do," Theo said. They shook hands, and then Theo hugged Jonas. "*Danke.*"

Still wearing his chef's coat and the rubber soled shoes he used in the kitchen, Theo made his way down the hall. The room door was closed, so he tapped it with his knuckles. "Mutti?"

"Come in, Theo. You're here, thank God," Liesel said. She rushed across the room to hug him tight. "Oma's very sick with pneumonia."

"That's what Jonas said." Theo approached the bed where his grandmother, looking both ancient and frail, lay. She wore an oxygen mask and had two IVs. A monitor to the left registered her pulse, oxygen levels, heart rate, blood pressure, and respiration. Although far from medically knowledgeable, Theo scanned them. She had a fever, both oxygen and respiration were low, and her heart rate and respiration were faster than he thought was normal.

"What happened, and why didn't you call me?"

"She's been weak all day, not well at all," Liesel said, and paused to cough. "She wouldn't eat much, and at supper, nothing. I noticed she was breathing hard and that her lips were bluish, so I called an ambulance. I knew you were busy at the restaurant, son."

Liesel sank down into a battered recliner on one side of the bed, and Theo, certain his knees might fold if he didn't, sat on a straight chair. "What did the doctor say?"

His mother shrugged. "He diagnosed pneumonia and said it can be very dangerous for elderly people. He admitted her, put her on oxygen, and she's getting antibiotics. If she responds to treatment, then she'll be fine. But if she doesn't…."

Her voice cracked, and she didn't finish the sentence. It wasn't necessary. Theo knew.

"Is she awake?"

"Sometimes."

Theo glanced down into his grandmother's open eyes. He leaned down to kiss her forehead, very gently, and said, "I love you, Grandmother."

The faintest flicker of a smile touched her lips and vanished. He thought she nodded before she shut her eyes.

"Where's Marlee?" Liesel asked in English, and Theo realized they'd been speaking German since he arrived, the local dialect that wasn't quite pure German after a hundred and fifty years.

"She's baking cakes for tomorrow, then she'll lock up for me," Theo said. "She's worked with me all day."

Liesel nodded. "You should go back to her, Theo. I will stay here with my mother."

He studied her face. She was almost as pale as Oma, and fatigue made the age lines on her face appear deeper. She smothered another cough, and he shook his head.

"I'll stay here—you need to go home. I'll see if Jonas can take you. You're still sick."

"I'm fine."

Theo shook his head. "No, you're not, and if you don't get some rest, you'll be in a room down the hallway."

"*Nein*, no. You have your restaurant to run, Theo."

"Family is more important. Besides, I'll be there working as usual tomorrow."

"Theo, go home and get some sleep."

He refused to yield and called Jonas to drive his mother back to the farmhouse.

Once alone, Theo slumped into the recliner and sighed. He hated to look at Oma, and worry gnawed at his heart. He prayed for a few minutes, then stepped out into the dim hallway to find a waiting room so he could call Marlee on his cell without disturbing his grandmother.

She answered almost before the phone rang. "Theo, how is she?"

To Marlee, he could be honest. "I don't know—she's not doing very well. She has pneumonia, and they have her on oxygen and antibiotics. I convinced my mom to go home and told her I'd stay."

"You're tired already," Marlee said. "Maybe you should close Bah Humbug! for the rest of the week."

Theo groaned. "I can't. I've already lost money with closing early on Friday and not opening on Saturday."

"Then let someone else stay with your grandma so you can get some sleep."

He scrubbed one hand over his face, thick-headed with fatigue already. "Maybe tomorrow or down the road that can be an option. There are other family members around, but not tonight."

"I could come, at least for a little bit."

Her concern and desire to help touched Theo. "Marlee, *liebling,* I appreciate you, but you've already worked your tail off for me today. You're the one who needs to go home and go to bed. I need to head back down to Oma's room. I'll see you in the morning. I'll try to be there by eight, so I can get started cooking. I love you, Marlee."

"I love you, too."

The atmosphere in the hospital room stifled Theo, and he wished he dared crack open the window for some fresh air. He couldn't get comfortable in the rump sprung recliner no matter what position he took, and he certainly couldn't sleep. His nerves were jangled, and every time he glanced at Oma, his stomach knotted. Theo hoped for the best and feared the worst as his mind raced. He had trouble focusing long enough to pray.

One minute he roasted, the next, he felt a chill. His chest tightened with anxiety until he wondered crazily if a little oxygen might help. Already tired when Jonas brought word, Theo's head ached with fatigue and his eyes burned. He tried to think about menus to shift his thoughts to something calming, but balked. Concentrating was hard. Thirsty, he wished for a cold bottle of iced tea, but he didn't want to leave the room in case Oma woke. He wanted her to know she wasn't alone, and he'd promised his mother he'd stay.

The soft hiss of the oxygen and the steady beep of the monitor seemed to grow louder, one more barrier that kept Theo from calm. Staff came and went, checking his grandmother's vitals. He was offered a blanket or a sandwich or coffee, all of which he refused with thanks.

A little past midnight, someone knocked lightly on the door, and he sat upright. "Come in."

He expected a nurse or tech, but instead, Marlee entered the room.

"I couldn't sleep," she said. "I hope you don't mind, but I brought you a few things I thought you might need."

Theo smiled for the first time since Jonas arrived at Bah Humbug! "I'm glad you're here," he said, voice low. He came to his feet and came to her in the dim room, then pulled her into his arms and held her tight. Her familiar scent, a light lavender, reached him, and he sighed. "How did you get in?"

"I asked at the desk, and they said, 'Oh, you're Theo's lady, go on back,'" Marlee said, snuggled against him. "I liked the sound of that."

"So do I," he replied, releasing her.

"You look so tired," she said. "I brought some pillows, a throw to use as a blanket if you need it, some cold tea, some ibuprofen, some snacks, and my Kindle."

"Thank you," he said. "I haven't slept at all. Maybe with the pillows and throw, I can. I'm so thirsty, but I didn't want to leave her long enough to get a cold drink. Plus, my head is splitting."

Marlee reached into the bags she carried. Then she placed pillows in the recliner, handed him a contoured neck pillow, and draped the throw over the back of the chair. She shook out several ibuprofen tablets and handed them to him, followed with a bottle of tea.

He downed the pills and took a long drink.

"Sit down," Marlee said, and all but pushed him into the chair. She placed the contour pillow behind his head and covered him with the soft throw. "Put your feet up, Theo, and try to sleep. I'll stay until you do."

"You don't have to."

Even in the dimness, he saw her lips shape a smile.

"No, but I am. And you don't need to come early. Liz is coming in to cook, and I'll be there to help her as much as I can."

"I thought she was sick."

"She was, but she's better now, and she promised to wear a mask, so she doesn't infect any customers. Autumn said she will be there, too. Even if she can't wait tables, she'll find things to do. Don't worry about the place."

Hard not to do when it was his livelihood, he thought.

"How did Liz know I needed her?"

"Jonas," Marlee said. "He called her and Autumn. Hush and get some rest, Theo."

"*Ja, ja, ja,*" he muttered under his breath, but he smiled and shut his eyes.

Sleep didn't come easy, but his headache eventually receded, and his taut limbs began to relax. Theo watched Marlee through half-lidded eyes. She perched on the edge of the straight-backed chair, reading and yawning. He pretended to sleep so she'd go home and get the rest she needed as much as he did.

When Oma stirred, he opened his eyes, but before he could rise, Marlee was at his grandmother's side. Although Oma couldn't really speak from behind the oxygen mask, Marlee seemed to understand.

"Theo's here, but he's asleep," she told his grandmother, reaching down to hold the old woman's hand. "Your daughter went home, but she'll be back in the morning. You need to rest, even more than Theo. If you'd like, I can hold your hand until you go back to sleep."

He watched, and a few silent tears slid down his cheeks as the woman he loved comforted his grandmother. After Marlee left, he finally slept for a few hours.

When Theo woke, momentarily disoriented, the headache had returned, and his stomach was uneasy. Someone had opened the drapes, and he could see it was not quite full daylight. He lowered the recliner's footrest and groaned.

"Ach, so you're awake," Liesel said.

With both hands, he scrubbed his face. "What time is it?"

"Around five."

"You're earlier than I thought," he said. "How do you feel?"

Liesel gestured toward the corner. "Thomas brought me so I wouldn't have to drive, and I'm good."

His cousin, Thomas Schubert, keeper of the family vineyards and winery, wore the faded overalls of a farmer. As fair as his sister Hanna, his face already had begun to tan from the sun.

"Thank you," Theo said.

"Don't mention it. I wanted to see how Oma is this morning anyway, but Tante Liesel says she seems the same," Thomas said. "I can't stay, though. It's a busy season with the grapes. I'm still tying new shoots to the trellises. I'm adding nitrogen and applying herbicide even though the blooms have started."

Theo nodded. There had long been an unspoken competition between them. Thomas appeared to think his grapes and wine making required more labor than Theo's chef skills and restaurant. Theo, who disagreed, had learned not to debate the issue.

"I can come back this evening and pick her up, if you want."

"That would be helpful," Theo replied. "Thanks."

Liesel sat down in the chair Theo had vacated. She fingered the soft throw with a tiny smile. "Did you go home for this and the pillows?" she asked.

"*Nein*," Theo replied. "Marlee brought them late last night."

"Marlee?"

Liesel replied to her nephew. "She is his *Schatzi*—you know, his girlfriend."

Thomas grinned. "Oh, now that explains a lot. I heard some talk, you know, about Scrooge and Marlee, but it didn't make sense until now."

Theo cringed as his mom shot him a stern look. He said nothing, but the reference made his blood boil, as always.

"She has such a good heart," Liesel said, defusing the moment.

"Yes. She did the baking for today for me and worked all day yesterday," Theo told her. "She'll be there today too."

"Are you opening?" Surprise made her tone rise.

"I must," Theo said. "But I will be here between lunch and dinner, and I'll stay tonight again too."

Liesel nodded and smothered a cough, which made Theo frown. "You may not have to, Theo. Hanna is coming, and some of the others said they will be here with Oma if needed."

The others meant more family. Besides Thomas, there were other Schuberts, a few still in the immediate area, others spread to St. Louis and beyond. Although Thomas and Hanna's parents had moved to southern Missouri, Theo had another aunt and two uncles, as well as several more cousins within a thirty-mile radius.

"Let me know. I'm willing, *Mutti*," he said. "Do you need anything? Coffee? Breakfast? I can go get whatever you want."

"I had coffee at home," she said. "I'm good for now."

"I'll bring you lunch when I come back."

"That would be very nice, my son. Are you leaving?"

Theo looked down at his wrinkled garments and nodded. "I am, so I can take a shower and get ready for the day. Thomas, thank you. Call me, either one of you, if you need anything or you have any news about Oma."

"We will," Liesel said as Theo leaned down to kiss her forehead.

Walking outside, he inhaled the fresh air, aromatic with the scent of soon to be summer. After the close environment of the hospital, it smelled like salvation.

At his apartment, he showered, drank coffee that was both strong and black, then sat down for just a moment to rest before he headed downstairs. Instead, he fell asleep, and when he woke, it was past ten and sunshine streamed through the windows.

With an hour until opening, Theo hurried downstairs and walked into chaos.

Chapter Fifteen

His kitchen was in disarray, with dirty utensils and pans covering most of the workspaces. Liz Vogel moved with frantic speed as she spread mashed potatoes over several pans of shepherd's pie. The normally pristine workspace had splatters and stains in multiple places. Liz wore neither hairnet nor chef's hat, enough to make Theo cringe. Nor was she wearing a mask. One stray hair in any dish served could be enough to damage his reputation. Her garments were as splotched as the floor, and on the stove, a pot bubbled dangerously close to the top. As Theo watched, the contents begin to spill over the top, and he dashed across the floor to jerk it from the heat before it spewed.

His quick action startled Liz, who screamed and dropped a spoon onto the floor. She clutched her chest. "You just took ten years off my life, Theo!"

He put the pot on top of a stack in one of the sinks. "*Gott in Himmel,*" he said. "We open in less than an hour, and the place is a wreck. Those shepherd's pies should have been in the oven long ago. Where's the *Maultaschen?*"

Liz looked blank. "The what?"

Theo balled both fists and held them at his sides with frustration. "The big dumpling things, the German special of the day."

She wiped her hands on her apron. "Oh, those. I don't know how to make those, Theo, so it's mustard braised pork chops."

He drew a deep breath. "Where did you get pork chops? I don't remember having enough on hand."

Her cheeks flushed. "Uh, I went down to the store and bought up all their family pack pork chops, Theo. I didn't know what else to do. You know I'm not a chef, just a cook. I am good at helping you when you explain what to do, but I can't make these dishes, not in huge quantities."

Retail, he thought, *she bought retail.* He would have to absorb the loss when he sold at his usual prices. And his customers who came to dine on German specialties would be underwhelmed by pork chops. A fiery rage threatened to erupt, but before he had a meltdown, Theo centered his thoughts.

"You're right, and I know that," he said. "And I appreciate you coming in for the day shift and doing what you could. Where's Marlee?"

"She left a few minutes ago to take some oatmeal cake and coffee to your mom at the hospital," Liz said.

"Okay. Let's get the shepherd's pies into the oven now, then let's get this mess cleaned up," Theo said. "Who's serving, Autumn and Constance?"

Liz stared at him with huge eyes. "That's all you have except you, me, and Marlee. Eva won't do days."

He sighed and made a mental note to hire more help, despite the additional cost.

Marlee returned at ten till eleven and greeted him with a smile. By then, he'd scrubbed countertops, prepared some side dishes, and mopped the floor.

"Hi, Theo." She crossed to where he stood and offered a kiss.

"Why didn't you wake me?" he asked without preamble. "I planned to be in the kitchen early."

His tone sounded harsher than he had intended, and he watched her smile dim.

"I thought you needed the rest," she said after an awkward pause. "I just left the hospital. Your mom loved the cake."

"That's good. How's Oma?"

"She seemed about the same. What can I do to help?"

"Wash pots and pans or wait tables," he said.

"I'll wash," Marlee said quickly. "I wouldn't want to dump someone's lunch in their lap."

Theo unlocked the door five minutes late, but except for the mountain of dirty pans, the kitchen had been restored, food was ready to plate, and the dining area passed his muster. A few customers were waiting, among them Todd Blevins.

"I was beginning to think you were closed again, Scrooge," he said as he walked past Theo. "Good thing you're not—there's a lot of tourists in town already."

Theo seated Blevins and his two companions at a table near the rear and listed the day's specials.

Blevins frowned. "Pork chops? I can get those anywhere, and they're probably better at Maybelle's."

Resisting an urge to tell him to have his lunch there, Theo forced a faux smile and headed for the kitchen. Autumn wore a special glove to protect her burn, and bustled through the noon rush. Constance seemed to drag a little, but Theo figured she was weary from working two shifts the previous day.

At three, Theo, who hadn't eaten since the previous evening, sat down with a piece of shepherd's pie, which he forced down without any appetite. Marlee joined him at the table.

"You look terrible," she said. "Are you okay?"

He forced a dry laugh. "No, I don't feel well."

Theo didn't, not at all.

"It's no wonder. You didn't have much sleep, and I know you're worried about Oma."

Theo marked that she used the family name for his grandmother, and liked it.

"True, but I'm also worried about this place."

"Why?"

"Everything is falling apart." He sketched for her the condition of the kitchen when he came downstairs. "I can't blame Liz—she tried—but pork chops? For once, Blevins was right about something—people can eat them anywhere. Plus, she paid retail. That eats into any profit, and after we were closed over the weekend, I'm concerned. I need more staff than I have. If you hadn't baked the cake, we wouldn't have had dessert. Thank you again."

Marlee grinned. "You're welcome. I brought you the last piece."

"We sold out?"

"Just about."

"That's wonderful," he said. He took a bite and sighed with pleasure. "That's delicious, Marlee."

"I'll bake something else for tomorrow. Your mom gave me a few recipes earlier. What's the specials tomorrow?"

Theo spread his hands wide and shrugged. "No idea yet. As soon as I finish, I'm going over to the hospital for a little bit. I'll figure it out later, I guess."

"Your mom said she wishes you'd close for a few days."

"I can't and told her so," he responded. "If I did, it would cost me in the long term. Even when I was so sick after jumping in the river, we stayed open. But then my mom and Oma were here, and I had a full staff. Mutti can cook—she ran the place for me—and now she can't, so we have to stay open. Bah Humbug!

has been open ten years this October. I'm tentatively planning a big celebration, but I have to stay in the black to do it."

"You've had this place ten years?" she said. "I didn't realize."

"And I hope to have it for many more. I need to go. I'll be back by four, so I can maybe add something else for dinner. I think there's plenty of shepherd's pie, but I may come up with a different special instead of mustard pork chops. Will you come with me to the hospital?"

Marlee shook her head. "I was there earlier, and I thought I'd start baking if I won't be in your way. If I do the desserts now, I can help you later with tomorrow's food."

It made sense, but he'd wanted her with him, even for the short time he would be gone and at the hospital — the last place he wanted to be, today or any day.

"All right. What are you making? I can tell you if I have the ingredients or not."

"Your mom suggested either an apple strudel or *pfeffernusse*, some kind of spice cookies."

"I don't have all the spices for the cookies, but I do for strudel," he told her. "Make a list, though, and when I order supplies or go to Jeff, I'll get anything else you'll need for desserts."

"Who's Jeff?"

Theo laughed. Even with everything happening in his life, Marlee made him happy. "Jefferson City," he explained. "There's a Sam's Club there. I'm heading to the hospital now."

She rose when he did. "See you when you get back," she said. "Kiss?"

"Any time."

Nothing much had changed at the hospital except Thomas was long gone, and one of his other cousins, his Aunt Trudi's daughter, had arrived. Liesel sat in the recliner with the throw wrapped around her shoulders.

"Are you cold, Mom?" he said.

She shrugged and coughed. "A little."

"You should go home early, get some extra rest."

"Theo, that's what I keep telling her," Clarissa said. "But she says no."

"It's good to see you," he told his cousin. "It's been too long. How's Oma?"

His mother fielded the question. "She's holding her own, but they have her sedated."

Theo frowned. "Why?"

"She gets agitated when she wakes up, doesn't want to be in the *Krankenhaus*," Liesel replied. "They want her to rest. The doctor said she's not worse, but she's not better, either." She coughed again, a hard barking cough.

"Have you eaten today? Besides the cake Marlee brought?"

"*Nein, mein sohn.*"

He shook his head. "You need to eat. I should have brought something from my place. Is someone staying with Oma tonight?"

"I am," his mother said. "Tomorrow, Hanna will be here, and she will."

"No," Theo said. "You're not. I will. I can do one more night."

Liesel touched his arm. "I will. I don't want to go back to the farmhouse—it's too far, and it's very lonely there. Thomas and his family are on the other side of the property. If Oma needs me, it's too far."

"Mama, you can stay at my place. You need to get some rest and take care of yourself, and it's closer. And you can get some good food."

She still refused, so Theo pushed. Just before he left to go back for the dinner shift, she agreed. "I will have Thomas bring me over there instead of home," she said. "But later, after supper."

Relief brought a small smile to Theo's lips. *"Sehr gut."*

At Bah Humbug! Marlee suggested bratwurst and red cabbage for the dinner menu, and he agreed. She had already taken enough bratwurst from the walk-in cooler, so he chopped cabbage and began frying it in a large skillet. As he worked, they talked.

"I could go pick up your mom," she said. "If she wanted. That way, your cousin wouldn't have to come back into town."

"Good idea. I'll call and tell him then," Theo said.

Logan and Lucas arrived at four-thirty, excited with only one more day of school left for the year. After careful instruction, he asked them to seat people, to hand them menus, and to take their drink orders. Although the boys couldn't serve if a customer ordered beer or wine, they could deliver soft drinks. When they proved capable, Theo let them help take full orders, although he or Constance delivered the plates to the tables. Autumn arrived and did some of the serving and some of the kitchen tasks, but Theo refused to let her do anything that might cause pain or infect her burned hand.

They had a full house and walking through the dining area, Theo heard more compliments than complaints. Grilled brats with a side of cabbage proved to be popular. More customers ordered some of his imported beers or local wines as well. With the sun shining and temps in the low eighties, some diners opted to eat outdoors, and the hours passed with less stress than earlier in the day.

In a lull, he phoned Thomas, who thanked him.

"It's been a long day," his cousin told him. "Are you staying with Oma tonight, then?"

"I am."

"You know, she really doesn't have to have someone there. She's sedated, and I know she's getting good care."

Theo sighed. "It's more for my mother. She'll insist on staying if someone else doesn't."

"True, true. Aunt Liesel needs a break. She's so tired, but every time she almost dozed off, she forced herself to wake up. I don't like that cough she has, either."

"Neither do I. If it's not better, I'll take her to the doctor."

Marlee departed to pick Liesel up just after six. When she hadn't returned by seven, Theo worried and phoned her. "Hey, it's me. Is everything all right?"

"It's all good," Marlee said. "We'll be there in five minutes or less. Your mom wanted to run out to the farm to pack a suitcase, and it took longer than I thought."

When Liesel arrived, Theo dished her up a hearty portion of bratwurst and cabbage. While she ate in his office, he carried her oversized suitcase upstairs, then stripped the bed and made it up with fresh sheets. He dashed back downstairs, plated more orders, and served them. As the number of customers eased downward, Theo had the Becker boys wrap silverware for tomorrow, then help with running the dish machine.

Somehow, in between everything else, Marlee had managed to bake multiple apple strudels. Once they were closed, Theo took time to eat some bratwurst and try the dessert. It was flaky, sweet, and delicious—almost as good as his mom's. He brought her a piece, and she nodded with approval.

"When are you going over to the hospital?" she asked.

"Soon," Theo said. "I have to prep for tomorrow."

Marlee popped into his small office. "What's the menu?"

"*Falscher Hase*," Theo replied. "But it's not rabbit, false or otherwise—"

"It's meatloaf," Marlee interrupted. "Isn't it?"

"Well, *ja*."

"I can make it. You know I make good meatloaf. What's on the English pub menu?"

"Pot roast," he said. "Braised in a little beer with potatoes and carrots and gravy. I'll start it here soon and let it cook low and slow all night. I'm going to serve potato pancakes, made with grated potatoes, with the meatloaf."

She nodded. "So, I'm making the meatloaf?"

"All right, you do the meatloaf, I'll do the pot roast, and you have the dessert made. Tomorrow, I will do the side vegetables and some gravy for both."

Liesel hacked, and Theo cringed. "I thought you would be going to sit with Oma sooner," she said, her voice a little hoarse.

"I'll be there in probably two hours," Theo said. "Mama, you should relax and get some rest. Do you have some cold medicine?"

"I have cough syrup," she said. "*Das geht dich nichts an!*"

"It does concern me," Theo replied. "I don't want you to get any sicker."

She glared at him and shook her head, but after a few more minutes, she told them both good night and headed upstairs.

Theo and Marlee worked in tandem. Sometimes they talked, sometimes they didn't, but they were in harmony, he thought. Cooking and spending time with her were balm to his anxious mind. Although still weary and fighting a headache, he unwound as much as possible.

When the pot roast was in the oven to cook overnight, and Marlee had the meatloaves ready for tomorrow's oven, Theo sighed. He scrubbed his hands, then changed into the casual clothes he'd brought down earlier—a pair of wash worn gray sweatpants and a favorite Kansas City Chiefs T-shirt.

Marlee held open her arms, and he walked into them for a much-needed hug. He held her close and then kissed her. When he pulled his mouth back, she cupped his cheek.

"Do you feel better? I know you said earlier you didn't feel very well," she said. "You look so tired."

He waggled his hand back and forth. "A little. I took some ibuprofen, so the headache's almost gone. I just hope I get some sleep."

"I hope so, too. I'll be here for a little while longer, and I'll clean up. I'll see you in the morning, Theo."

Theo nodded. "Yes, I'll be here early so I can drive my mom back to the hospital. I just hope tomorrow is a better day. Don't stay here too long—go home yourself. I love you, Marlee, and I don't even know how to show how much I appreciate you."

She leaned in and kissed him, just a brush of her lips. "I love you too, Theo."

He fished a bottle of water out of the small fridge and left, tired and disheartened. For weeks he'd impatiently waited for Marlee's arrival and dreamed of spending special moments with her. Now all he wanted was about twelve hours of unbroken sleep, no financial worries about profit, and most of all, for his grandmother to recover.

Theo wanted his everyday life back.

Chapter Sixteen

He slept fitfully and poorly. Every time he managed to doze, someone entered the room to tend to his grandmother. First, he was cold, then after covering up with the throw that now reeked of his mother's Tabu perfume, he became hot. The strong scent revived his headache, and the long night stretched out endlessly.

At six, his cell rang, and he grabbed it, half awake.

"Theo, when are you coming to pick me up?" Liesel said.

Thick-headed, he took a few moments to understand the question. "Now, I guess. I'll be there in ten minutes."

By seven, he was in the kitchen, grating potatoes after dropping Liesel at the hospital, staying long enough to hear the doctor's somewhat encouraging report on his grandmother, and splashing through a short shower.

Moving on auto pilot and fueled with strong, black coffee, Theo had most of the vegetable work done before Marlee arrived. He had checked the pot roasts, added the potatoes and carrots, then returned them to a warmer oven.

Theo greeted her with a distracted kiss.

"You didn't sleep much, did you?" she asked. "Go grab a nap. It's early, and there's time."

At first, he argued, then realized he acted as stubborn as his mother. *At least I come by it honestly,* he thought with a faint flash of humor. "All right, I will if you promise to wake me by ten. I have to fry the potato pancakes then. And the meatloaves have to go into the oven."

"I will, and I'll do it," Marlee said.

Theo put his arms around her from behind and kissed the back of her neck. "I waited so long for you to move here, but this isn't what I thought we'd be doing," he said. "I wanted to take you places, show you things, spend fun time together."

"That'll happen eventually," Marlee answered. "I want all that too, Theo. Life happens, and we just have to roll with it. Summer's hardly started, and we'll have time to do all those things before school starts."

"I hope so," he said, as she turned around so he could kiss her properly.

"I know so," Marlee told him. "Go take a nap."

He went upstairs and crashed on the couch. With his phone alarm set for ten, he slept until it woke him. Then, bleary eyed and fuzzy headed, he headed downstairs. Unlike the previous day, his kitchen remained in order and Marlee, although a teacher, not a chef, had things under control.

The servers were all there, Autumn, Eva, and Constance. Liz would come in around three to help with the evening shift, Marlee told him, and the Becker kids as soon as the last day of school ended.

Theo's mood improved, especially after he got busy frying the potato pancakes, then plating meals once they opened for lunch. He heard more compliments than complaints, many for Marlee's meatloaf. He wouldn't be a chef if he didn't taste it and found it, as expected, delicious.

Around two, however, as the number of diners slacked, Marlee came to the kitchen with an indignant look, lips pursed into a pout.

"There's a woman asking for you," she told him. "I told her you're busy, but she insists she must see you."

"Is she a customer?"

Marlee shrugged. "She ate lunch, so yes, she is. I asked her if there was a problem, but she said she will only talk to you. She wouldn't tell me her name, and she told me she wasn't talking to 'the help.'"

He sighed. "All right, I'll go out in just a minute. Let me get Table 8's order ready."

The kitchen doors flew open and Hanna, blonde, dressed in a short sundress that stopped well above the knee with slender spaghetti straps holding it up, strode into the room.

"Didn't your new hire tell you I'm here?" she said. "She tried to tell me you were busy, but I know you're never too busy for me."

He loved his cousin, but he had often fought with her growing up. She could be an angel, or she could be trouble. Marlee glared at him, and he reached out one hand to her. She took it and stood beside him.

"Marlee, this is my cousin, Hanna Schubert," he said in a tone as dry as good Sauvignon Blanc. "Hanna, this is my lady, Marlee Dupree. She's not an employee, by the way, although she's worked harder than any I've ever had to help out."

Hanna's fair skin turned scarlet as she heard the rebuke in his voice. "Oh, Theo, I'm sorry," she said. "I didn't know."

"You don't owe me an apology, but you do owe one to Marlee," he replied. "Mama said you were coming, but I'd forgotten when. I'm glad you're here to help with Oma."

His cousin moved farther into the kitchen and pulled up a stool at one of the prep counters. "How is she?"

"Still very sick. They have her sedated, so she'll rest and not get worked up. Oma hates the hospital, but right now, it's the best place for her. Who picked you up at the airport?"

"No one—I rented a car." She held up a keyring with a grin. "I need wheels while I'm here."

Thank goodness, Theo thought. He lacked the time or energy to play chauffeur. "I suppose you're staying at the farmhouse. My mom has been staying here nights."

"No, I booked a room at the Frau Haus with Fritz Lautner. It's more convenient."

Hanna had yet to make any amends to Marlee, and Theo shot her a hard look.

"Oh, and Marlee, I'm sorry if I offended you, thinking you worked for Theo."

"None taken," Marlee said. "Theo, I was about to fix a to-go box for your mom and run it over to her. I doubt she's eaten."

"Good thinking. Let me put one together with the meatloaf, potato pancakes, some applesauce, and some dessert."

"I'll take it to her," Hanna said. "I was planning to go over there anyway."

Theo didn't like the edge in her voice or her possessive manner, but he wanted to avoid a fight. "Sure. Have you eaten?"

She nodded, and he cringed as she flipped her long hair over one shoulder, imagining fine hairs flying in all directions. Everyone, including himself, wore a hairnet when in the kitchen, and she knew that.

"I did. The meatloaf was superb, the best you've ever made."

"Don't tell me—tell Marlee because she made it. She made the strudel too."

"I stand corrected," she said.

"And Hanna, the hairnets are in that box right behind you," he said. "If you're staying in here, get one on, *verstehst du?*"

"*Jawohl, mein Vetter.*"

He nodded and watched as she pulled her hair into a ponytail and netted it. Marlee hovered, then headed back to the dining room. Theo chatted with his cousin about how long she planned to stay—which proved to be indefinitely—and made small talk. Then Theo handed her the meal he'd prepared for his mother.

"Make sure she eats," he said. "And tell her when she's ready to leave for the night, call me or Marlee so we can pick her up."

"I will," Hanna said. With Marlee out of the room, her abrasive manner had eased. "Are you sick too? You look awful."

"Just tired. I was away over the long weekend and came back thinking I'd get caught up on sleep. But Oma got sick, and I've stayed with her the past couple of nights."

"Maybe you should close for just a day or two—"

"No!" He spat out the word with force. "I've been told that multiple times by my mother, Marlee, Jonas, and I can't. They closed early last weekend when I was out of town, but I can't, or I'll have no profit. This is my business, my living."

Hanna held up both hands, palms facing him. "Okay, okay, I'm sorry. I was just thinking of you, Theo."

"I appreciate that. But Hanna?"

"What?"

"If you want to make my life easier, keep in mind Marlee's out of bounds. No snark, Hanna. You're my cousin, but I love her. It's not a competition. You came to help, so be a help, not a hindrance."

She frowned. "I'll try, Theo."

He shook his head because that wasn't enough. "You will. You're the one who thought I should date."

"True, but—"

"And it's Marlee."

"All right."

"Take Mutti her dinner before it's cold."

Marlee returned once Hanna had gone. "Is she always like that?"

"You're straight to the point, but yes, she usually is. But she's also like a sister to me, even though sometimes we fight like enemies and always have at times. Did you think she was an old girlfriend?"

Her frown shifted into a smile. "I did, Theo. I thought maybe she might be a recent one. I'm glad she's your cousin instead."

"Me too. But Marlee, there's no one in my past to compare to you," he said. "I love you. You do know I mean that?"

She nodded. "I do, and I love you too, Theo Scrooge. It's almost three—let's eat!"

By the time Theo reopened Bah Humbug! for dinner, they had planned out menus for the remainder of the week. Gingerbread, using his mother's recipe, was ready to bake, and Theo had everything under control. Logan and Lucas pleaded for pizza, and he caved, vowing it would be the last time.

Hanna delivered Liesel to the back door around six-thirty.

"*Ach du Lieber Gott, Ich bine mude,*" she told Theo as she came into the kitchen.

"I know. I'm tired, too, Mutti. Are you hungry? There's pot roast, potatoes, and carrots."

"I'll eat a little, then I'll be ready to go upstairs. If you want your bed back, I can sleep on your couch."

"No, no, you keep the bed—the couch is fine. I'll be down here for quite a while anyway after we close with Marlee."

Although weary, Liesel was in good spirits, which cheered Theo. She lingered long enough to eat with them, then climbed the stairs to his apartment. Once the evening dinner hour ended and the work was done, Theo sat down at a table with Marlee and a just opened bottle of his favorite sweet red wine. He had just poured their glasses when Jonas rapped at the door. Theo rose to let him in.

"We were just pouring some wine," he told his friend. "Would you like to join us? Or would you like to eat?"

"I'd take a beer and some food," Jonas, still in uniform, replied. "I'll eat whatever you have. I'm not picky, but I'm starving."

As he ate a plate of meatloaf, Jonas brought up his upcoming wedding. "It's a week and half away," he said between bites. "Theo, you need to go get fitted for your tuxedo tomorrow. Is everything ready for the reception here?"

Theo hadn't thought about it for months, but he nodded. He had a file with all the notes and would review it tomorrow.

"Yes," he said. They would close at five that day, he recalled, for the reception. The cake would be delivered from a local bakery, but Theo would provide the meal.

"How's your grandmother?"

"She's hanging in there," Theo said. "I think the fact she's not grown any worse is a good sign."

"Are you up for a game of chess and more wine?" Jonas asked. "My bachelor days will be over soon."

"Too tired," Theo said. "Plus, I need a little time with Marlee. Except for working our tails off, I've hardly seen her since she got moved."

Marlee spoke up. "You can play chess if you want, Theo. It might help you unwind."

Jonas laughed. "No, no, it's all good, I understand. Thank you for the food and the beer. Call me if you need anything — and get fitted for the tux tomorrow, please."

Theo promised he would.

Once Jonas departed, he yawned and stretched. "I'd ask you to come up, but my mother's probably asleep by now," he said.

"Come over to my place then. You haven't been there since we unpacked. We can watch a movie or something. It's still early."

"I'd like nothing better."

"Then let's go before anyone else knocks at the door or calls."

He grabbed another bottle of wine, some cheese and some crackers, and they left. Theo wanted to laugh, but he smiled instead.

Marlee's apartment, now in order, offered a homey comfort. Theo eased down onto the couch and tucked a pillow behind his head. He exhaled.

"I needed this."

"We both did," she said. She opened the wine and poured it into a pair of chilled goblets from the freezer. He started to rise to prepare the snacks, and she waved her hand. "Stay there, Theo."

They watched several episodes of *Poldark,* and Theo enjoyed it, although, after the first one, he had trouble staying awake. His fatigue, the wine, and the contentment combined to put him to sleep. The last thing he recalled was Marlee easing off his shoes and covering him with a blanket.

He woke hours later to his cell ringing and was too befuddled to find it for a couple of minutes. When he did and realized his mother had phoned, he came wide awake and called her back, fearing bad news.

"Mama?"

"*Wo bist du?*"

"I'm at Marlee's. I came over to watch a movie, and I guess I fell asleep. What is it?"

Theo heard her long sigh. "*Danke Gott.* You weren't on the couch or downstairs. I called Hanna, and she hadn't seen you."

Theo shut his eyes with relief, followed by immediate frustration. "I apologize. I didn't plan to go to sleep and thought I'd be home long before now. What time is it?"

"Almost four."

He groaned. His inner programming always dictated that once he woke, he was up for the day. "I'll come to pick you up. Do you want me there at six or seven?"

"Six is fine."

"I'll be there. How about if I buy you breakfast at Maybelle's before I drop you off at the hospital?"

"I can get something at the hospital if it's too much trouble.'

"It's not, or I wouldn't ask. I'll see you then."

Theo almost wished he'd offered to collect her now, but the restaurant wouldn't be open until six, and he didn't fancy spending additional time at the medical center. A peek into her bedroom confirmed that Marlee remained asleep. He thought about heading over to his restaurant, but his mother would almost certainly hear him and come downstairs. He wouldn't mind the company, but he craved a good, hot breakfast prepared by someone else.

He made coffee with Marlee's one cup maker and drank it. Because he was bored, Theo stepped outside in front. Although the sun was no more than an orange glow above the horizon, it was humid and still. *Storm weather,* he thought. Although May often delivered the worst storms each year, the month had been quiet, and they were overdue for a major blow. He checked his phone for the latest weather forecast and frowned. A special weather statement had been posted for the area, calling for strong to severe storms, possible tornadoes and high winds, hail, and heavy rain.

"Ugh."

"What is it?"

Marlee stood behind him at the front door, mug in hand.

"The weather may get messy later," Theo replied.

"It might storm?"

"Eighty percent chance it will, and I don't doubt it," he said. "It's humid already, and there's almost no breeze."

She shuddered. "I don't like storms."

Theo didn't either, but he smiled and said, "It's just weather. As long as the power stays on and the river doesn't flood, it should be fine."

The line that divided her forehead into two deepened. "Does it flood?"

"Most of the time, no," he said. "The last big flood was in 1993. I was in grade school, but I do remember it. If it flooded the same, all of downtown would be inundated, including my place, so let's hope it doesn't."

Theo came back inside and kissed her, letting his mouth linger over hers. When he loaded his pockets with his billfold and keys, Marlee looked sad.

"You're leaving? It's not even five-thirty yet."

"I need to pick up Mutti," he said. "And I promised her breakfast at Maybelle's. I thought I'd go put some chickens in to roast—specials are fricassee and a pub curry. They'll be ready to work with when I return."

Marlee yawned. "I'll be there around nine, probably. Are Thursdays busy?"

"They are in June. Friday and Saturday will be the busiest. I'll see you there, *liebling.*"

With that, Theo departed to begin another day, one he hoped would hold fewer surprises and troubles than the past few had delivered. That would be a welcome change.

Chapter Seventeen

The severe thunderstorm watch issued around the noon hour became a warning that called for heavy rainfall, damaging winds, cloud to ground lightning, small hail, and the possibility of a tornado. The rain also brought the possibility of flash flooding. That didn't worry Theo much, but the chance that the river could flood did.

Hanna drifted into the restaurant around four, this time wearing casual khakis and a plain pink T-shirt. "I'm hungry. What are you serving?" This time, she had her hair up in a tight bun and paused to pull on a hairnet.

"Same menu as always," Theo said. "Specials are fricassee or curry or bratwurst with potato salad. Aren't you early?"

"Fix me a plate with fricassee. I can get brats anytime. I may be a little early, but I told Aunt Liesel I'd go get her at five and bring her back here for the night. She was concerned about the storms."

"So are we," Theo replied. "They've already issued warnings."

"I'm not worried about it. Remember the big storms when

we were kids?" Hanna said, taking a full plate from him. "We used to sit out on Oma's porch to watch, and more than once, we got in trouble for running out into a storm."

Theo chuckled. "I'd almost forgotten until now."

"They made us stay inside when it rained after that," she recalled. "We played checkers and Monopoly, and you tried to teach me chess."

"You never did grasp it, did you?"

Hanna giggled. "No, but I learned a lot of other things. Aunt Liesel would make those gingerbread cookie things—"

"*Lebkuchen,*" Theo said. "The boy and girl cookies or the hearts."

"Those were the best."

Marlee interrupted their trip down Memory Lane with a question. "Theo, how far are we from Sedalia and California?"

"Two hours from Sedalia, and more than a day unless you fly," Hanna quipped.

Marlee glared, and Theo frowned. His cousin knew very well Marlee referenced the small town, not the distant state.

"Yeah, two hours from Sedalia, about an hour from California," he said. "Why?"

"They're reporting winds somewhere between sixty and seventy miles an hour," she said, her voice tight. "The supercell is moving east—that's toward us, right?"

"*Ja,*" Theo replied. "I need to go put my truck in the garage. Hanna, you'd better go get Mutti now."

Marlee had been glued to her cell all day, checking the latest updates. Her tension thrummed in the air like electricity, and he wished he could ease her fears. Under normal circumstances, weather didn't worry him, but her anxiety was infectious. Already stressed with his family and business issues, Theo was wired.

"Let me finish eating, and I will," Hanna said. "There's

plenty of time."

"Not if you want to bring her here, then get back to stay at the hospital with Oma before the weather moves in," Theo answered.

She quibbled, but she went once she'd finished the last few bites on her plate.

Marlee, who had been unusually silent, sighed. Theo, who had suspected there was more wrong than stormy weather, turned to her.

"Was ist los?" he asked, then remembered she spoke little to no German. "What's wrong?"

"Nothing is like I expected," she told him. "Do you have a few minutes to sit?"

Theo nodded. "I do. Everything's ready to go, and with the storms coming in, hopefully, it will be a light dinner crowd."

Once they were seated at the table, he considered his, the one closest to the kitchen door. He leaned forward and grasped her hand. "Tell me."

"I anticipated coming here so much. I daydreamed about it, thought about all the fun things I thought we'd do together," she told him.

He thought he knew where her dissatisfaction came from.

"And all we've done is work. Marlee, I'm sorry. I love having you with me in the kitchen, but if you'd rather have the free time, it's okay. I can deal with that."

She groaned. "That's not the main problem, Theo. I enjoy it too, and I understand life doesn't always go the way we expect. You had no way to know your grandmother would be sick and end up in the hospital or that you'd be short-staffed. It's that we don't talk or laugh or joke. We talk about food and what to serve. You tell me to bring this or that. And you're focused on whether not you're making a profit, Theo. It makes you seem mercenary."

"I have to make a profit if I want to stay open, and yes,

it gets hectic in the kitchen," he replied after a long moment's thought. "I'm not trying to ignore you or be rude. I'm sorry that I have been. At your place, we talked."

A faint smile flirted with her lips, then faded. "That's true, but not here, Theo. You kiss me on occasion if you think about it, and otherwise, I feel like an employee. You talk to me about as much as you do to Constance and a lot less than you do with Hanna."

Theo blew out a long breath. He should have known—Hanna, although his close cousin, could be a major pain. It didn't help that she hadn't treated Marlee with friendly respect.

"I've only seen her twice since she arrived, and you were here both times," he said, selecting his words with caution. "There's no comparison, Marlee, and I agree she's been out of line. I called her down yesterday, and that remark about California was unnecessary. It hasn't been the way I want either, Marlee, but it will be. I love you, and if I haven't paid you enough attention, I will."

Her smile emerged, and she leaned across the table to kiss him. "I love you, too, Theo. I haven't had time to get adjusted yet, either."

"Are we good?"

She nodded. "Totally."

"Let's plan on doing something fun on Sunday," Theo said. "We'll figure out what later, but we'll spend the whole day doing whatever you'd like."

"Perfect!"

Theo put his truck up out of the weather and scanned the sky. Dark, low clouds were to the west, and he knew they would be on top of them soon. As he watched, lighting flashed in the clouds, then he saw jagged branched bolts illuminate. Against the black clouds, it was a spectacular display. The first rolls of thunder boomed as he headed inside.

"Is that thunder?" Marlee asked.

"Yes, it is. The storm is almost here. I wish Hanna would get Mama here before it hits."

Although he'd been open for the evening trade for more than an hour, no customers came through the door. Although that would cut into how much he made for the night, Theo didn't mind much. He stepped outside as the wind began to rise from a dead calm to gusts that blew odd bits of trash along the street. The gusts were strong enough Theo thought he might lose his balance, so he turned to go inside. As he did, Hanna's rental car pulled up, and his mother exited before Hanna turned around and drove toward the hospital. Liesel swayed in the strong wind, so Theo rushed down to grab her hand.

"Let's get inside," he yelled over the sound of the gale. "Before it rains."

Rain fell in torrents almost as soon as they were inside. It drummed on the roof and lashed against the windows. Jagged lightning split the sky, and thunder growled as the fury of the storm hit.

Marlee came out of the kitchen with a worried frown. "This is just the leading edge," she said. "They just extended the warnings until seven. Just in case, is there a basement?"

"There is," he answered.

"I wish I was at the farmhouse," his mother said. "That stone house is solid."

"So is this brick building," Theo said. "It's stood for decades."

A burst of hail hit, the clatter sounding like ten thousand marbles pitched from the sky. At first, the pellets were marble sized, but they became larger.

"I'm glad I put up the truck," Theo said.

Marlee's expression became alarmed. "My car's parked on the street."

Theo refrained from pointing out the obvious—it was either already damaged or not.

"It should be okay," Theo told her. "Since we don't have anyone in the house, let's eat. Tell me if you want one of the specials or something from the menu."

As they ate, the storm continued, but when they were almost finished, the wind dropped, and the rain stopped.

"It must be almost over," Marlee said with relief.

Theo checked the weather app on his phone and tensed. Before he could share what he saw, Jonas drove up, siren blaring, and came to a stop outside the entrance. He dashed into Bah Humbug! with his soon to be bride, Shannon.

"The weather service just issued a tornado warning," he said. "Mind if we head for your basement with you?"

Marlee made a dismayed sound. "Theo?"

"We're going," he said. "I just saw it myself. Grab your purse. Mutti, let's go downstairs."

He led them to the door that led to the lowest level and turned on the light over the stairs. He used the area primarily for overflow storage. A few discarded tables and chairs were stacked against one wall. A few boxes were tucked away in one corner, and some racks that dated to when the building was used as a grocery stood against another wall. A single light bulb dangled from the ceiling to provide light, but although dim, the space was dry and comfortable.

Theo set down chairs for everyone and added a table. "Come sit down," he said.

Marlee stood beside him, trembling. "Theo, I'm afraid."

He wrapped his arms around her. "Don't be. Nothing will probably happen. We have warnings like this all season long. It's better to play it safe and wait it out down here."

Jonas pulled out a chair for Liesel, then one for Shannon, but the sheriff didn't sit down. "Marlee, this is Shannon," Jonas said. "She's one of the librarians at the high school, so you'll be working together this fall."

Marlee turned around and forced a smile. "It's good to meet you. Maybe we can have lunch or something soon, and you tell me about the school."

"I'd like that," Shannon said. "As long as it's after the wedding and honeymoon."

"And I know a perfect place for lunch with great food, good atmosphere," Theo quipped.

Jonas laughed. "The four of us could go out for dinner sometime," he said. "Try one of the other restaurants, or even go up to Jeff City."

"Maybe Sunday." Theo had promised Marlee they would do something, and it was his single day off.

Shannon shook her head. "That's too close to the wedding—it's next Saturday. Maybe when we're settled."

Theo convinced Marlee to sit down. Below ground, he couldn't tell if the storm had ended or not, but when the electricity went out, he figured it wasn't over. After a few seconds of total darkness, the emergency light he'd mounted on the wall came on. None of them said much. Theo hoped they wouldn't emerge to find destruction, and that the power would be back on soon.

Twenty long minutes later, Jonas told them that the warning had been cancelled. One by one, with Theo bringing up the rear, they emerged from the basement. He held his breath until he confirmed his place was still standing. He emerged outside to survey any damage and found many limbs down. Looking up the street, Theo noticed damage to a few signs. Bits of small debris, including posters and trash, littered the ground.

"Everything's still standing," he said.

"Wind, but not a tornado," Jonas stated.

Marlee joined Theo outside. "So, it's all good, then?"

"It should be, as long as your car doesn't have any major

hail damage and the power comes back on soon."

"How soon is soon?" Marlee wanted to know.

"The sooner, the better, at the latest within a day or so," Theo replied.

"What happens if it doesn't?"

"I lose all the food in the freezer and cooler. Not a good scenario."

But he had every confidence that the electric company would have the power back long before it became a problem. He couldn't afford to take the hit if they didn't, so Theo had to believe they would.

He was wrong.

Chapter Eighteen

Power was restored in other areas of town before it came back on at Bah Humbug! Theo's electricity returned on Sunday afternoon, too late to save several thousand dollars worth of fresh food stored in the walk-in cooler and the freezers. He'd been so certain the utility company would have it back before anything spoiled that by the time he decided to act, it was too late. Besides, he could find no place large enough to put his stock on hand.

Without power, he couldn't open Bah Humbug! so he lost several days of revenue. Already concerned about finances, the combined events stressed Theo to the point he suffered severe headaches daily.

Oma improved enough to go home on Monday, and although he had a delivery scheduled to arrive, he offered to drive her home to the farmhouse, which hadn't lost power. Wearing the portable oxygen that would now be a daily feature, his grandmother needed a boost to get into the seat of the truck that had once been her husband's. Theo lifted her in his arms, and once home, he carried her into the house.

She weighed little in his arms, he noted, and although

she'd recovered from the pneumonia, Theo thought she remained pale and seemed weak. Liesel suggested he take her upstairs to her bedroom, but Oma rejected the idea.

"I don't want to be up there alone," she said. "Or make you run up and down the stairs all day long."

"The doctor said you need rest."

"I'll rest downstairs."

Theo intervened. "Oma, it may be hard for you to climb the stairs to go to bed."

"This is true, *Herr Doktor* Theo," Oma said. The flash of her usual sarcastic wit made him happy. "So maybe you could bring the bed downstairs for me."

He wanted to groan but didn't.

"And where would we put it?" Liesel asked.

"In the library," Oma said. "It would be temporary only."

Downstairs, there were several rooms—a large parlor used as a living room, a family room just off the kitchen, a dining room, and a room they'd always called the library. When his mother's family still ran the winery, it had been an office as well. It was a snug, pleasant room at the east end of the house, with a view overlooking the fields and grape arbors.

His mother and grandmother debated the possibility, but in the end, Theo provided the muscle to take apart the bed upstairs, carry it down, then reassemble it. He turned down Liesel's offer to help, but he wished Marlee had come with him. She'd opted instead to go to lunch with Shannon—in Jefferson City.

Once Oma was settled, she asked Theo if he would make her some good German potato soup. He spent the afternoon cooking in the large, open kitchen, where he'd first learned, from his grandmother and mother, to prepare many of the dishes he now served.

The familiar tasks of dicing potatoes, onion, and celery for

Kartoffelzuppe took Theo's mind from his woes. He shared some soup with them for an early supper before he headed back into town.

His delivery had arrived in his absence, restocking his supplies of perishables, including produce, milk, butter, eggs, sour cream, meats, and frozen foods. The freezer, which he'd worked hard to clean after the spoilage, now held the various meat and other ingredients needed to create his dishes. Autumn had signed for the food in his absence.

"Thank you," he told her with a hug. "I appreciate it."

The young woman grinned. "It's not like I had anything else to do."

She had pitched in to help clear out the ruined foods, working side by side with Theo, Marlee, and Hanna. The Becker kids had helped, too, along with Constance when she could. It had been a mess, he thought with a shudder, and the dumpster out back brimmed full.

"We'll open tomorrow," he told Autumn. *"Danke Gott."*

Theo spent the evening alone, planning what he'd cook the next day and lamenting the financial hit he'd taken. It could be worse, and he could weather it, but it still concerned him. To cope, he began brainstorming for ideas that might help cut costs.

Marlee phoned around nine. "I'm back," she told him.

The sound of her soft voice soothed some of his anxiety.

"I missed you. Did you have fun?"

"We did. I like Shannon. We talked a lot about the school."

"Good, good. If you're hungry, I have some potato soup I made for Oma."

"No, thanks. We ate at a buffet in Jefferson City, and I'm still stuffed," Marlee replied. "How is your grandmother?"

"She's better, happy to be home."

Marlee had never turned down an offer to eat something he'd prepared. Theo tried to blow it off, but he couldn't help but be a little miffed.

"I'm glad. Does that mean Hanna went home?"

"*Ja,* early this morning." He hadn't realized she still had an issue with his cousin. "Where did you eat?"

"It was a Chinese buffet in a shopping center," she said. "I don't remember the name, but I ate way too much cashew chicken."

"You sound tired, *liebling.*"

"I am, Theo, and my tummy's grumbly. I did have fun, though, and I bought a dress for the wedding."

He'd hoped she would come over or that he could go to her apartment, but Theo thought she needed some rest.

"So, you are going?"

Marlee had said previously she wasn't because she hadn't been invited. "I am. Shannon invited me to come. You'll be there, right?"

"Of course. I'm the best man, and then the reception will be here at the restaurant. Would you like to go with me?"

For the first time, she sounded upbeat. "Yes, Theo, I definitely would."

"Then it's a date," he said. "I'll let you get some rest. See you tomorrow?"

"I'll come over, sure," Marlee said. "Good night, Theo."

"Sleep well, Marlee. I love you."

On Tuesday, Theo made roast chicken with spaetzle and an English chicken pot pie with puff pastry. He didn't have any desserts and thought maybe he could get by without any for a day or two. Although he feared he might have lost customers while closed, business was brisk by the time Marlee strolled into the kitchen around twelve-thirty.

Theo greeted her, hair mussed beneath his chef's hat, plating food and stirring pots. He grinned at her. "I'm glad you're here. I really missed you yesterday."

"You look worn out," Marlee said after a quick hug. "Having a rough day?"

"A crazy busy one," he said. "I'm frazzled trying to keep up. There's no dessert, and every other diner wants dessert."

"Didn't your mom make something?"

He shook his head. "No. And worse, she doubts she'll be able to make daily desserts anymore. She wants to focus on Oma more."

"I can't blame her for that."

"I don't," Theo said as he put up an order with two pot pies and three roast chicken meals for Amber to deliver. "Oma's much better, but she's weak and needs more care. But desserts aren't my forte. I guess I'll have to start ordering from a bakery or something, but that's going to cost a fortune."

He had done the math the night before and calculated that it would cut his profit margin per meal served by at least ten percent. His hands were tied, though, because the desserts had always been a popular item, and customers expected them.

As he rushed around the kitchen from one station to another, both his energy and anxiety were high. Theo longed to take a break and sit for five minutes, but he didn't think he could. The pressure was on, and he wasn't coping well.

Marlee caught his arm. "Slow down, Theo, before you have a nervous breakdown or hurt yourself."

"I don't have time."

"Make time," she said, and steered him toward his office. "Take deep breaths. Your heart is pounding. I could feel it when we hugged."

"Marlee, I have to—"

"Calm down," she interrupted. "You have to calm down, Theo, or you won't be able to function. Do you want to have to close early? No, I didn't think so. And I doubt you want to be prescribed anti-anxiety meds."

"I don't."

"Then breathe and relax. I've never seen you like this—what's the matter?"

"Nothing. There's just so much to do and not enough time to get it done. I still need to hire a couple more people, and I'm concerned about money."

Marlee pushed him into a chair. "Sit for five minutes. We'll talk more later because I know it's still lunch rush, and you do have to get back in the kitchen. Would it help if I make a dessert, something simple?"

Theo sighed. "Maybe for dinner, but it would make baking a rush."

"I'll make a cookie fluff," she said. "Call it a trifle if you want to be fancy. It's just a whipped dessert with sandwich cookies, some condensed milk, cream cheese, and whipped topping. I can go get the ingredients and have some made in no time."

"You don't have to, Marlee."

She put a finger across his lips. "I want to, Theo. And I really want you to chill out a little. I'll run to the store and be right back, okay?"

"*Jawohl, Ich verstehe.*"

Marlee was back with the ingredients and had the trifle made before the lunch hours ended. She made a larger batch for the dinner hour, then convinced Theo to sit down to eat as soon as Bah Humbug! closed.

Once he'd finished a good-sized piece of chicken pot pie, she served him the trifle.

"It's good," he said.

"You sound surprised."

"Not really. It just didn't take long to make. Mama spends hours baking."

"Well, you needed something quick. If you want, I can

make a few desserts like I did last week, but just for the summer."

"I do," he said. "I can't tell you how much I appreciate this."

Marlee pitched in during the evening hours and helped, doing anything Theo needed. She served tables, she refilled beverages, she delivered beer and wine to diners. She scrubbed pots and pans in the industrial size sinks and loaded the dishwashers. By the time he closed, Theo's eyes burned with fatigue, and he longed to sit down. His head thumped with a world class headache as well. Once he'd finished clean-up, he turned to Marlee, where she stood in the kitchen.

"Let's go upstairs and have a glass of wine," he said. "I need to unwind."

"You do," she replied. "First, though, you need this more."

Heedless of his now dirty chef's coat, she pulled him into an embrace and kissed him, long and slow. As Marlee's mouth caressed his, Theo could feel some of the tension in his shoulders and back ease. He exhaled with pleasure and cradled her close for a few moments.

Upstairs, he opened a bottle of the best Riesling from the family winery and poured it into a pair of stemless glasses he kept in the freezer. Theo pressed one of the frigid glasses against his forehead for a moment, savoring how good it felt on his aching head.

"Do you have a headache?" Marlee asked, popping up behind him.

"*Ja*," he said.

"Wouldn't you rather take something for it instead of wine?"

Theo shook his head. "No, the wine will help."

She took a glass, and he touched his to hers.

"*Prost!*"

He took a sip of the sweet wine and sighed as it traveled

down his throat. Marlee led him into his living area, and they settled onto the couch. Theo shut his eyes and savored the wine. She sat beside him, one hand resting on his thigh, and he took comfort from that too.

"Do you want to watch a movie?" she asked. "Or listen to music?"

"No movie," he replied. He didn't think he could stand the moving pictures or the excitement. "Music, sure."

She rose, sorted through his many CDs, and put Mannheim Steamroller on the stereo. The combined sounds of the sea and their unique blend of music ranked among Theo's favorites, assisting him to unwind. Marlee refilled the wine as they listened.

After an hour or so, Theo stirred. "I need to plan tomorrow's specials," he said.

"It can wait."

"It really can't," Theo told her, then, in response to her expression, shifted it. "Well, it shouldn't."

"Make it easy and have the same two specials for both meals," Marlee suggested.

"I have been, and I often have."

"You need to do it each day. After all, how many people come for both meals? And if they do, you still offer a menu, right?"

He did, and she made sense. "You're right."

"So have bratwurst on a bun and bangers and mash tomorrow," she told him. "I'll be here early, and I'll make some desserts for you. It'll work."

Theo couldn't argue and didn't. He would take anything that simplified his life.

"All right," he conceded. "It will. I'll do German potato salad with the brats. There's still the rest of the week and the wedding reception."

"And there's tomorrow," Marlee said. "Besides, don't you

already know their menu?"

"It's written down," he said. "A lot has happened since Jonas and Shannon made their reservation. They made it long before I ever met you."

Her smile was sweet. "In another life, then."

"Yes, it was."

"We can think about all those things tomorrow," she told him. "We'll be like Scarlett O'Hara."

The reference eluded him. "What?"

"Scarlett, in *Gone With The Wind*," Marlee replied. "It's how the book ends, she'll think about everything tomorrow, at Tara. Haven't you ever read it?"

"No, I don't believe I ever did."

"Or watched the movie?"

Theo shook his head.

"We'll watch it together sometime, then. But for now, don't worry about the wedding reception or the menu or money or hiring more help. Just take some chill time."

He laughed, but it was hollow. "I don't think I remember how."

"Well, lucky for you, I'm a teacher, so I'll teach you. How's your head?"

"Still hurts."

Marlee scooted down a bit and patted her lap. "Come lay down your head, Theo, and I'll do something to help."

He doubted it, but he gave her the chance, sprawling out along the couch with his head in her lap. Although it seemed silly, when Marlee began to massage his temples with her fingers, Theo shivered.

"What is it? Do you want me to stop?"

"No, it feels amazing," he told her.

As the headache waned, he became drowsy, but Theo fought it, wanting to spend the time with Marlee awake and aware.

He lost the battle, though, and slept, waking late into the night on the couch. Marlee, covered with a throw, slept in the recliner, her breathing deep and even. Theo marveled that she'd stayed, but he was glad she had.

Although he thought about waking her, he went back to sleep, and when he woke in the morning, she had gone. A shower, a shave, and clean clothes restored some of his spirit, and he went downstairs to find Marlee baking pineapple upside-down cakes. The delicious aroma filled the kitchen and reminded Theo of similar cakes with pineapple Oma used to make.

The burdens he'd been carrying lightened, and he greeted Marlee with a kiss, then tied on an apron to begin this day.

Theo felt confident it would be a good one.

Chapter Nineteen

On Tuesday, four days remained until Jonas's wedding. When Theo reviewed the details, he was reminded there would be a rehearsal at six on Friday evening, then the wedding on Saturday at three, followed by the reception set to begin around five at Bah Humbug! As best man, he would need to be present at the rehearsal, leaving his place in the hands of his staff, and on Saturday, he would need to close earlier than he'd anticipated — by one at the very latest. If he hadn't just reopened after the storm fiasco, Theo might have considered being closed on Saturday, but he didn't want to miss that day's trade even for a half day.

Marlee, however, disagreed. "It's your best friend's wedding," she told him. "He'll only have one, and you're in the wedding party. I'd suggest closing after lunch on Friday and staying closed, then not opening Saturday. I imagine Shannon wants to decorate for the reception too — she can't do that with customers in the house."

Theo argued but soon conceded. Closing would make the preparation of the foods to be served much easier, and the last thing he'd want would be to cause problems with the wedding.

So, at his direction, Marlee made a sign for the door and posted it.

The only complaint came from Todd Blevins, who was vocal and a little vicious. "Well, that's a rip, Ebenezer," he told Theo when he paid for his lunch on Tuesday. "I was planning to bring the wife here for dinner on Friday and some golf buddies on Saturday. I guess we'll go to Maybelle's or the Munich Steakhouse instead. Surprised an old miser like you would take a chance to be closed. You didn't even close when your poor old grandma was in the hospital, did you, Scrooge?"

His fingers clenched into a fist, and Theo longed to punch Blevins's obnoxious mouth but didn't. Instead, he ignored what the man had said and asked if he wanted a beer.

"Yeah, bring me two to start, and the bangers and mash, then."

Theo headed for the kitchen and sent Autumn out with the beer. He counted to ten, contemplated hitting something, then took long, deep breaths.

"That Blevins guy again?" Marlee asked as she sliced one of the cakes.

"Is it that obvious?"

She scrutinized him and nodded. "Definitely. Just ignore him, Theo."

"I'm trying."

On Wednesday, he held interviews during the hours Bah Humbug! was closed between lunch and dinner. He hired two servers—a young man named Albert, who had just moved to town who said he'd been a waiter at an Olive Garden in Kansas City, and Bethany, a newlywed who wanted to earn extra money toward buying a house with her husband. Theo also hired a prep cook to help with some of the basic tasks. Lacey would work a split shift—sometimes days, sometimes evenings. He also hired Logan and Lucas Becker to bus tables.

"You both have worked hard," he told them. "You've more

than served your time, so if you'd like to work this summer, I'm happy to bring you on as paid employees."

"That would be freakin' awesome, Theo," Lucas said.

"Sure," Logan said. "Do we get pizza for this?"

His question made Marlee laugh, and although Theo said no, she quietly paid for a pizza to be delivered for the Becker boys' supper.

The hectic week might not have been the best time to train new hires, Theo reflected late on Thursday. By then, he had food for the reception in hand.

After close, he and Marlee shared a rare beer to taste it for Saturday night. Both preferred wine, but Theo found the bock beer to be palatable and tasty.

"They're having wine too, right?" Marlee asked.

"*Jawohl,*" he replied. "That's simple—I'll get it from Thomas. And pick up the breads from the bakery, the meats and cheeses from the supplier in Jeff. The rest I'll cook, and I'll start on that tomorrow afternoon after I close. The wedding cake will be delivered on Saturday morning."

And, Theo remembered, he also had to pick up his tuxedo, ask Jonas if he wanted a bachelor party—although if he did, he had no idea how he could organize one at this late moment—and write a speech or toast for the reception party.

He sighed, and Marlee smiled. "It'll be over soon enough," she told him. "On Sunday, you can rest, and maybe we can do something fun."

"I hoped we would last week, but that didn't work out."

She shrugged. "We'll figure it out, Theo. After this week, it's just summer, right?"

"Summer means peak tourist season," he said. "It will stay hectic until Labor Day, then there's Oktoberfest and the tenth anniversary party I want to have here."

"Remember—don't think about tomorrow," she said.

"That's all a long way off. Do you want to come over and watch a movie at my place?"

"I'm too restless," he replied. "Let's take a walk down the riverfront. It's late enough there won't be many people out—"

"Or kids on bikes."

Theo laughed, and it felt good. "Or that. Let's try not to end up in the river, though."

"Definitely. But you're here to save me if I do."

Although her tone remained light, he saw how much she meant it in her eyes.

"Always," he said, and kissed her.

They strolled hand in hand down the waterfront, the area illuminated by retro looking streetlights every six feet. The night air smelled of blooming flowers and water. Beside them, the never quiet Missouri River gurgled with its own song. Theo delighted in holding her smaller hand in his, and his spirits lifted.

Midway down, they stopped and sat down on a bench. He put his arm around her, and after a few quiet moments of reflection, he kissed her, slow and sweet. From her soft sigh, he thought she enjoyed it as much as he did. A gentle breeze wafted over them, and he let it clear the cobwebs from his head. In those moments, he let go of his financial worries, his fears, and his stress.

Despite everything that had happened in recent weeks to cause Theo distress, the one thing he did not doubt was that he loved Marlee. More than that, he envisioned a life together. Jonas's wedding plans fired Theo's imagination to dream of a day when he might be the groom and Marlee his bride, but he didn't speak of it to her, not yet. She'd barely had time to settle into the town, a place so different than where she'd been raised. School wouldn't start for another two months, and Theo had no wish to distract her from her career. He'd lived in the same place where he'd been born, for good or bad, all his life except when he gained his education. Hermann was familiar — it had been his cradle and remained his foundation. Theo had trouble visualizing life elsewhere. He knew he'd never fit seamlessly into Marlee's hometown, not the way he fit here. *I belong here, and I'm wise enough to know it.*

Theo longed to ask her to marry him, but he waited. This was not yet the time, he reasoned, although he would someday. Maybe in the fall, maybe after the holidays, when life slackened to an easy pace, and he didn't have to think about being Scrooge.

He kept his thoughts and focused on the woman in the moment. For now, that was all he felt he had the capacity to do.

On Friday, Theo tried to hold fast to the sweet moments of the previous evening but found it hard. Although he would serve at the noon hour only and had kept the specials simple, the morning became a hectic whirl. Marlee picked up his tuxedo for him and delivered it to his apartment. She pitched in and worked as hard as he did, harder than most of his staff.

His mother dropped off apple strudel she'd made for the wedding reception and lingered. Theo thought she must miss her daily time at Bah Humbug! as much as he felt her absence. Mutti had been part of the place since he opened, and although Theo talked to her by phone daily, there remained an empty spot each day that she and Oma had always filled.

"We'll be at the wedding," Liesel told him. "But we won't come to the reception. Oma still tires easily, and it might be too much. How are you? *Du bist war mit den Nerven völlig am Ende.*"

"*Mir geht es Gute,*" he told her. "There's some stress, *ja,* but it's all good."

Her sharp eyes peered at him, and Theo would swear she had the ability to see past the façade into his soul.

"So you say, but you don't look so well. On Sunday, take time and do something with Marlee."

"That's what I plan," he said with a smile he didn't have

to force.

Liesel nodded. "Tell me, what are you serving at the reception besides my apple strudel and the wedding cake?"

"Various breads, rolls, cold meats including ham, turkey, German style bologna, pastrami, and cheeses," he said. "All that I will pick up from the bakery and the butcher. I'm preparing *frickadellen,* bratwurst balls, potato dumplings, braised red cabbage, *spaetzle,* potato soup, wedding soup, onion pie, and half chickens, roasted until the skin is crisp, with lemon pepper. I'll set it up like a buffet for easy serving, with a separate table for the wedding cake."

"That sounds like a feast, a good one. Don't work too hard, though, my son."

He laughed but with little mirth. "I'm doing some of it today after we close and before the rehearsal, the rest tomorrow morning."

"Tell Marlee she can sit with us," Liesel said, and kissed his cheek. "I'm going home now, and I will see you tomorrow."

All afternoon, until almost five, Theo worked like a fiend, preparing the side dishes and starting the soups. He had a hundred half chickens seasoned and ready to prepare before he hung up his apron and went upstairs to shower and change. Marlee had left an hour earlier to do the same.

In faded blue jeans and an old button-down plaid shirt, Theo picked her up fifteen minutes before the rehearsal was scheduled to begin and drove the few blocks to the church. Although Marlee had no formal role in the wedding, she'd promised to take some photos and offer input if needed.

Although held in the sanctuary, the mood was light-hearted and casual. Shannon marched down the aisle with measured steps on her dad's arm, hands poised as if she held a bouquet. At the altar, Jonas found his spot and situated Theo where he would stand during the wedding. He handed Theo the wedding ring and made him promise not to lose it.

"I'd have to kill you if you do," Jonas said. "That thing cost a fortune."

"I'll keep track of it," Theo promised.

Afterward, the couple treated all present to pizza and salad in the parish hall. When Shannon pulled Marlee aside, Jonas nudged Theo.

"It's hard to believe that by this time tomorrow, she'll be my wife," he said. "It's awesome but surreal, too."

"I can imagine. Come by after this, if you want, and we'll drink wine while we play chess," Theo said. "I hope you don't mind. I didn't organize a bachelor party."

Jonas shot him a grin. "I'm glad you didn't, Theo. That kind of stuff's not my style. I'm having enough of a time figuring out how to act on our honeymoon. I've never been on a cruise before, and I hope I don't get seasick."

"I probably would," Theo said, and put a hand to his stomach. "But you'll be fine."

Theo and Jonas played chess into the early morning hours, drinking a sweet Moscato and smoking a rare cigar each. Neither smoked under normal circumstances, but it seemed to be part of the bachelor party tradition, so they did. Jonas won twice, Theo took three games, and they quit. As he showered away the smell of the tobacco, Theo reflected he would miss those evenings with his best friend a great deal.

On Saturday, despite cutting his hand, spilling cream all over the kitchen floor, and fighting a slight headache, Theo got the food prep finished with plenty of time remaining before the wedding.

He'd always found Marlee attractive, but when he picked her up to head for St. Morand's, she shattered his expectations. Her mid-calf light periwinkle blue lace dress suited her, and it matched almost exactly the blue of the tuxedo jacket Jonas had chosen for his groomsmen. The sleeveless dress flattered Marlee. She wore her hair in an updo crowned with fresh flowers, a white magnolia with two tiny rosebuds and some baby's breath.

"You're lovely," he told her as he leaned in for a kiss, careful not to smear her make-up.

Her wide smile rewarded him. "We match," she said. "You look very handsome, Theo."

He resolved to be sure the photographer snapped a photo of the two of them—he wanted to keep this memory forever.

Each moment of the wedding kindled a desire in Theo to marry Marlee. From the front of the church, he watched her with his mother and grandmother, marveling at her beauty. He didn't fumble the ring, and the ceremony proceeded without a hitch.

Theo had a few anxious moments at Bah Humbug! The wedding cake arrived, late but intact, and he changed from the formal wear into his chef's garments. By the time the reception began, he had the food in place and the tables in position. He'd asked Amber and Constance to help serve. Marlee joined him in the kitchen, and he paused for a kiss before the festivities got underway.

Before they could eat, Theo stood for the best man's speech.

"This is a wonderful occasion," he said. "I wish Jonas and Shannon every happiness. Jonas and I have been best friends most of our lives, since when we started kindergarten. We grew up here in town, two blocks apart, and he spent as much time at my grandparents' winery as I did. He's my brother from another mother. We've fished and hunted and played chess. Now, he starts a new chapter of his life as a husband, something I hope to do someday as well. Shannon was a fit for him from their first date. I think I saw that even before Jonas did. Let's raise a glass to Mr. and Mrs. Jonas Kaiser!"

After the food, which the guests praised, the three-tiered wedding cake was cut and served. Before the newlyweds left for their honeymoon, Shannon tossed the bouquet, and Marlee caught it, her mouth wide open with surprise. Her cheeks were pink as she inhaled the floral fragrance.

Once all the guests had gone and the place restored to order, Theo plugged in the fairy lights at the outdoor dining area, moved back the tables and chairs, and played waltz music on his phone.

"Would you like to dance?" he asked Marlee, and she nodded.

Theo could waltz like Fred Astaire thanks to Oma, who first taught him, and lessons in his grade school days. Marlee followed his lead, and they twirled to the music without talking, in harmony. At least he thought they were until she spoke.

"Did you mean what you said?"

"What was it?"

"That you someday hope to start a new chapter of your life as a husband."

He did—but not now.

"Yes, I meant it."

Marlee rested her head against his shoulder. "That's good to know," she murmured. "Because I want to be married, Theo."

Neither said any more about it, but Theo felt he'd been given notice, and although he planned to marry Marlee in the future, her words made him tense. Panic seized him, but he said nothing. Now, he thought, was not the time.

It was almost midnight when they stopped.

"What do you want to do tomorrow?" she asked.

"It is tomorrow," he replied with a chuckle. "We can do whatever you want. Normally I would go to church, but the wedding was a Mass, so I don't plan on it. We can have a picnic or whatever you'd like."

"Could we go to St. Louis on the train?"

Her request blindsided him, but after a moment, he

nodded. "We can," he said. "It shouldn't be a problem to get tickets. What would you like to do in Saint Louie?"

"I'd like to go to the Gateway Arch. I was there once when I was in third grade. Can we, Theo?"

"Yes," he said. "Let's go inside, see what time the train leaves, and buy the tickets."

Nothing, Theo vowed, would prevent him from the outing with Marlee. He needed the break as much, if not more than she wanted it.

They went to the Arch and rode to the top, although the tight car made Theo more than a little nervous. Afterward, they walked hand in hand through Laclede's Landing. They dined at a French bistro, enjoying crab cakes as their starter, lobster bisque, and one of the best steaks Theo had enjoyed in a long time. The cost shocked him, but he paid and managed not to protest.

"That was lovely, Theo," Marlee told him as he kissed her goodnight at her apartment. "Thank you."

"It was," he replied.

He had enjoyed it too, but now that it was over, he had to turn his mind back toward his business. *I can't be spending that kind of money,* he thought as he climbed the stairs to his apartment, *or I'll be broke before fall.*

Chapter Twenty

A week after the wedding and their St. Louis trip, summer arrived with a hot and humid vengeance. Temperatures soared into the upper nineties, hitting the century mark and shattering old records. Theo switched from his winter black chef's uniform to short-sleeved white versions for summer, but as the heat rose, he contemplated cooking in white T-shirts for the duration. If he didn't fear it would look unprofessional, he would have.

Marlee baked desserts early, utilizing his kitchen before it became too hot. Theo envied her the shorts and tank tops she wore. He rose before dawn to join Marlee as she baked, despite the fact he was often up until midnight or past. The long hours and the heavy, humid heat sapped his energy, and already slender, Theo grew thinner as the summer passed.

His appetite waned. Theo had never been one to enjoy eating in sweltering weather. The heat, however, didn't appear to bother the tourists, who came in record numbers. Although good for the community and Bah Humbug! the result kept Theo burning the candle at both ends, running to keep up and never quite making the finish line. Sleep proved elusive, and when it came, it was often a few short hours till he had to rise.

"*Du bist dürr gemacht,*" Liesel told him one week when she brought Oma for Friday lunch. That had become the outing of the week for them — shopping, maybe a hair appointment, a stop at the library, and lunch before heading home. Other than that, they came to church each Sunday. "*Bist du krank?*"

"*Nein, Mutti,*" Theo had replied. "I know I'm thin, but I'm fine, not sick at all. It's this heat and my busy schedule." Her snort indicated she didn't believe him, not entirely, and it didn't help that Marlee expressed the same opinion.

"You're running yourself ragged. You don't take hardly any time off. It's summer. It's supposed to provide some downtime."

"That's for teachers," Theo told her, his tone gentle. "The rest of us have to work, especially in a tourist town."

"You're too skinny, and you don't eat enough," Marlee nagged. "I'm lucky if you have time to do something with me on Sundays. If I wasn't doing the desserts, I don't know when I'd see you. And when school starts, it's going to be a challenge."

"I love you, and I'll always make time for us," Theo said, and meant it. What he didn't say was he didn't sleep enough and that he existed on caffeine and stubborn determination. Nor did he mention that he worried about money daily, still concerned about recouping the losses from the storms and anxious about the added expense of additional employees. His desire to build a life with Marlee fueled his fears. Theo dreamed of buying a house and creating a home with her. He wanted kids, but until he thought he could afford all those things, he remained silent.

Just before the Fourth of July, when Marlee had almost talked Theo into a getaway trip to Union Station in St. Louis, he sliced his index finger to the bone while chopping onions. Theo, working at his usual breakneck pace, didn't even realize he'd been cut until the blood spewed onto the cutting board. When the bleeding wouldn't stop, he had to. The new prep assistant, Lacey, took over while Marlee drove Theo to the hospital for stitches. Even so, wearing a special glove to protect the wound, Theo was back in the kitchen within two hours, a little paler than usual. The wound was sore, and Marlee scolded him, but he continued working—it was necessary. Instead of the trip to St. Louis, Theo took Marlee to see a movie, then out for dinner in Jefferson City.

Marlee's baking time grew shorter the closer the calendar moved toward the first day of school. Long before that first day, she reported to school for a series of meetings, some for new hires only, others for all staff. She had a classroom and curriculum to prepare, so her focus shifted. In early August, her efforts to keep up flagged, and Theo, who had done little baking since culinary arts school, began to experiment with various desserts.

He decided he could make decent gingerbread, some cookies, cheesecake, and one or two cakes. The time needed to do so, however, didn't exist, so he spent a Sunday baking and freezing the results. Normally he never missed Mass, but he did to bake, which made Marlee unhappy and upset his mother.

"Don't work so hard," Liesel told him when she stopped by after church. "Spend more time with Marlee. You're neglecting her."

Theo bristled as he put three cakes into the oven. "Everything I do is for her," he told his mother. "I love her, and I hope to marry her. But I want to have something to offer her—a solid business making money to provide for her and a home, something more than a few rooms above the place."

"Have you told her this? Have you asked her to be your wife?"

He hadn't and wouldn't, not until it was the right time, and told his mother so.

"Ach, *Gott*, there's never a perfect time—not to get married, not to have children. Or find a house. Have you looked at any?"

"A few."

Theo wanted something like the farmhouse, but those properties were out of his reach. He would settle for one of the many vintage houses in town or simpler places like the house where he'd grown up. After his father's death, he and Mutti had moved to the farmhouse with his grandparents.

"Don't wait too long, my son," she said, and kissed him. "I have recipes, if you want them."

"*Danke,*" he replied. "I have Oma's pineapple cake in the oven now."

Marlee arrived around one, bringing two carryout meals from Maybelle's. Theo inhaled the delicious aroma of fried chicken through the containers and grinned.

"You brought lunch," he said. "I was going to stop and make something, but this is better."

"I thought it would be easier," she said. "I missed you at church—so did your family."

"Mutti's already chewed me out. I would have been there if I didn't think this was necessary. Let's eat."

She suggested they eat outside, but Theo shot that idea down, citing the heat. They ate upstairs at his kitchen table, and he had to admit that the change of scenery was welcome. For once, his appetite returned, and he ate the meal, savoring each bite. Afterward, he stretched out on the couch for a power nap, planning to spend no more than ten or fifteen minutes, but Theo fell asleep. By the time he woke, it was almost four.

"You should have woken me up," he said, sitting up and scrubbing his face with both hands.

"You need the rest," Marlee replied with a small smile. "Let's go swimming."

"Swimming? Where?"

She laughed. "The public pool in the park. Come on, summer's almost over, and we've never been swimming."

The last time Theo swam there, he'd been in ninth grade. Spending the remainder of the afternoon among a bunch of splashing kids didn't appeal, and he didn't think he owned a pair of swim trunks. "I'd rather go fishing."

Her expression was priceless, a combination of shock and horror. "I don't want to get that close to the river, Theo."

"Not the river, Little Bear Creek. Jonas and I have fished there for years," Theo told her. "I could use the break. Do you like to fish?"

"I haven't been since I was a kid, but I always liked being around the water," she said. "I don't have any fishing gear, though."

"I have plenty, more than enough for us both. Let's go fishing."

He changed into faded jeans and an old T-shirt, then dug out his rattiest worn-out athletic shoes. With more anticipation than he'd had for anything in weeks, Theo dashed downstairs to the basement and dug out his gear. He loaded the truck, and after a quick stop at a local convenience store that also sold nightcrawlers and bait, they headed for the creek.

On the way, Theo turned on the AM radio to the oldies station and sang along. Happiness surged through him, almost a high, as Marlee scooted across the seat to sit beside him. She sang too.

Once at the creek, he savored the summer heat for the first time, tempered with the shade trees that lined the banks. A light breeze made the leaves dance. The combined smell of the water and the loam were pleasant. Best of all, the fish were biting, and between them, they reeled in a decent number of striped bass. Theo cleared his mind and did not think about money or the pub or anything but the moment and Marlee.

He planned to remain until dark, but at dusk, his cell phone rang.

"Don't answer," Marlee said.

"It's my mother," he replied, and did.

"Are you busy, my son?"

"I'm fishing with Marlee."

"Wunderbar! That is good, Theo. Would you like to come to supper and bring Marlee too?"

"I'm filthy, but sure, we can."

"It's just pot roast and potato dumplings," she said. "Come over, then. We will wait."

Theo ended the call and turned to Marlee. "Are you okay with having supper at my mother's?"

"Sure."

"Then let's wrap up and head over."

He put the fish they'd caught into a cooler. Tomorrow, maybe, he would prepare them for Marlee.

At the farmhouse, he quickly scaled, gutted, and cleaned the fish, then sealed them into plastic bags for transport. Theo left them in the refrigerator and scrubbed in the bathroom adjacent to the kitchen. Then he joined the ladies at the table.

The roast was delicious, a taste from childhood, and Theo savored it. For the second time in one day, he ate with gusto. Although they stayed too late and he ate too much, the evening turned out to be one of the few he'd enjoyed in recent months. The day had been a sweet respite, and he relished it. He told Marlee so when he dropped her off at her apartment around nine-thirty.

"This was the best day I've had in a while," he told her. He ached to take her in his arms and kiss her, but he knew he stunk with sweat and fish and the outdoors. "We didn't go swimming, but thank you."

"It was better than swimming," she said. "Theo, it was awesome. We need more days like this one."

"I agree. Tomorrow I'll cook the fish we caught, just for us."

"I'd like that, but I have meetings till five."

"So, I'll cook a late meal after close if you can wait."

Marlee could, and so after a quick brush of their lips, Theo headed home to shower up and sleep. For once, he rested well and woke refreshed. His specials were *kassler rippchen,* pork loin he had slow smoked out back on Saturday, served with kraut and potato salad, or an English pork pie. In the heat, he tried to keep the menus relatively simple, and both dishes sold out midway through dinner. The pineapple cakes were also popular, and he managed to save a piece for Marlee.

Theo had debated whether to cook the fish they'd caught with a mustard cream sauce or to fry it. He fried the bass until it was crisp, then topped it with bacon to serve with a butter lettuce salad he threw together, unless Marlee wanted a different side dish. She arrived just before he closed at seven, and as soon as he had everything in order in the kitchen, Theo hurried upstairs. He carried both the salad, a special salad dressing made with cream, lemon, and sugar, and the dish with the prepared fish.

As she'd waited, Marlee had set the table, and so he served the meal.

"How was your day?"

Marlee shrugged. "Long. School starts on the twenty-fifth, in eight days. I hope I'm ready."

"You will be," Theo told her. He admired her ability to organize, and he had no doubt she would do well. "I can't believe the summer is almost over."

She frowned. "It went quickly, but I had hoped we'd have more time to do things together. I'll be in class all day once school starts. That plus meetings and grading papers and events will eat up a lot of time."

Theo experienced a moment of regret. He'd thought they would do many things together, but there was always the restaurant to run.

"The tourists will slack down after Labor Day," he told her. "At least until October, then it's Oktoberfest every weekend, and I'll have my tenth anniversary celebration. I haven't decided which weekend I will."

"Your mom said your birthday is in October, too."

She had, and Theo almost wished she hadn't. Traditionally, in Germany, it wasn't proper to mention a birthday until the very day, but he figured Mutti wanted to be sure Marlee knew when it was.

"The twenty-third," he said.

"That's a Saturday this year, I think."

"It is."

"Why don't you have the anniversary celebration that day?"

His first thought was to reject the notion, but Theo considered it. The idea had potential. Although normally he wasn't one to want attention on his birthday, it could enhance the celebration.

"That's not a bad idea," he said. "It could work."

Marlee smiled from across the table. "We could celebrate alone on Sunday."

Without thinking, Theo shook his head. "No, no, that's not a good idea. Mutti will have a cake, probably. During Oktoberfest, I value my Sundays off."

Her bright expression faded, and he wondered why.

"Oh."

During the remainder of the meal, Theo talked about Oktoberfest and his plan this year to offer the same specials for the month, all German.

"It would make menu planning simpler. I would just cook larger batches."

"What would you offer?"

"A mixed wurst plate, bockwurst, knockwurst, and

bratwurst, for one," Theo said. By then, he'd grabbed a notebook to jot down a few of his ideas. "I think also maybe sauerbraten on my birthday, or maybe rouladen. Yes, rouladen, one of my favorites."

"Maybe you could offer free birthday cake that day, too," Marlee said it deadpan, but although he saw no evidence she might be upset, he thought it was a sarcastic remark. "Only the best for the paying customers." Then she finished her last bite of the fish and wiped her mouth with a napkin. "That was delicious, Theo, thank you. I'm going to head home now—I must get up early. Some of the other teachers and I are making a trip to St. Louis for some classroom supplies. We'll probably be gone all day, so if I come here, it will be evening."

His dinner rested uneasy. Somehow, without realizing it, he'd upset her, Theo thought, but had no idea what he might have said or done.

"I didn't know you had planned a trip. I could have taken you."

She laughed. "When? You won't hardly put a toe past the door of this place, Theo. I didn't ask because I figured you'd be too busy, and I wouldn't dare suggest you close early or leave your staff in charge."

Her sharp words kindled his anger. "I spent yesterday with you, and it was wonderful."

"It was, and that just makes all the days we've wasted this summer worse. I'll probably see you Wednesday. I don't have any meetings, but I do want to decorate my classroom. Maybe you can come over and help me."

He took the olive branch she offered and swallowed his ire. "I'd like that, Marlee."

"We can talk about when later," she said. "Thank you for the meal. You're an excellent chef, Theo. I'll take the cake with me for later."

When she stood, so did he. Theo opened his arms, and she stepped into his embrace. He kissed her, his mouth urgent and almost desperate in his desire to prove to her how much she mattered, that he loved her.

Theo walked her downstairs and to her car parked behind the place. He kissed her again and stood, watching as she drove away. She didn't look back, and that somehow made him sad. Theo cleaned up after their meal, spent time in the kitchen making sure all was ready for the next morning, then went to bed, his mind filled with Oktoberfest. After all, he had a business to run, he thought, and Marlee had to understand that.

Chapter Twenty-One

The school year began on a hot, August Wednesday. Although tourists still arrived daily and many came for a meal at Bah Humbug! Theo always felt like summer ended when school started, although he knew that wasn't the case. Labor Day would slow the tourist trade, and the heat would linger into September most years. It wouldn't be fall until the first frost, and the leaves began to change into bold shades for autumn.

Theo had seen less of Marlee than he liked since the fish dinner, but he wasn't sure why, although she'd been tied up with school responsibilities. The day after her trip to the city for supplies, she'd come and shared lunch with him after he closed for the afternoon. Although he'd wanted to hear about the expedition, she said little about it.

"I was talking to Lisa—you know, my landlord's wife," she said over a serving of cottage pie. "The florist."

"Yes."

"She asked me why you don't take an early morning stroll along the river like you used to do, and I told her I had no idea. I didn't even know you did that."

"I do it more in winter and spring," he replied, trying to remember when he last had taken that walk. "It's been so busy."

"I'd love to join you if you wanted to start again. As long as it was early enough, I could do it before school, Theo."

"Sure. As soon as it cools down a little, we will."

Theo meant it, at least in the moment, but Marlee sighed. "Whatever."

After the first day of classes, he didn't see Marlee until Saturday, although they talked on the phone each night. Although he'd planned to start his morning walks again, it didn't happen. By the time the weather turned cooler, it was too dark early in the mornings.

On Saturday nights, he spent time with Marlee. On Sundays, they went to church together, and then he baked. He had become proficient with a few desserts and had begun baking breads too, which were a hit. In his odd moments, he continued planning for the tenth anniversary bash and Oktoberfest.

"What's the festival like, this Oktoberfest?" Marlee asked on one of their rare evenings together. They sat cuddled on her sofa, listening to music. It was the last weekend of September, and outside, a chilly rain fell.

"It's wild and crazy and fun," Theo said. "The whole town comes alive with everything German, every weekend. There are German bands with oompah-pah music, street vendors, a car show, arts and crafts, dancing, historical exhibits and events, especially at the museum, beer gardens, special tastings at the wineries, horse and wagon rides, and more. I think you'll like it, Marlee. I wish I'd had more free time to spend with you during it."

"I wish you did too," she said, and he thought her voice sounded sad. "How's the anniversary party plans coming?"

Theo shrugged. "Good, I suppose. I'm going to attempt to make Black Forest Cakes for the event and offer slices free for my birthday."

The first week of October, in advance of the weekend and the festival, Theo made a trip to St. Louis to buy some supplies for the events. Most of the time, he could get all he needed from his usual suppliers or with a trip to a wholesale club in Jeff, but this time there were things that were easier to find in the city. There was another reason for the trip as well, one he shared with no one except Jonas, who approved.

Theo visited a family-owned jewelry store in downtown St. Louis, the place where Opa had bought a ring for Oma decades earlier. From their vast selection, he chose rings for Marlee, for the day when he would summon up the courage to ask the question. The solitaire engagement ring was fashioned to resemble a blooming rose with a diamond mounted in the center. That ring nestled into the wedding band. Both had fine details with intricate vines and smaller blossoms. The price was double what he'd hoped to pay, but Theo bought it, paying outright for it. Although happy with his purchase, once home, he began to worry about the expense and thought he might wait until he'd replaced the money spent in his savings. He locked the ring away in his office, safe for a future time.

He'd thought he would show it to his mother and grandmother, but didn't. Lately, they'd been more than a little critical of the time—or lack of it—he spent with Marlee. Because of that and Marlee's attitude, Theo made an effort to break away from Bah Humbug! long enough to share some of Oktoberfest with her.

For his tenth anniversary bash, he ordered maroon mums for each table, and spent most of the day receiving congratulations and birthday wishes when he wasn't in the kitchen. Because it was his birthday, he left the restaurant to his staff after five, with a lot of trepidation, and let Marlee take him out to the local steakhouse.

Blevins was there and commented. "Well, if it isn't old Scrooge himself, out on the town. Now that's an amazing sight to see," the man boomed. "Must be the lady paying because we all know what a miserly skinflint Scrooge is. I was beginning to think you'd moved away — never see you out and about anymore."

"Ignore him," Marlee hissed across the table. "Don't ruin the meal."

Theo did as she asked, but it took great restraint.

At his place afterward, they watched one of Theo's favorite movies.

"Happy birthday," she told him as they shared a sweet red Moscato. "How old are you anyway? You never said."

"Thirty-six," he answered. "I'm on my way to being an old man."

"Hardly," she said with a laugh. "So, you opened the place when you were just twenty-six? Tell me about it."

"Growing up, I never thought I'd stay here," he told her. "Jonas was going to join the Navy SEALS, and I was going to travel the world. But, after my dad died during my senior year, I realized I wanted to cook. I'd helped my mom and grandmother in the kitchen for years, so becoming a professional chef seemed like the next step. I went to MU — a commuter student — and earned a degree in business and culinary arts. As you know, I worked for Sarge at his diner while I was in school. Afterward, I worked at a bistro in Jeff for a short time, then this building went on the market. It was a wreck, hadn't been used in years, but I bought it and came home to open my own place."

Theo didn't mention he'd originally planned to move far away from his hometown or that he'd returned because he'd been worried about his grandparents aging and their health issues.

"And you named it Bah Humbug! I've always thought that's funny considering how you feel about the whole Scrooge thing."

Theo laughed. "It was my Opa's idea, first. He suggested calling the place Bah Humbug! I thought it was a joke, really, but then he paid for the sign, and so I decided to use it. At the time, I decided it would be the perfect, if sarcastic, name for the place. Originally it was just going to be a German restaurant, but there were several others here at the time, and with the name, I decided to serve English food too."

"What were you planning to name it?"

"*Gemutlichkeit*," he said, and in response to her blank look, added, "It means good cheer, comfort, good times. But it's a mouthful, and a lot of people wouldn't have known the meaning. My other ideas were Taste of Germany, Wurst Case, and Old World."

"I like Wurst Case," Marlee told him. "But I like Bah Humbug! even more."

"I do, even though it's Scrooge's line. But it gave me a chance to showcase English cuisine, too, for my dad's memory. After all, Scrooge is an old English name."

"Was your dad English?"

"Three generations back. He grew up in St. Louis, not here."

Thinking about the past turned his mood dismal. Birthdays usually bordered on bitter as well, with too many thoughts of what might have been. He said something along that line to Marlee, who stared at him.

"Theo, most people wish they had what you do," she told him. "You have a family you're close to, a business that provides your living while doing something you love and have a talent for doing, and you live in a picturesque, wonderful town. Anything you think you've missed wouldn't be worth losing all of that, would it?"

"I don't know." Even to his own ears, he sounded peevish. "I always wanted to travel, to see more of the world than this little corner. I've never made it to England or even Germany. I went to New York once but never to Los Angeles. I love the ocean, and I've been to the beach just a few times. I've only been to the Rockies once, and that's when I was ten years old."

"Theo Scrooge! I don't know what's gotten into you, but you still have time to go those places if you really want to go, and you don't appreciate what you have. Think about all the people who work a nine to five job or labor in a factory and struggle to make ends meet." Her voice became sharp as she spoke. "You've never been alone, have you? It sucks. Yeah, I have my brothers, but I wish my parents were still alive. Or my grandparents, three of which I didn't know well. I teach school and love it, but I answer to a principal, even to a school board."

Her unexpected outrage surprised Theo. He hadn't wanted to make her angry, just to share his thoughts.

"Marlee, I'm sorry — "

"You should be," she told him.

She stood up and left the room, returning with two wrapped packages. The bright birthday paper filled him with remorse — he hadn't known she had gifts for him.

"Happy birthday, Theo," Marlee said, and thrust the packages into his hands. "I should have bought something different, I guess. I'm afraid these may just fuel your resentment."

"Don't be mad," he said, his voice soft. "Thank you. No one else has given me presents yet."

"Don't be such a spoilsport. I never dreamed you were so unhappy."

"I'm not."

She lifted her eyebrows and shook her head. "Go ahead, open them."

There were two books, both travel books about Germany. As he flipped through the pages, both were filled with color photographs and information that intrigued him. "*Danke,*" he said. "These are marvelous. I've always wanted to go there. Thank you, Marlee."

Her expression remained somber. "I'd thought that maybe someday we could.... Oh, nevermind. I can't get you to go with me anywhere in Missouri, let alone Europe. Well, happy birthday anyway, Theo."

He reached for her, and for the first time, she pulled away.

"It's late. You probably have baking to do tomorrow anyway."

"It will wait," he said. "We'll go to church, then out to the farmhouse for a birthday dinner, then I may bake. I don't have to, though, Marlee."

He did, though, if he wanted desserts to serve on Monday. The other option was to buy from the bakery, but he hated to spend the money.

She rubbed her forehead. "I have a headache, and I'm going to bed. I'll see you in the morning if you're going to church. If not, call me, and I'll drive myself there."

"Marlee, *liebling,* I'll pick you up in the morning. I'm sorry you don't feel well."

Theo leaned down for a kiss, and this time, she let him within her space. His lips lingered on hers, and she kissed him back.

"I love you," he said.

Marlee made no move to walk him to the door, just stared at him with forlorn eyes. "I love you too, and happy birthday."

At his place, he drank some wine to unwind but still couldn't sleep. Marlee's sharp words had hurt—and he didn't think he deserved them. He'd been sharing, after all, and thought that's what she wanted him to do. Theo realized, though, he'd managed to hurt her, and that hadn't been his intention. He picked up the books with an appreciation for the care she'd taken to select them. Her remark about someday that she didn't finish bothered him. If she thought they could one day visit Germany together, maybe they could, and he would love it, although he doubted he could leave his business long enough to manage a trip.

And, though he'd squelched his anger, Blevins's words returned to haunt him. His insinuation that he wanted Marlee for her money, to buy dinner, rankled, but then Theo realized he'd never thanked her for the meal. As late as it was, he dialed her cell but reached voice mail.

Theo slept little and not that well. He woke to cloudy skies and a chill rain. Although Marlee accompanied him to church, she said little, and he thought she seemed paler than usual. His mother and grandmother opted not to come because of the weather, and as soon as Mass ended, Marlee pulled Theo aside.

"What's wrong?" he said.

"I still have a headache," she said. "I ache all over, and I think I may be coming down with the flu. I just don't feel very well, and I wouldn't want you or anyone, especially your grandmother, to catch it from me. I've probably already exposed you, and I'm sorry. I hope you don't get sick. I need to go home, Theo."

He put his hand across her forehead and frowned at the heat of her skin. "You're too warm," he said. "I'll get you home. Whatever you need, I can go get it for you."

She asked for some juice, some over the counter medication, and a box of tissues. Theo brought it all along with some soup he had frozen earlier.

"I'll stay if you need me to," he told her. By then, she'd changed into her pajamas and had crawled into bed.

Marlee shook her head. "It would be nice, but no, go celebrate your birthday and have dinner. I'll call you later, but don't call me in case I'm asleep."

The warm welcome at the farmhouse was short-lived as

soon as he explained Marlee's absence. Liesel packed a meal to go with Theo's favorites — beef rouladen stuffed with mushrooms and onions, spätzle, and green beans cooked with ham. She also cut several generous pieces of the apple strudel she'd made and sent him home.

"You shouldn't have come, Theo," his mother scolded. "Oma can't afford to be sick. I hope Marlee is well soon and that you don't get it."

He went home, after making apologies, with his gift — a new watch — and the food. After he ate, he had little else to do, so he baked gingerbreads and tried his hand at baking a rustic rye bread. If it turned out well enough, he thought, he'd serve it.

Marlee, who called late in the evening, missed the entire week of school, but refused to let Theo visit in case he became ill. On Wednesday, he woke with a pounding headache, his body as sore as if he'd gone twelve rounds in the boxing ring.

"I should close," he told his mother in a phone call. "I can't afford to, though."

"You can't afford to infect half the town, either."

"I won't," he told her. "I wouldn't wish this on anyone."

On Friday, most of his staff called in — either sick or afraid they would be. Theo had to close until Monday. Half the town had it — the schools had closed for two days. Theo, who for once would have welcomed a little coddling and some loving care, found himself alone. He'd never been sick before without someone, usually his mom, to provide some support. His mother dropped off an onion pie with the idea it would help eradicate the virus, and he crept downstairs to retrieve it from the back door.

On Saturday afternoon, Marlee came over, shaky but recovered. Theo was still in bed, but she made him rise and take a shower and remade his bed with fresh sheets. She prepared hot tea for him, and warmed up some of the onion pie.

"I'm glad you're here," he told her. "It's been lonely. Do you feel better?"

"Much. I'm just a little weak and so tired. Once the fever breaks, you'll improve."

"*Ach Gott, mir is schlect,*" he moaned.

Her capable, caring hands tucked pillows behind his head. "Poor Theo. I wish I could have been here sooner to take care of you."

"Me, too."

"Your soup was very good, though. Tomorrow I thought I'd bake snickerdoodles for the restaurant. Are you opening on Monday?"

"I've got to, losing too much money now."

She felt his face for fever. "How many of your staff are sick too?"

"Half of them, I think."

"Where's Amber? She's usually reliable."

Theo closed his eyes for a moment. "She's living in the dorms at MU," he said. "She'll work over the semester break, but not now."

Marlee stroked his cheek. "You probably should keep the place closed until you're a hundred percent, Theo."

He shook his head. "Can't."

"You're stubborn."

"I'm German."

"Half German," she said. "Although I do believe the English are just as pig-headed. Just don't be mercenary—your health is important."

Lying there, feeling more lifeless than lively, Theo still found the energy to protest. "It's just the flu."

"Yeah, yeah, yeah. People die of 'just the flu.'"

"I won't."

She kissed his forehead. "No, it might cost you money. I'm

going to go and let you sleep, but I'll be here tomorrow to bake cookies if that's all right."

"It's more than all right," he said. "I appreciate it. I do love you, Marlee."

"I know, and I love you. Get some more rest. I'll be back in the morning. If you need anything, call me."

By Sunday morning, his fever had gone, and he crept downstairs to watch Marlee bake cookies. He also decided to finish out the month with the same specials but opened on schedule Monday with a short crew. He might have returned to full strength quicker if he hadn't worked so hard before he had recovered, but it was mid-November before he regained his health.

Marlee returned to the classroom, and they saw far less of each other than he would like.

Thanksgiving loomed, but he had little interest in it. Marlee had announced that she would spend the holiday in St. Joe with her brothers. Theo offered to cook the meal for his immediate family at Bah Humbug! and did—roast goose with chestnut stuffing, dumplings, red cabbage, and the rye bread he'd almost perfected. For dessert, he made a German-style pumpkin pie, one richer in spices but without evaporated milk, which made it more of a custard filling.

His mother, grandmother, Thomas's family, and Hanna joined him for the meal. They all praised it, but Theo missed Marlee. They talked on the phone, but it wasn't the same.

The ring he'd bought her remained locked in the safe, and the question he'd meant to ask months ago remained unasked.

Christmas season loomed large, his least favorite of the year, and Theo tried not to think about it, to ignore the Scrooge remarks that came his way, and hope that he'd end the year well in the black, not red.

Chapter Twenty-Two

In December, the town transformed into a magical place, with holiday lights and Old World style decorations. There was a European style street market with vendors and horse drawn carriage rides. Theo began serving mulled wine and a variety of Christmas cookies, most of which his mother baked for him. Marlee had been enchanted by the holiday scene, and although she'd asked him to spend time with her, Theo had begged off, busy with the restaurant.

School would dismiss for the winter break the Wednesday before Christmas, and Theo had promised Marlee that he would deliver the gingerbread cut-out cookies she'd made with his mom to school, then stay for the history club party. Although he couldn't bring wine to the high school, he had offered to bring some of the grape juice that the family winery also bottled.

"That would be wonderful," Marlee had told him. "I'll pick up some plastic flutes or something."

He'd written it in his seldom used planner and on the dry-erase board in his office so he wouldn't forget. The cookies, each one hand-iced and decorated, were in two plastic cake carriers on his desk.

"The party is at one-thirty," Marlee told him. "School dismisses at one—it's a half-day. You'll bring the cookies and stay for the party, right?"

"Of course," Theo said.

But on Wednesday morning, the weather forecast distracted him, calling for an Artic blast of cold air that would deliver sub-zero temperatures, with wind chills dropping as low as twenty-five and thirty-five below zero, ice, then a sizeable amount of snow. Since it was already cold, he decided to change the day's specials to German wedding soup and Scotch broth, so Theo hit the ground running with his soup making. He pulled several trays of black bread from the freezer to thaw as well. The recipe was one he'd added after he mastered baking rye bread.

"It's going to be a white Christmas," Autumn, home for semester break, told him with a big smile when she arrived. "Isn't it wonderful?"

Theo thought it was anything but, and said so.

"Oh, come on," she said with a laugh. "Don't be a Scrooge. I mean, shut the door. You decorated for Christmas this year. I 've never seen that before."

The decorations were all Marlee's, and remained a sore point for Theo. "That was Marlee's idea, not mine," he said.

On the Sunday after Thanksgiving, Marlee had come over, unpacked her multiple boxes of decorations, and transformed Bah Humbug! into a Victorian Christmas wonderland. Plaid clad carolers with wide bonnets and muttonchop whiskers were captured forever in song. Wreaths festooned with red ribbons hung on the front door and entrance to the kitchen. A tall Douglas fir stood in one corner—he'd had to remove a table to make room—decorated in Victorian style with bead garlands, lace, flowers, feathered, and a few handblown German antique ornaments. Marlee had bought those, but the angel that topped the tree had been in her family for two generations. She'd even hung a sprig of mistletoe, which Theo had enjoyed to full advantage with Marlee. Unlit white candles were also on the tree, but he would never light them due to the fire risk. At home, his mother would light similar candles briefly on Christmas Eve.

Each table had a red candle inside a glass hurricane lamp with a ring of artificial holly. Marlee had wanted to use real holly with berries until Theo told her it was poisonous, not something he wanted around the food he served.

Unlike the disastrous time Theresa Duncan had decorated Bah Humbug!, the overall result had festive appeal, even for Theo, although he hated to admit it. Customers liked it, and to keep the peace, Theo allowed the decorations to remain. He even did his best to keep his negative comments to a minimum.

Temperatures hovered around freezing until almost noon, when they plunged into the low twenties, and a freezing rain began to fall. People rushed out to buy milk, bread, and other groceries, and from the number who filled his tables, wanted a hot meal at lunchtime. Theo was stunned to learn they had people waiting for a table and hustled to fill orders, keeping one eye on the clock.

It was after one-thirty when the rush slacked off, and, aware he was running late, Theo shucked his apron and grabbed the cookies. He had to stop long enough to scrape his windshield and rear window on the truck, and by the time he entered the high school, it was after two. He stopped to sign in at the office, then made his way as quickly as possible to Marlee's classroom.

"I'm here," he announced as he came through the door. Ten or twelve students were in the room, a couple seated on a table, legs dangling and feet swinging.

Marlee scowled, then tried to hide it with a smile. "You're late," she said. "What happened?"

"The lunch rush was crazy," he said. "There was freezing

rain coming down, and I had to scrape the windshield before I could come."

Her expression lightened a little. "Is it slick?"

"A little in places, nothing too bad," he said. "But I don't like the forecast—bitter, sub-zero temperatures and snow."

"Maybe we'll have a white Christmas," she said with a grin.

Theo shook his head and put the cookie containers on her desk. "I hope not," he replied. "I'll be glad when it's just January, and things go back to normal."

Theo had forgotten some of her students were present. One boy, perched on top of a desk, eating chips from a bag, snickered. "Oh, right," he said with a chortle. "Peeps, remember Ms. Dupree is dating Scrooge."

All the kids laughed, and Theo fumed. He expected Marlee would call them down, but after a moment, she laughed too.

"For those who haven't met my guy, this is Theo Scrooge, and he owns Bah Humbug!"

"Hi, Scrooge. Do you hate Christmas?" one of the girls asked, a candy cane in her mouth.

"Seen any ghosts yet?" another student quipped.

Not for the first time, Theo regretted naming his place Bah Humbug!, even though most of the time, he liked Opa's suggestion. But it evoked Scrooge, and sometimes—no, most of the time—he resented that.

Theo ignored them. Marlee opened one of the cookie containers and started handing them out. She gave him a gingerbread boy wearing a red and white Santa hat.

"Merry Christmas," she said, with more than a little sharp edge to her voice.

"*Frohliche Weinachten*," he returned. Theo wanted to kiss her to erase the sting of her words. He knew all too well she had issues with his dislike of all things Scrooge and Dickens, but her tone shocked him. She sounded furious.

"Whatever." Marlee turned away from him and pulled out a stack of disposable cups. "Who wants some grape juice?"

Theo nibbled at a gingerbread cookie and drank a little juice. The kids played games and then started singing Christmas carols. Marlee joined in, but Theo didn't, which earned him yet another sharp sideways stare. By just after three-thirty, he'd had enough. Although present, he had no part in the festivities. He'd imagined participating, but Marlee's mood kept him from trying, and it wasn't his thing, anyway.

"I need to go," he told her at four. The days he'd missed when he had the flu had served to increase his financial worries. "I have to get things ready for the evening rush. Are you coming by?"

She shook her head. "No, Theo, not tonight. I have things I need to do, too. I'll probably see you tomorrow."

"Probably?" He couldn't believe she wasn't joining him, or that she wouldn't confirm tomorrow. Since she'd moved to town, they'd seen each other every day, even on the hectic, crazy ones. But since school started, it had been less and less.

"Maybe," she said with a shrug of her shoulders. "Don't worry, I know exactly where to find you."

Her indifference made him sad, but he wouldn't start a scene in front of her students, who watched with avid interest. All they needed was popcorn, he thought, to call the tension between them entertainment. "Walk me out?"

Theo craved a few moments alone with her and figured he could get a kiss, but Marlee sighed, shaking her head.

"I really can't leave the kids," she told him. "I'll see you, probably tomorrow. There's no school, so I'll have all day."

"They're teenagers, not toddlers," Theo replied, stung into speaking.

Marlee said nothing, just pursed her lips together tight.

He couldn't think of anything more to say that wouldn't make things more tense, so he left.

At Bah Humbug! he made sure enough soup remained for the evening meal. He thawed a few more loaves of black bread. Fewer customers came to dine because the temperatures continued dropping, and the wind kicked up, so it felt even colder.

More sleet mixed with light snow fell, and Theo closed early to give his staff more time to get home over the deteriorating roads. He waited until all customers had finished their meals and no one else came in. He locked the door at seven-thirty, then opened it for Jonas a few minutes later.

"Everything all right?" he asked. "You closed early."

"It's the weather. Everybody's going home to hunker down," Theo told him. "All the customers were finished, so I decided to shut down. Are you on duty, or do you have time to play a little chess?"

"I'm on duty, but I'll eat if you have anything left. Where's Marlee?"

"There's plenty of soup, either German wedding soup or Scotch broth. It was the last day of school, and she said she was heading home."

"Wedding soup sounds good," Jonas replied, then, in a more serious tone, asked, "Did you two have a fight?"

Theo spread his hands wide. "I didn't think so, but she acted mad when I took cookies over to her classroom today. I was a little late, but it couldn't be helped. We were busy."

"True. But Theo, I've noticed she's not around as much."

"She's got school. It's not like last summer." He handed his friend a bowl of soup and sat down across from him at a table.

Jonas blew on a spoonful, then tasted it. "That's good. You know, I don't remember you having a lot of time for her last summer, either. Theo, I'm not trying to make trouble. You know

I'm your friend."

"You're like my brother."

The sheriff nodded. "True, and that's why I'm saying this. I don't think Marlee's happy these days. You seem preoccupied and distant. I've watched her here, seen her smile fade when you pass by her without speaking or make her wait before you have time for her."

Stung by the unexpected chastising, Theo said. "I love her. You know that, and so does she."

"I'm not so sure she feels very loved these days," Jonas said. "Shannon's noticed that Marlee seems sad. She also heard that Marlee's talking about not renewing her teaching contract at the end of the year."

That was unwelcome news to Theo. "Why not?"

"I have no idea. It's just what she heard. I've noticed Marlee's not here as much, and I know you've been focused on this place."

"I have to be, or I don't make a living," Theo replied. "Everything hinges on being successful here. I plan to ask Marlee to marry me soon, and I'd like to think I can provide for her."

Jonas lifted an eyebrow. "You haven't asked her? I thought you bought the ring in October."

Theo had. He had spent hours shopping and chose a bridal set with a floral motif.

"I did."

"And you haven't given it to her yet?"

"No."

"Why not?"

Theo shrugged. He lacked a decent answer. For one, the ring, which he'd paid for at purchase, cost far more than he'd expected, and he'd had some notion about recouping the money before he asked Marlee to marry him.

"I just haven't gotten around to it yet. I wanted the moment to be the right one, something special."

Jonas snorted. "This is what I'm talking about, Theo. You bought the rings, but you haven't asked her the question because you're so wrapped up in this place you don't think about anything else."

"That's not true!" Anger harshened Theo's tone.

"Maybe not, but you somehow started putting Bah Humbug! first, and that's not good," Jonas said. "I don't know if you've noticed, but Blevins and his friends are having a field day with it, saying that, after all, you are a Scrooge, so why wouldn't you be all about the money."

Furious now, Theo came to his feet. "That's not me, and it never has been."

"I'm just pointing out what I've noticed and what's being said, my friend. I don't want you to lose your lady over being mercenary."

Fear tinged his anger now, and Theo lashed out. "I think you'd better go before things are said that I can't forget," he said. For now, he had his temper under control, but Theo could feel it rising and knew he would blow up soon.

Jonas rose and extended his hand. "Thank you for the soup," he said. "No hard feelings?"

They shook hands, and Theo replied, "None, Jonas. Be careful out there."

Then he spent another hour working on the books and paying some bills.

Afterward, Theo did a last check of his place, then turned out the lights before heading upstairs. He poured a glass of wine to relax, but it didn't help. His mind whirled with the day's events, with Marlee's unexpected anger at school, and at the things Jonas had said. He reflected back over recent months but didn't believe it. Surely Marlee wasn't considering leaving. It had to be gossip, he thought, and anything Blevins mouthed wasn't reliable.

He reached for the phone to call Marlee, but she didn't answer. His call went straight to voice mail, and he left a message, now more than a little uneasy, although Theo told himself she must already be asleep.

"Hey, *liebling,* I love you. Good night and stay warm. I'll see you tomorrow."

Theo thought he'd go to bed early, but sleep proved elusive, and instead, he stared out the window, watching the snow fall and wondering just when everything in his life had become so difficult.

He came up with no answers, and fell asleep just a few hours before he would have to rise, stomach aching and mind uneasy. But everything would resolve when he saw Marlee. It had to, he thought — it must.

Chapter Twenty-Three

Although it had snowed and sleeted through the night, little accumulated, but it was bitter cold. Theo woke and remembered the things that had disturbed him. Determined to make this a better day, he woke, showered, and drank a cup of coffee before heading downstairs. It was early, not quite six, but he was surprised that Marlee hadn't called him back.

He made more coffee, ate a bit of breakfast, then phoned her. This time, she answered. "Good morning, Theo."

Taking heart since she didn't sound angry, he said, "Morning. It's very cold, but are you coming?"

"I probably will later," she said. "Right now, I'm snuggled in bed, reading. What are you serving?"

"Cabbage rolls, if I can get down to the store to buy some fresh cabbage, and Cornish pasties for the English," he said. "I don't have a dessert yet, but I'll pull something together, maybe a trifle."

"That sounds good. There's only three more days until Christmas. Your mom invited me, but I wasn't sure if it's at the farmhouse or at Bah Humbug!"

"I think at the farmhouse," Theo said. He realized he didn't know, and that perhaps Jonas had a valid point that he wasn't paying full attention. "We did Thanksgiving here, though, because I cooked. I need to call her and find out."

"What does your family eat for Christmas dinner? I know you had goose at Thanksgiving, so will it be turkey or ham or what?"

"Probably *Schweinebraten*," he said. "German pork roast with potato dumplings, noodles, maybe red cabbage, a stollen or *Lebkuchen* for dessert. It depends on how many are coming to dinner. Sometimes there's *rouladen* too, and apple sausage stuffing."

Theo had no idea what his mother planned, if she would cook or if she might want him to do the honors. *I need to find out, also see if she's bought the food or not. If not, I need to get busy.*

"That all sounds good."

He savored the sound of her voice and stayed on the phone, although he should have already been on the way to buy cabbage.

"On Christmas Eve, we always eat supper together, then go to Midnight Mass. This year that will be weather permitting with the forecast, especially since the church is on the highest hill in town. You're invited for that too."

She yawned. "Okay. I'll see you later, Theo. Love you."

"I love you too."

He headed down to the market, which had just opened, and bought cabbage. Then he returned and got busy. By mid-morning, he had the pasties made and ready for the oven and the cabbage rolls underway.

Theo put together trifle using pre-made angel food cake, whipped cream, and strawberries from the freezer. Normally he avoided using anything he hadn't made, or that wasn't from scratch, but he figured it wouldn't hurt, just once.

A few diners braved the cold, but the dining room was far from full. Between the weather and the upcoming holiday, Theo wasn't surprised, and figured he'd freeze whatever he had left to use at another time. Autumn arrived to serve, but she was the only one, but between them, they managed.

Marlee arrived at noon, coming in through the back, dressed for winter in jeans, boots, and a plaid flannel shirt. She wore a coat with a hood but shucked it in his office. Theo was plating two orders when she came from behind and put icy hands on his cheeks.

"Guess who?" she said with a giggle.

Theo turned around and swept her into his arms. He kissed her until she squealed for breath, then he kissed her again. "It's good to see you, Marlee."

She grinned at him. "You're in a wonderful mood. I like it."

"Of course, I am — you're here. Are you hungry? We're not busy, so tell me what you'd like, and I'll take a break with you."

Marlee chose one of the pasties, and so Theo ate one too, but he split a cabbage roll between them so she could taste it. As they ate at his table near the kitchen, he said, "I apologize for being late yesterday. I didn't intend to be."

She dismissed his apology with a wave of one hand. "It's all past. I shouldn't have let the kids keep on with their Scrooge talk, either. Since you're not busy, do you think you could close a little early?"

"Why?"

"I'd like to run up to Jefferson City and do a little last minute Christmas shopping at the mall," Marlee told him. "It would be fun, and we haven't done anything together in weeks."

"It's too cold," he said. "Plus, there's snow coming."

"You have a heater in your truck, don't you? And more snow's not predicted until tonight, is it? Let's do it! Maybe we could even catch a movie while we're there."

Her smile sparkled, and Theo wanted to agree, but he didn't see how he could. With Christmas falling on Saturday, he had already planned to be closed on Friday and Monday. That schedule would repeat in a week for New Year's, and he wanted to get the highest profit margin possible for the year.

"We'll do it next week on New Year's Eve."

Marlee's happy face faded. "I can't go Christmas shopping next week," she said. "So, that's a no?"

"It is. If business stays slow, though, I might close early, and we could watch a movie upstairs or at your place."

Theo expected her to be pleased, but she frowned. "I don't want to watch a movie or stay in town, Theo. I want to do something different, get out of here for a few hours, and shop."

He tried to salvage the conversation. "What about shopping local? We've got some excellent small shops here in town. I don't know what you're looking for, but you can probably find some things here."

She tossed her silverware on top of her plate, even though she hadn't finished the pastie. "I'll see you later, Theo," she said, and reached for her coat.

"Where are you going?"

Her lips were pressed in a tight line, and her eyes were hard as she glared at him. "I'm going shopping, Theo, with or without you. I'm going to live a little, have some fun, see some different scenery."

Her wrath upset him. "If you can wait till all the customers are gone, maybe I can go after all."

Marlee shook her head. "Don't bother, Theo. I'm sure you have some cooking to do, or accounting, or something that revolves around this place."

He made a desperate attempt to explain. "It's not that I don't want to go, Marlee. It's just that I have responsibilities here.

I'd love to go."

In his heart, Theo knew he wouldn't enjoy the trip. He would like the movie, sure, but he wasn't a mall fan, and he loathed walking up and down, stopping in one store after another. But he'd do it for her. His mistake was failing to realize how much she'd wanted the outing.

"Never mind. It's too late, Theo," she said. "But think about this. When's the last time we actually went somewhere besides church on Sunday and did something besides hanging out at your place or my apartment? I'm going now. I'll see you later."

Theo held her coat while she slipped into it. "Don't go off mad, Marlee. I could close tomorrow — we could go then."

"No. I have plans for tomorrow. Just think about what I said."

She had made up her mind, so he yielded. "Be careful. Highway 94 is a two-lane with a lot of curves."

Marlee turned around to face him. "I will," she said.

"Will you call me when you get back, so I don't worry?"

Her expression softened a fraction, and she sighed. "All right, I will." She stepped forward and brushed his lips in a quick kiss, then touched one hand to his cheek in a brief caress. "I love you, Theo."

"I love you too."

Her mouth twisted into a knot, and he thought he saw a glimmer of tears in her eyes. Marlee didn't respond as she turned and headed for the back door. He watched her go, sad and frustrated. Maybe, he thought, Jonas had a point after all.

I should have gone with her without question, been spontaneous and fun.

The reality, though, was that he couldn't just walk away from the restaurant. Autumn was the only employee present, and she'd go home after lunch, and with any luck, Constance would come in. He regretted his reluctance to go, but since he couldn't change it, Theo plodded through the rest of his day.

He planned a simple menu for Thursday and called his mom to ask about Christmas.

"Mutti, so who's cooking for Christmas, me or you?" he asked.

"Theo, we decided we both would," Liesel replied. "I thought you were coming out on Christmas Eve with Marlee, and you'd both stay the night. If the snow misses, we'll all go to Midnight Mass, but if the roads are slick, we'll stay here."

He didn't remember discussing any of it, but said, "Yes, that works. What's the menu?"

"*Schweinebraten* with noodles and stuffing, red cabbage, bread, and the desserts," she said. "Marlee said she'd make a turkey breast too and bake some kind of cake. Theo, *bist du in Ordnung?*"

"*Ja*, I'm okay."

"*Bist du krank? Bist du verrückt?* "

"*Nein.*"

"That's good, then," she said in a dry tone. "I just wondered. Oma's going to bake *Milchbrötchen.*"

"That's good. How is she doing?"

Since her illness in the early summer, his grandmother's recovery had been slow but steady. For the first time, she'd had to admit she was aging and did less, with his mom's blessing.

"Very well, thanks for asking," Liesel replied in the same dry tone she'd been using throughout the conversation. "I have all the food for the dinner, I believe. And your cousin Thomas brought over some wine. All you'll need to do is show up and help cook, if you will."

"Of course, I will." Theo's emotions were more than a little riled. *It must be everyone throw down on Theo day.* "I'm looking forward to it."

Liesel made a wordless sound. "I hope so, my son. I know how you are about Christmas. I remember when you loved it."

He had once, but preferred not to remember it. The holiday had been tainted by all the Scrooge jokes, and Theo never could forget his dad had died in December. Although his death happened earlier in the month, it still cast a shadow over the celebration that year. Theo, at eighteen, would have preferred to forget all the festivities, but his mother had insisted that they had to keep Christmas, so they hadn't skimped on any of the traditions.

"That was a long time ago," Theo said. "I was just a kid."

"Christmas is for all ages," she replied. "But you lost the joy of it, and that has always made me sad."

That revelation startled him. "Don't be sad because of how I feel, Mutti."

There was a pause in the conversation, and then she said, "Do you remember your father?"

Blindsided by the unexpected question, he said, "*Jawohl,* you know I do."

"Sometimes I've wondered. Your *Vati* liked Christmas so much. He would laugh and play, eat and drink too much, but he had fun every minute. He never got upset when people said Scrooge. You don't think some teased him about it too?"

Theo hadn't. A sharp pain in his belly almost doubled him over, almost as if he'd been punched there. *Gas pains from the cabbage rolls,* he told himself, *just gas.* No way could it be an emotional gut reaction.

"No, Mama. But I remember him, and I recall very well how he died not long before Christmas. I never understood how you could celebrate that year."

"Ah, Theo, how could I not?" Liesel said in a soft tone. She sounded as if she might start crying. "I'll let you go now. I know you're busy. Just bring Marlee and *das Geschenke* on Friday, and you will stay, won't you?"

"I will," his voice came out in a croak. "I'll talk to you later."

Temperatures continued dropping through the day, and by early evening hovered just above zero. The wind kicked up and blew, rattling against the windows. Wind chills were predicted to be well below zero during the night. Theo closed at six because the few hardy souls who'd come out for dinner had eaten and gone home to stay warm.

Theo opened a bottle of a sweet white Riesling and drank it, one glass at a time, as he went over his accounts. The early closings cut some of his profit margin, but overall, he was in the black and had no real reason to worry. Still, he did, though, and he still had an occasional pain in his belly. The wine, he thought, would help. Somewhere in the first book of Timothy, he thought Paul had written a few lines, something about taking a little wine for thy stomach's sake.

He'd drunk half the bottle when he heard someone enter the back door, which he hadn't yet locked.

"*Wer ist da?*" he called out. "Jonas, is that you?"

Marlee stepped through his office door. "It's me, Theo. I'm back."

"I'm glad. Did you enjoy your shopping expedition?"

She shook her head. "No, not really. It was a drag alone. And I wanted to apologize. I know I was a little bitchy earlier, and I didn't mean to be."

"I'm sorry I disappointed you, Marlee."

Marlee sat down in the only other chair in the room. "I would say it's okay, but it's not. It's happened before, but this is the first time you realized it, so maybe that's a start. I came by instead of calling because I have something for you. It's not a Christmas gift, not really. And I have something to say that would be even harder to say on the phone."

"What's wrong?"

Her subdued manner frightened him. He'd never seen her so quiet. She spoke in crisp, even tones without much emotion.

She sighed and put her face in her hands for a moment. When she took them away, tears tracked down her cheeks. "Everything, Theo."

"I don't understand. Tell me what's the matter."

Marlee reached out to take his hands in hers, but the gesture didn't comfort him at all.

"This is hard, so bear with me, please. You've changed, Theo, and not for the better. When I first met you, when you dived into the river and saved my life without thinking, that was unselfish and brave. I started to fall in love with you that night. Then afterward, we had such good times, and you made me feel so special, so loved."

"I love you, Marlee, so much."

She raised one hand in a stop gesture. "Just listen to me, Theo. We met, and then all spring we talked on the phone, and when I was here, it was wonderful. I made the commitment to move here, which you'll remember I had planned before I even knew you. I moved here, and it was good. It got so crazy at first because you were shorthanded here, but I enjoyed helping you, working with you side by side. But then everything started to change. Your grandmother got so sick, Hanna came, and then that storm caused all the damage. And somewhere through all that, your focus shifted from me and your family to how much money you were losing or making."

Marlee drew a deep breath. "I thought the summer would be so wonderful, that we'd do things together and have fun. But you were always working, always griping about money and profit and this place. If I didn't see you here, I hardly saw you. We didn't go out to eat or to visit wineries except once, or make more than our one special day trip to St. Louis, or have picnics at

Starkenberg or anywhere else. We went to Jeff City, what, twice? We ate here, I came up to your apartment, or you came over to mine. We watched movies or listened to music. Sometimes you were so tired, you fell asleep. I've been so lonely, Theo. In the middle of a relationship, I'm lonely, and that's not good."

The tears streamed down her cheeks as she spoke, and matching tears burned in Theo's eyes. "Why didn't you tell me? If you'd said something…."

Her smile was bittersweet, a brief flash of sun during a heavy rain. "I did, Theo, or I tried. You didn't listen. And I shouldn't have to tell you."

She pulled a paperback book from her purse and laid it on his desk, a copy of *A Christmas Carol*.

"I think this is part of the problem, Theo. You take it so seriously when anyone mentions Scrooge or compares you to him. You get angry, unreasonably so. And it's gone so far that you have issues with Christmas. I've tried to understand, and I just can't."

The book lay between them like a coiled rattlesnake, volatile and dangerous.

"Why are you doing this?" he asked, his voice breaking as his belly pain increased.

"I'm trying to save what we have, what we *had* before it's too late," she told him as she grasped his hands in hers. "I do love you, Theo, more than you can imagine, but something has to change, or we won't make it. I've even thought about not renewing my teaching contract for next year, but I don't want to give up yet. I'm doing this because the Theo I've seen in the last few months is more like Ebenezer Scrooge than you could imagine. Not Scrooge after he learned hard lessons and changed, but the mean, miserly man no one liked. The story isn't only about that. It's a story about redemption and love, about second chances and happiness. I know you haven't read it, Theo, because you told me so—bragged about it. For the sake of our love, for the chance we can still have a future, please read it, or at least watch one of the movies or something. Then maybe you'll understand, and we can move forward. I know you won't want to, but please do it for me."

Marlee let go of his hands and pushed back the chair. "It's not a long book, Theo. When you finish it, if you have anything to say, call me or come over. I'm hoping you can read it before Christmas. I'd like to have a happy holiday with your family at the farmhouse."

He noticed she'd never taken off her coat, and she pulled her purse back onto her shoulder.

"Are you leaving?"

She nodded. "I am, Theo."

A cramp knifed through his guts, and he moaned, then pressed his belly with one hand.

Marlee frowned. "Are you all right?"

"My stomach's giving me grief," he said. "It'll pass."

She walked around the desk and bent down to kiss him, a brief gesture. Then, without anything else to say, she left.

Theo sat still. He listened as her footsteps led her to the door, heard it close behind her, then he put his head down on the desk and wept in a way he hadn't since he was a child. He loved her, really loved her, and it was as if she'd just ended their relationship. *She didn't, though, not yet—she gave me a chance, one chance.*

After a long time and another glass of wine, he calmed. His brain began to process all she had said. If there was still a chance, he had to take it. Theo picked up the book, handling it with care as if it were a stick of dynamite that might explode in his hands. And then he opened it and began to read.

Chapter Twenty-Four

At first, he hated every word and wanted to mock the Victorian prose, but Theo pressed onward and kept reading. He developed a headache, but he read until he began to nod off to sleep. Then, Theo carried the book upstairs and went to bed. First, however, he put a note on Bah Humbug's door to say they would be closed on December 23, 24, 25, and 26. He woke early and made coffee, then began reading again. Theo failed to check the weather forecast or pay any attention to anything but Scrooge's story. He didn't realize it had begun snowing during the night and that heavy snow continued to fall. He finished it by noon, and when he did, Theo sat and pondered the story. Marlee had been correct, he mused—it wasn't at all the tale he'd thought it to be. And after Theo read it, he decided he had to watch the movie. Theo searched until he found a version playing on one of the streaming services he had and watched it. Now familiar with the story, he shed a few tears, and his love for Marlee swelled his heart until he thought it might burst. She had risked everything to get Theo to understand. After the movie, he showered and dressed. Theo phoned Marlee, eager to hear her voice, but the call went to voice mail. He tried again without any luck, so he decided he'd go to her apartment. Theo picked up his keys and wallet, stuck the box with the engagement ring into his front pocket, then dressed in winter gear. It wasn't until he opened the door to head outside that he realized it had been snowing and that it was already deep. Although it wasn't quite four o'clock, it was nearly dark due to the low, heavy gray clouds. Frigid air caused him to shiver despite the coat, hat, and heavy clothes he wore.

Theo started across the back lot, and his feet slid. A thin sheet of ice lay under the snow, making walking or driving treacherous. He almost turned around to go back inside, but his desire to share his new views on Ebenezer Scrooge with Marlee outweighed safety concerns. He had just climbed into the truck, fortunately, parked inside the shed, when his phone rang.

"Hey, *Liebchen,* I'm on my way over."

But it wasn't Marlee. It was Liesel.

"Theo? Is Marlee with you?"

"No, but I'm on my way over to her apartment now."

"Are you certain she's there?" Her voice had a cautious tone.

"No, but I expect she's home. I thought maybe the weather was messing up the cell phones because she didn't pick up when I called."

The realization he was talking to his mom on his cell negated that.

"Theo, she was on her way here hours ago," Liesel said, heavy concern in her voice. "I asked her if she'd like to come out a day early because of the weather instead of waiting until tomorrow, so she said she was on her way. She was going to stop at the store for a couple of things, but still, she should have been here a long time ago."

He shuddered with a chill that wasn't from the cold. "How

long ago did she leave?"

"I talked to her around one, and she was on the way to the farmhouse," Liesel said. "Theo, I'm worried for her."

"So am I. I'll find her, I promise."

"*Sich vorsichtig, meine Sohn,*" Liesel said. "*Gott sei mit dir.* Find her and bring her home."

"That's what I'm going to do."

Theo ran back upstairs and grabbed some blankets. Then he headed out into the snowstorm. His truck started on the first try, and he backed out to let it warm. As it did, he tried calling Marlee again without success. Then he called Jonas.

"Sheriff Kaiser."

"Jonas, I need your help."

"What's the matter?"

The old friendship negated the near quarrel that they'd had.

"Marlee's missing. She headed out to the farmhouse three hours ago and never made it. I'm leaving now to find her before she freezes to death."

In a somber voice, his best friend said, "Theo, it's not a good idea. We're short staffed and busy. There have been slide offs and accidents everywhere. The roads are very bad, and the main storm is about to hit. When it does, it will be whiteout conditions. You're better off to stay there, and I'll put Marlee on the list. What does she drive?"

"A 2012 Buick, a blue one," Theo said. "But, Jonas, I'm still going after her. If it was Shannon, wouldn't you?"

"Yeah, I would. Be safe, brother, be safe, and I hope you find her."

To rule out any chance Marlee might be at home, Theo drove over the slippery streets past her apartment, hoping to find her car there, but it was gone. Every few minutes, he tried to call her without success. Since his mother had mentioned Marlee planned to stop at the store, he circled past each local grocery, but she wasn't there either. As Jonas had told him, the snow increased from moderate to heavy, falling onto the snow packed pavement.

Theo remembered that after his father's accident, his uncle Konrad had said if Ted Scrooge had used snow chains, he might have been able to trek safely across the icy bridge. Whether or not that was true didn't matter now, but Theo remembered the advice and made a detour to the local automotive store. They were about to close, but he bought chains. Theo installed them in the parking lot, struggling against the snow, and when he drove forward, they cinched in place. To reach Marlee, he would need every advantage, and it wouldn't help if he slid off on the way.

Traveling in town was challenging enough, but when Theo turned from the main road onto the winding narrow lane that led through vineyards and hills to the farmhouse, travel became perilous. He inched forward, tires spinning on occasion despite the chains, and peered through the driving snow, searching both sides of the road for Marlee or her car.

As he drove, Theo prayed aloud to St. Jude, repeating the familiar prayer. He offered prayers to St. Michael the Archangel and said a decade of the rosary from memory. Although inside Opa's truck it was warm, the chill of fear settled over Theo.

Although he never doubted that he loved Marlee, he realized now, after facing up to his longtime aversion and reading Dickens's holiday classic, how close to losing her he'd come and that now her life might be in danger. Theo also realized that whether or not he made a large profit margin, whether Bah Humbug! succeeded or failed, neither mattered compared to Marlee. She and his family were important, not dollars and cents.

His thoughts flew as fast as the driving snow that fell. Since she'd failed to arrive at the farmhouse, Theo figured she must have slid off the road. If Marlee remained inside the car, she would be cold but probably all right. But if she exited the vehicle to seek help or try to walk to the farmhouse, Theo understood she could die.

As the road took him between vineyards where empty arbors were covered in white, he struggled to keep the old truck on the road. The closer he came to the house, the more the road had an increasing incline and curves.

He almost lost control on the first curve, the truck sliding as he fought the wheel to keep it steady. The truck turned a full round until it faced the way he'd come, leaving Theo's heart pounding, his breath short, and his hands within the gloves wet with sweat. With extreme caution, he turned back the way he needed to go and plodded along with enough speed to move forward but slow enough to avoid sliding into the ditches.

Five miles that on a normal day over dry pavement took fifteen minutes became an hour-long trek. Theo had just passed the sign that indicated the winery was just ahead on the left when he eased the truck to a stop. On the right side, right before the driveway that led to the farmhouse, he saw something blue in the ditch.

Theo exited the truck, and his feet slipped. He went down hard, but clawed back upright, then walked toward the car with a penguin like waddle. From a few feet away, he confirmed it was Marlee's. The snow was marred with what appeared to be footprints, filling rapidly in the falling snow, and his gut clenched tight. The wind cut through his heavy coat as if he wore a light jacket and lashed his face with bitter cold. Theo fumbled in a pocket and pulled out a ski mask, then pulled it on with difficulty.

He climbed down into the ditch with clumsy steps, falling more than once. At the car, he tried to peer inside, but the windows were covered with frozen precipitation. Theo thought he could see a figure in the driver's seat, but he couldn't tell for sure, so he jerked at the door handle, praying it wasn't locked or frozen shut.

It took some effort, but the door swung toward him, and he saw Marlee slumped in the seat. Her eyes were shut, and what he could see of her face was very pale. At some point, Theo speculated, she'd been outside, because she had snow caked on her coat and jeans.

"Marlee!" he said, his tone sharp. "Marlee!"

She didn't appear to hear him, and he touched her. Marlee didn't move or respond. Risking frostbite, Theo removed a glove to caress her cheek. Her skin was frigid. He needed to get her to warmth, and soon. For a moment, he considered calling for help, for an ambulance or one of Jonas's deputies to take her to the hospital, but he recalled Jonas had said they were busy. Either action would take precious time, which Marlee didn't have. He had to act, and now.

Theo put his arms around her and pulled her toward him. She didn't stir, and he repeated her name several more times. He tried and failed to lift her into his arms, so he pulled her across his shoulders in a fireman's carry position. The effort left him breathless, and he feared he might not be able to support her weight. Theo staggered out of the ditch toward his truck, reciting silent prayers that he'd get there without falling. Once he reached it, he managed to slide her onto the passenger seat. As soon as he got behind the wheel, he covered her with blankets and drove as fast as he dared toward the farmhouse.

Even with the truck's heater going, Theo shivered all the way. At the house, he couldn't make out exactly where the drive was, so he drove as close as he could to the front entrance. As he climbed out of the truck, Liesel opened the door.

"Theo, did you find Marlee?" she called over the wind.

He nodded, then realized she probably couldn't see the movement.

"She's in the truck," he said, teeth chattering. "I'm bringing her inside, so stand back. Don't come out here—it's too cold."

"Is she all right?"

"Don't know yet," Theo gasped as he opened the passenger door. He did his best to wrap Marlee in blankets, draping one over her face. This time he managed to lift her in his arms and carry her the short distance to the front door. Once inside, he turned toward the formal parlor to the left, but Liesel shut the door and interrupted.

"*Nein*! Bring her back to the family room. It's warmer with the wood stove going."

Theo summoned up enough strength to carry Marlee through the house to the smaller room off the kitchen. Half the size of the parlor, the cozy space did have a woodstove, as well as a couch, several chairs flanking a table that held a hurricane lamp, and a card table with four folding chairs. He put Marlee down onto the couch, a wide rose colored vintage piece that belonged to his great-grandparents. She still had not stirred, although he could see she was breathing.

"You need to get out of those wet clothes, Theo, and get warm," Liesel said.

He nodded, shaking with cold. "Her clothes are wet too. I think she must have gotten out of the car and tried to walk, then got too cold and got back into it, which probably saved her life."

"I'll get something she can wear while you go change. I think you have some things in your old room."

Theo did, clothes he kept here for the occasional hunting or fishing trip. He wanted to stay with Marlee, but it made sense. He needed to warm up, too, or he wouldn't be able to care for her.

He phoned Jonas on the way up the steps and told him. Jonas rattled off some tips about home care for hypothermia before he hung up.

"Stay there," he advised. "The roads are in terrible shape, and it's still coming down."

By the time he returned, his mother and Oma had managed to put Marlee into an ankle length flannel nightgown, with heavy socks on her feet. They had piled blankets and quilts over her, where she lay prone on the couch. One of them had pulled her hair back into a ponytail, and Marlee lay on her right side.

"Did she come around at all?" Theo asked. He had donned some old camouflage pants and a thermal shirt.

"She stirred when we were changing her clothes," Liesel said, a worry line dividing her forehead. "She seemed a little confused, but she asked for you, Theo. Maybe she should be at the hospital."

"I doubt we could make it there," Theo said. "I talked to Jonas, and he thinks if it's just mild hypothermia, she'll be okay once she gets warm. She needs something to drink too, but nothing with caffeine or alcohol."

"I'll make some chamomile tea," Oma said. "Theo, do you want some?"

"I want coffee," he said.

Most of all, he needed Marlee to open her eyes and to be fine.

Theo knelt by the couch facing her. He picked up her left hand and stroked it gently, noting it remained cool.

"Hey, *liebchen*," he said. "Marlee, it's Theo. You're at the farmhouse, you're safe, and you'll be warm soon. I love you, and I read the book."

When there was no immediate response, he feared her condition might be worse than he'd thought. Theo put down his head and prayed in German for a few minutes. Then he said her name again, his voice low and tender. "Marlee, I'm worried. I love you, and I need you. Talk to me, *Liebchen*."

Her eyelids quivered first, then she said, her voice hoarse and reedy, "Theo?"

"I'm here." Relief swept him with such power he swayed

on his knees, dizzy.

"Theo, I'm so cold."

"I know you are, *meine Geliebte,*" he said, almost whispering. "But you'll be warmer soon."

"Where are we?"

"At the farmhouse, in the family room."

She blinked and shook her head as if to clear it. "I think I slid off the road."

"You did, but I found you."

"Theo, I love you." She sounded sleepy.

"And I love you, too. Do you think you could drink some tea? Oma's made some."

Marlee nodded and struggled to change position. Theo helped her shift until her head and shoulders were propped against a bank of pillows resting against the arm of the couch. He settled her covers back around her.

She sipped the tea and made a face. "Sugar?"

Theo added more and helped her to taste it again.

"Better."

With his help, she drank all of what was in the cup.

Her pallor faded as she warmed, and she became increasingly more alert. "Is it Christmas Eve?"

"Tomorrow," he told her. "It's December 23, Thursday."

She sighed with relief. "Then I haven't missed it."

Theo smiled. "No, you haven't. Merry Christmas, Marlee. I read the book and watched the movie."

Marlee's eyes widened. "You did?"

"*Ja,* I did. And you were right to tell me to read it, Marlee. We'll talk about it when you're warmer, but I love you, and you can call me Scrooge any time you want. Just not Ebenezer, please."

Her face lit up with delight. "That's wonderful. Oh, Theo!"

Marlee's hand in his remained cooler than normal.

"You're still chilled. Let me throw more wood into the stove and keep you covered. Sleep, *Liebling*."

"I will," she said. "I'm so tired. But it's going to be a merry Christmas."

Theo grinned and kissed her. "*Jawohl*, it is. Get some rest."

Her eyes were closed before he could stand. Once Theo could, he drank coffee, finally, and ate a little bit of soup his mother brought. Then he settled into one of the recliners in the room, grabbed a quilt, and he, too, slept.

Chapter Twenty-Five

Theo had never known a happier Christmas, not since childhood. Although the final total of a foot and a half of snow on the ground resulted in Midnight Mass being cancelled for the first time he could recall, all was good. By midday on Christmas Eve, Marlee had recovered enough to join his mother and grandmother in cooking for the holiday feast. Jonas had called a tow truck to retrieve Marlee's car, then deliver it to the house. Theo had carried in her bags, suitcase, and the items she'd bought at the store.

Theo hovered, unwilling to let Marlee out of his sight for long. He couldn't resist touching her or delivering frequent kisses. Together, he, Marlee, Mutti and Oma worked prepping dishes for Christmas Day. Theo took over the kitchen to create crumb-topped salmon filets for supper, paired with a shrimp pasta salad and rice pilaf. To add some color, he also served broccoli with julienned carrots in a butter sauce. He sang Christmas carols as he worked, some German, others English, so Marlee could join him in song. Watching, Liesel smiled.

After the evening meal, in traditional German fashion,

they decorated the fresh Douglas fir in the parlor, delivered by Thomas before the snow, and decked it with handblown heirloom ornaments from Germany. There were also a few from Theo's childhood. He had all but forgotten the custom of receiving a special ornament for each year of his life until Liesel brought down the keepsake box where they were stored.

Theo clipped the candle holders to the branches, and his mother added the slender white candles. It was another Old-World custom his family kept. The candles would be lit for a short time. As they decorated, they sipped some spiced mulled red wine that Theo concocted.

"It's good to have you here for this," Liesel told Theo. "It's been years since you helped with the tree."

He hadn't since his last year of high school, the year his father died. Theo had been present for Christmas, but he hadn't assisted with decorating. Most years he hadn't even lent a hand with the food preparation.

"I should have been here, doing this every year," Theo replied.

"You're here now, *mein Sohn,*" Liesel told him. "Let's light the candles."

He lit each candle with care, then dimmed the lights, so the tree glowed in the darkness. The candlelight illuminated Marlee's face, more beautiful to him than any decoration.

Theo picked out the smallest package under the tree, the unwrapped ring box, and knelt before Marlee's chair. His mother and grandmother wore small smiles. Both knew what he planned, but Marlee had no idea.

Her eyes widened when he went to his knees. Theo took her right hand in his.

"Marlee, I love you. I've loved you almost since the day I first met you. I'm so glad you are part of my life, and I'm sorry I lost my focus. I got caught up in my business, and with money, so much I almost forgot what's the most important. You were right to call me Scrooge, to hand me the book to read, and you saved me, I think. You caught me before I was lost or lost you.

"When I realized you were out somewhere in the snow, that you should have arrived hours before, I was afraid, more than I have ever been. Nothing mattered but finding you safe. And so I have a question. Will you be my wife?"

Theo opened the box to reveal the rings, and the diamonds sparkled in the light from the tree. Marlee caught her breath and made a tiny sound.

"Yes, Theo, yes, I will," she cried.

She held out her left hand, and he slid the engagement ring onto the third finger. Theo kissed first her left, then her right hand, then rose to kiss her lips in a lingering kiss. Marlee came to her feet, and he held her tight.

"I was beginning to think you would never ask," she said after a few moments.

They all laughed. He kissed her again before they exchanged the rest of the gifts.

The other gifts were small but thoughtful, each selected with care — a warm shawl for Oma, her favorite lavender perfume for Liesel, shirts and fishing gear for Theo, and a hand-stitched quilt for Marlee. Each gave the others at least one gift, sometimes two. Theo also had given Marlee two books to help her learn some basic German. Marlee, despite her recent issues with their relationship, had bought him the leather jacket he'd coveted.

Although it was early, Marlee appeared tired, so Theo suggested that they wrap up the evening.

"We'll be up early in the morning," he said with a grin. "Marlee needs her rest, this time in a real bed, not the couch."

"She will have the blue room upstairs," Liesel said. "It's ready, and her bags are there, but we're not yet done with gifts."

Theo glanced under the tree where no more packages

remained. "We're not?"

"*Nein, mein Sohn,*" she said. "This is a gift long planned, a gift for you."

She stood up and left the room, returning in a few minutes with a large manilla envelope, and handed it to him.

"Before you open it, you must know this—we planned this for a long time, your grandparents and me," Liesel said. "It's signed by all of us, you will see. I would have given it to you sooner, but we waited until you showed *die Vernunft,* some reason and sense. As long as you cared more for your business, it wasn't time. But now, I think, it is."

He undid the flap on the unmarked envelope and pulled out a stack of papers. When he began to read, Theo drew a sharp breath and turned his gaze to his mother.

"Mutti?"

Liesel nodded. "It's just what it looks like, Theo."

Emotion brimmed in his heart until it almost overwhelmed him. Tears blinded his eyes and knotted tight in his throat.

"You're giving me the farmhouse?"

"It was already done a long time ago," his mother said. "It is what Opa and Oma both wanted."

"*Du bist der Sohn unseres Herzens,*" Oma told him. "You always were our Theo."

Theo clutched the papers in his hands. He held the key to his dreams, the reality of having a home to bring a wife and where he could raise a family. It had already been there, he mused, in his grasp but unknown.

"*Danke, danke, danke,*" he cried as he came to his feet. He swept his mother and grandmother into a hug, and they clung to him, tears in their eyes. Theo opened his right arm to bring Marlee into the circle, and she joined them in a group hug for the people he loved the most.

He had many questions, though, and asked them. "Will

you stay here with us, then?"

"*Nein,*" Liesel said. "We will move to town. It will be better, for Oma and for me. We're older now, and it will be good to be close to things—including your restaurant, Theo."

Wrapping his head around all of it was difficult.

"But where will you live? I don't want you to have to buy a house or live in a small apartment. I'd offer you mine, above Bah Humbug! but it's up too many stairs and too tiny."

Liesel's smile shone brighter than the candles on the tree. "We'll live in the house where you grew up, Theo."

"I thought that was sold, after we moved here, after Dad died."

She shook her head. "No, we kept it—rented it out, but the lease is almost up with the current tenant. Opa said we should hang on to it for this, for what we're doing now. It's perfect for us, a bedroom each, just a few stairs to come into the house front and back, and near the park. I have good memories there. We will be content."

He would have been happy there, too, but the farmhouse was beyond anything he ever had dared to dream. It was what he'd wanted but never hoped to have. He turned toward the tree for a moment to collect himself. Marlee put her arms around him from behind.

"Theo?"

"Can you live here?" he asked as he turned to face her. "Will that work for you?"

"I love this house," she told him. "I have from the first time you brought me here, so yes."

Their eyes met, unblinking.

"If I learned anything in the last two days, it's that I will do whatever makes you happy," he told her. "I want to live here, more than anything, but if you didn't, then I would go where you wished, even to another town. If you'd rather I would give up my place, I'd find another job, maybe as a chef for someone else. I don't have many other skills, but I'd try."

"Theo Scrooge, I love you, and I want to live here, in this house, in this place, with you, and raise our children here," Marlee said. "I'm happy to be a chef's wife and Scrooge's wife. I like Bah Humbug!, and you cook much better than I do."

"I love you, and we'll live here. But now, you need to go to bed and get some sleep. Tomorrow will be a big day."

Marlee nodded. He lifted her into his arms, and despite her protests, he carried her upstairs to the blue bedroom. If she'd allowed it, he would have stayed to tuck her into the canopy bed piled with soft blankets and a Delft patterned comforter in blue and white. The blue canopy matched it, but she insisted she could go to bed on her own, so he kissed her and went downstairs.

Theo lingered long enough to extinguish the candles on the tree and to spend a few minutes with his family. Then they too retired for the night, and he sat alone, heart full, until he thought he could sleep.

On Christmas Day, the snow remained too deep to travel, and services at church were cancelled. They enjoyed a delicious meal, something each of them contributed toward, with roast pork, a glazed turkey breast, noodles, potato dumplings, and more. Oma made rolls that were sweet enough to serve at breakfast but were a treat for the holiday feast. There was apple strudel, a Black Forest cake, and many cookies.

For the first time in years, Theo spent no time thinking about profit or his business. He would reopen on Tuesday, he had decided. He focused on his family, his wife to be, and relaxed enough to enjoy the holiday.

On Sunday, he and Marlee sat down with a calendar for the coming year. Neither wanted to wait long but agreed they couldn't marry during Lent or until after Easter.

"I need time to find a dress," she said. "And make plans.

But I know I want to be married here, in Hermann."

"That's perfect."

"How about two Saturdays after Easter weekend?" Marlee asked. "April is a pretty month, and it will be about a year since we met."

"April works. We'll reserve the church, and unless you want the reception somewhere else, it'll be at Bah Humbug!"

"Oh, like Jonas and Shannon had."

"Better!" Theo told her. "And I think I'll just stay closed until Friday, New Year's Eve, then we'll have an engagement party. What do you think?"

"I love it! But do you really want to be closed until then?"

"*Liebling,* the snow's not going to melt very soon, and I'm changed."

Marlee's wide smile delighted him. "Just checking, Theo Scrooge," she said. "Just a test."

"Did I pass?"

"Definitely."

When the roads cleared enough that he could, Theo drove into town. He put a notice on the front door at Bah Humbug! that announced they would remain closed until Friday and that an engagement party would begin at five. Food and beverages would be on the house.

He hadn't even returned to the farmhouse when his cell began ringing. Jonas was first to call with congratulations. "Theo, I'm so happy for you both! I was beginning to think you'd never ask her."

"That's what Marlee said," Theo replied with a laugh. "We'll be married in April. Will you be my best man?"

"Of course! That's wonderful news. We have some of our own, too. We're going to have a baby, due in March."

"*Herzlichen Glückwunsch!*"

At the party, Theo played the host with pleasure. His

guests dined on rouladen and fricassee. The dessert was a seven-layer Prince Regent cake, a Bavarian specialty and a labor of love from Liesel.

Although the guests were long gone by midnight, Theo and Marlee greeted the new year as they would spend it— together.

Epilogue

By summer, after the wedding and the honeymoon were memories, Mr. and Mrs. Theo Scrooge settled into their new life. The old stone farmhouse had become home, personalized with a few changes that Marlee made. His mother and grandmother settled into his childhood home as if it'd been tailored for them.

At Bah Humbug! Theo streamlined the menus to offer six German and six English entrees plus the daily specials, which were now for both lunch and dinner every day. He added a few American items, too, including Marlee's meatloaf. Diners could choose from rouladen, fricassee, schntizel, a wurst plate, bratwurst on a bun, or *marsch*. On the English side, cottage or shepherd's pie, bangers and mash, fish and chips, steak pie, bacon butty and chicken croquettes.

He shortened the hours as well—there was no evening meal served Monday through Wednesday. Theo also had winter hours that were not as long as those in the tourist season. During the school year, that gave him more time to spend with Marlee, and once the summer break began, Marlee worked with him again, doing some of the desserts and a few breads.

When the wedding pictures came back, Theo hung one of the wedding party at Bah Humbug!, and another with the bride and groom in a place of honor behind the cash register. Marlee, after searching for a gown on both sides of Missouri, had worn his grandmother's early 1950s vintage gown and fragile veil. The lace trimmed dress with a full skirt had suited Marlee, and fit as if it'd been made for her.

Scrooge jokes no longer upset Theo—he laughed when they were made. It wasn't long until Todd Blevins stopped because if they didn't wound, there was no fun in it.

Most of all, Theo had discovered happiness. He fit into his skin, and his niche in his corner of the world suited him. The old English surname now brought him pride, a facet of his heritage, and he thought that his dad would be proud.

Marlee was—he saw it in her eyes, but the joy overwhelmed it, and they were happy.

The last thing he did was to frame a quotation from the end of Dickens's novel, one he now understood and even lived. It hung beside the kitchen door at Bah Humbug! where Theo saw it often each day.

Scrooge was better than his word. He did it all, and infinitely more; and to Tiny Tim, who did not die, he was a second father. He became as good a friend, as good a master, and as good a man, as the good old city knew, or any other good old city, town, or borough, in the good old world. Some people laughed to see the alteration in him, but he let them laugh, and little heeded them; for he was wise enough to know that nothing ever happened on this globe, for good, at which some people did not have their fill of laughter in the outset; and knowing that such as these would be blind anyway, he thought it quite as well that they should wrinkle up their eyes in grins, as have the malady in less attractive forms. His own heart laughed: and that was quite enough for him. – from "A Christmas Carol," Charles Dickens

And for Theo, his own heart laughed too, the lost laughter

restored to him along with love. And for Theo, like old Ebenezer, it was enough.

Lee Ann Sontheimer Murphy is a former newspaper editor and reporter who makes her home in the Ozarks. As a widow with three grown children, her focus is on writing romance novels that range from sweet to heat, from contemporary to historical. She has written more than twenty-five novels and novellas along with a variety of non-fiction and freelance works. A native of St. Joseph, Missouri, where the Pony Express began, and outlaw Jesse James met his end, she is a graduate of Crowder College and Missouri Southern State University. She lives in what passes for the suburbs in far southwestern Missouri, a little north of Arkansas and just east of Oklahoma.

www.ingramcontent.com/pod-product-compliance
Lightning Source LLC
Chambersburg PA
CBHW030120180626
46812CB00002B/499